The emerald hills and violet valleys of Wales seem the ideal place to start over after murder—and divorce—shattered Eilidh's life in the Scottish Highlands. But within the stone walls of an ancient castle, a family's dark, violent past threatens much more than her newfound tranquility...

For the past two years, Eilidh has called the quaint Welsh village of Thistlecross home, embracing her new life as estate manager of a restored fifteenth-century castle. But the long-anticipated arrival of her employer's three estranged sons and their wives transforms Thistlecross Castle from a welcoming haven to a place seething with dangerous secrets. When the escalating tensions culminate in murder, Eilidh must sift through a castle full of suspects both upstairs and downstairs. She can trust no one as she follows a twisting maze of greed and malice to ferret out a killer who's breaching every defense, preparing to make Eilidh the next to die.

Books by Amy M. Reade

The Malice Series

The House on Candlewick Lane
Highland Peril
Murder in Thistlecross

Novels

Secrets of Hallstead House
The Ghosts of Peppernell Manor
House of the Hanging Jade

Published by Kensington Publishing Corp.

Murder in Thistlecross

A Malice Novel

Amy M. Reade

LYRICAL UNDERGROUND
Kensington Publishing Corp.
www.kensingtonbooks.com

First Electronic Edition: February 2018
eISBN-13: 978-1-5161-0016-3
eISBN-10: 1-5161-0016-6

First Print Edition: February 2018
ISBN-13: 978-1-5161-0019-4
ISBN-10: 1-5161-0019-0

For my parents ~ all of them

Acknowledgements

As always, I would like to thank my family for their constant support along this journey. They give me the time and space I need to write, endless encouragement, and their honest opinions. Without them this passion of mine would be much more difficult.

I also must thank Carol Thompson, who won a charity raffle in which the prize was the chance to name a character in this book. Carol chose the name Rhisiart Tucker, and I think it fits perfectly.

I would also like to thank my editor, Martin Biro, for helping to make this a better book, and all the professionals at Kensington whose work helps make my dreams come true.

Glossary

Ach-y-fi: a Welsh expression of disgust (Och-a-vee)

torch: flashlight

Iechyd da: Be well (Yech-ee-dah)

cracking: excellent

CV: Curriculum Vitae, a type of résumé

dummy: pacifier

jumper: sweater

Pronunciations

Eilidh: Ay-lee

Rhisiart: Ree-see-art

Sian: She-on

Chapter 1

Arthur Tucker sat on the floor, slumped sideways, head resting against the sharp edge of the nightstand. His eyes were closed. Blood seeped from a wound above his left ear.

Minutes earlier, in a drunken stupor, he had tried to crawl into bed and missed the mark, hitting his head on the nightstand and causing the deep gash on his scalp.

In rising pain and panic, he called for help in a voice that, though feeble and confused, somehow remained imperious and harsh.

A person stood in the shadow of the doorway, watching with ambivalence as the lifeblood flowed out of Arthur. The person had every intention of calling for an ambulance, but not until Arthur was good and dead.

It took longer than the person expected for Arthur to finally take in one last, ragged breath. Blood had stopped spreading beside him and was already beginning to congeal. The person watching from the doorway waited another minute or two, then walked over to Arthur, careful to avoid stepping in the blood, and felt his wrist.

No pulse. It was over.

The person went downstairs and called for an ambulance.

* * * *

"Eilidh, I'm going to need quite a lot of help with this."

I smiled at Annabel, who tended to ask for quite a lot of help with everything, though she was perfectly capable of doing most of it herself. She had a way of making me feel needed, which I loved about her.

"That's what I'm here for," I answered.

"I'll make a list while you run into the village and pick up my package at the dress shop."

My room was at the end of a long stone hallway, punctuated at regular intervals by old iron sconces which had been wired for electricity. I passed Brenda on the way to my room, bustling by with a broom and dustpan. I greeted my eighteen-year-old coworker cheerfully.

"How are you this afternoon, Brenda?"

She scowled. "*Ach-y-fi*. It's always somethin' around here."

I didn't want to get involved in whatever the problem was this time, so I kept walking. The arched wooden door to my room creaked softly when I pushed it open. Every time I went into my room I was transported back to the first time I had seen it—between the stone floor and the damp stone walls, I was sure I would freeze to death. That was before I noticed the fireplace. And I didn't really have a choice, so I bucked up and told myself—and Aunt Margot—it would be an adventure to live in an ancient castle, updated, of course, with all the modern conveniences.

And I had been right. Living on Annabel's estate, in her magnificent home, for the past two years had indeed been an experience of a lifetime. Not only had I learned all about the job of being the manager of a big estate, but I had made friends and come out of my shell. Since I had come to Wales alone, divorced, and bewildered, I had been forced to mature quickly.

I was lost after I divorced Callum. Far from feeling free and exhilarated, I sank into a miasma of despair. How was I going to support myself? Where was I going to live? I couldn't stay in Cauld Loch, not with all those people whispering behind my back, or worse, pitying me.

It was my Aunt Margot, Greer and Sylvie's mum, who came to my rescue, who lifted me out of my depression when she convinced me to take a job in the village of Thistlecross, in Wales. Her longtime friend, Annabel Baines, was looking for someone to help manage her estate, Thistlecross Castle. Aunt Margot, with her typical good sense, had realized that Annabel and I had certain things in common that would make us natural friends.

I was hesitant at first, not knowing anything about managing property and employees. My previous jobs in Scotland had been as an antique shop and gallery assistant for my cousin, Sylvie, and her husband, Seamus, and as a clerk in a potter's shop. But Aunt Margot wouldn't take no for an answer, and I'm grateful she insisted that I step out of my comfort zone and into the responsibilities of being Annabel's assistant.

I grabbed my purse from the heavy mahogany armoire in my room and walked back to where Annabel was waiting for me in the sitting room, my footsteps echoing through the corridor.

She was sitting at an old desk, its burnished wood shining in the lamplight of the late afternoon. "Let me see," she said, tapping her pencil against the jasmine-scented notepaper. I could smell it even from where I stood. "I've started making a list of what we need to do before everyone arrives tomorrow evening. We're going to be busy."

I smiled, knowing *I* would be busy and that Annabel would take a more supervisory role. "Do you want to talk about it now, or do you want me to pick up your dress first?" I asked.

"The shop closes at five," Annabel answered, glancing at her wristwatch, "so you'd better go there first and we can talk when you get back."

I hurried outside to the small parking area where we kept the cars. It never ceased to amaze me that I was lucky enough to work in such a magnificent place. The four-story castle, built like a fortress, was made entirely of stone, with a huge turret at each corner, though one of the turrets, crumbling and unused, led to an ancient part of the castle that was decrepit. No one ever ventured into that wing, as it was too treacherous. The blue-gray slates on the many levels of roof had a matte look to them. They looked wet from this distance.

Most of the rooms on the upper floors of the castle were unused, though there were a few Annabel loved to visit. She made sure those rooms were comfortable and beautifully furnished. Many of the rooms were used only for storage. I had been amazed at the amount of space necessary to store the castle's supply of Christmas décor, as well as the light furniture and bedding which Brenda swapped out at the beginning and end of each summer.

Maneuvering my car past the stone walls of the enclosure, I headed down the mile-long drive, past the rolling hills that made up the "front yard" of the estate, and made a right to take the main road into the village. Thistlecross Castle had been built in the fifteenth century to protect Thistlecross, which was larger at that time. The village was quaint and charming, with stone houses situated side-by-side and colorful wooden signs hanging over the pavement in front of the shops and the local pub. A swollen stream tumbled along behind the homes and shops on the main street.

I parked in front of the ladies' boutique where Annabel bought most of her clothes and made my way inside.

"Hello, Mrs. Carrington," I called.

"Is that you, Eilidh?" came a voice from the back of the shop. "I'll be with you in a moment, dear."

I smiled. Mrs. Carrington was the village grandmother. She always had a kind word for everyone so I didn't mind when she called me "dear."

I browsed through the dresses I couldn't afford while I waited. Mrs. Carrington appeared, struggling with a big box wrapped in pink paper and tied with a pink satin ribbon. "Here's Annabel's dress. Just in time, isn't it?" she said, hefting the box onto the counter. I reached out to help her.

"Yes. Her kids arrive tomorrow evening and I know she's looking forward to wearing this," I answered.

Mrs. Carrington fixed me with a shrewd look. "Do you think this is a good idea?" she asked. Mrs. Carrington wasn't just the village grandmother—she was the village gossip, too, but she always seemed to gossip in the most innocent and pleasant manner. She never seemed petty or mean.

I needed to choose my words carefully when I answered her, or they would be repeated all over the village until they made their way back to Thistlecross Castle and Annabel's ears.

"Annabel is very much looking forward to seeing her boys," I said. "We're hoping everything goes smoothly."

Mrs. Carrington winked at me. She knew I couldn't say more than that. I took up the box and the elderly lady went around the counter to open the front door of the shop for me. I stashed the box in the boot of my car and waved to her as I drove off toward the castle.

Once I was back at the castle, Annabel was excited to open the box and see the dress. She had picked it out over a month previously and had been anxiously awaiting the alterations from the tailor. She ripped off the pink paper and lifted the dress from the folds of tissue paper hiding it from view.

"Isn't it gorgeous, Eilidh?" she exclaimed, holding it in front of her. It was a beautiful tea dress, made of crushed black velvet with three-quarter length sleeves and an empire waist. I had been there when she first tried it on in Mrs. Carrington's shop. It looked just perfect with her silvery-gray short hair and the simple jewelry she favored.

"I love it," I said. "Are you going to check the alterations before dinner?"

"I should; you're right." Annabel slipped the dress over the crook of her arm and carried it out of the room. I could hear her low heels clicking on the stone steps leading to her suite of rooms on the first floor, one story up. It wasn't long before she returned, looking aristocratic and regal in her new dress. With the money she had from the sale of her first husband's textile business and from her second husband's vast land holdings in Wales, she had enough wealth to buy Mrs. Carrington's entire store, as well as every other establishment in Thistlecross, but she was always thrilled to get a new dress. She turned around slowly in front of me so I could get the full effect of the twirling skirt.

"Perfect!" I exclaimed and she grinned.

"I'll take it off and we'll eat soon. Maisie said dinner would be at six."

I put my handbag away and returned to the sitting room to wait for Annabel. I assumed she would want to review her list as soon as she could. There was so much to do.

When she came back and had seated herself at her desk, she lifted her notepaper and invited me to sit down in one of the armchairs in front of the desk.

"What's first?" I asked.

She scanned the paper. "Have you come up with ideas of things for everyone to do while they're here?"

"Yes," I answered. "I thought they would enjoy horse riding—everyone except Sian, that is—and I have looked into some cooking classes."

"Wonderful! Anything else?"

"I've talked to two local guides who are willing to take them up into the foothills for a day-long hike if they're interested, plus I thought about hiring a hot air balloon and setting up a time for them to go beachcombing. I remember Sian has always enjoyed that."

"Those are excellent ideas, Eilidh," Annabel praised me. "Can you take care of all the reservations?"

"Already done, as long as you have no problem with the days I've chosen for each activity."

"Whatever did I do without you?" Annabel asked, giving me a fond look.

"What's next on the list?" I asked.

We talked about meal preparations and room readiness, which would be handled by Brenda and her mother, Maisie. We talked about which local doctor would be available in case Sian required medical attention. We also discussed what Annabel would do while her guests were occupied.

We took a break from the house preparations while we dined. Maisie was a wonderful cook and it seemed somehow disrespectful to discuss business over one of her meals. As we tucked into creamy leek soup followed by plates of breaded cod with steamed vegetables, we talked instead about my cousin Sylvie's planned visit to the castle, coincidentally scheduled at the same time as Annabel's guests. I was excited for Sylvie to visit; I hadn't seen her since leaving Scotland. Aunt Margot had visited, of course, mainly to see her old friend, but I knew I would have more fun with Sylvie around. As much as I loved Aunt Margot, her idea of a fun activity was not the same as mine. I had hoped my other cousin, Greer, could visit, too, but she couldn't take the time away from her job. She was a professor of art history at the University of Edinburgh and she had to take holidays when school wasn't in session.

"Sylvie will be staying in the coach house, correct?" Annabel asked.

"Yes. She'll be here day after tomorrow," I answered. I know Annabel worried a bit that I might not have the time to take care of her guests while Sylvie was visiting, but I assured her that I would make myself available every hour of the day. I didn't expect her guests to require my services too much, since all their activities would be arranged in advance and guides and other activity leaders would be readily available to offer any assistance they might need.

Annabel took a bite of the fish Maisie had prepared to delicate, firm white perfection, then set her fork down and fixed me with a concerned look.

"I'm nervous," she said.

I had been waiting for this. I wondered how long it would take Annabel to voice her feelings about the impending arrival of all her guests.

"I know you are, but we've talked about this many times," I reminded her. "Everything is going to be just fine and you needn't worry about a thing. I'll be here to help, and I know Sylvie will be happy to help, too. You leave everything to us."

"I know all that, but I can't help feeling apprehensive about the visit," Annabel said. "After all…" Her voice trailed off. Maisie had bustled in from the kitchen, bearing a tray of fruit and cheese. "Oh, thank you, Maisie. Could you please bring the tea?" Annabel asked, then she turned to me and said in a low voice, "I need something to settle my stomach."

When Maisie left the dining room I asked Annabel, "What were you saying?"

She looked down at her hands, which were resting on the edge of the table. "Oh, it's nothing. Never mind."

I knew Annabel had been close to explaining why she was nervous for her three sons to visit, but she had apparently decided against telling me. She had come close so many times before, but hadn't been able to bring herself to share the secret she held.

But I knew the secret—Aunt Margot had told me. She thought it important for me to understand the complex relationships between Annabel and her sons.

I watched a movie in my room that night before going to bed. I thought about Annabel, alone in her big suite of rooms upstairs, probably pacing the floor out of nervousness over the arrival of her sons.

The next morning dawned cool and softly bright, the fog slowly shredding into tiny wisps that remained close to the ground, giving the estate an ethereal look in the watery sunshine of the early morning.

I yawned and stretched, savoring the quiet. There would be a storm coming, I knew, and its arrival would coincide with that of Annabel's sons. In the meantime, there was plenty of work to be done. I made sure Maisie and Brenda were caught up with their work in the kitchen and the guest rooms and then confirmed the various reservations I had made for the family over the next several days. I double-checked the office hours of the local doctor in case Sian required his services. I spent a good part of the day trying to calm Annabel's nerves. She was in quite a state by late afternoon. I almost wished she hadn't insisted upon this reunion—it was doing nothing for her state of mind.

The doorbell rang at precisely four o'clock. Annabel, in her favorite armchair in the sitting room, gave a start. She had instructed Brenda to admit the guests and show them to the sitting room. She twisted a scarf nervously in her hands, looking at me with uncertainty in her eyes.

"They're here. What should I say?" she asked in a loud whisper.

"They're your sons, Annabel. You'll know just what to say when you see them," I assured her, hoping I was right.

The door swung open without a sound and Brenda stepped into the room. "Mrs. Baines, Andreas and Sian are here." She stepped aside to allow Annabel's eldest son and his wife to enter the room.

I was glad I was sitting off to the side, where I could watch Annabel and her son and daughter-in-law without being obtrusive or seeming nosy. Andreas Tucker, a tall man with hair the color of onyx and a cleft in his chin, gave his mother a hug and Annabel held out her hand to Sian, who grasped it lightly and gave it a quick squeeze. Sian was tall and pretty, with wavy light brown hair and fair skin that seemed to glow. Her belly, which had grown substantially since I had seen her last, only added to her voluptuous beauty.

Brenda watched Andreas and his wife greet Annabel, then turned to leave the room, looking back over her shoulder and straight at Andreas before closing the door behind her.

"How was your trip? And how's that little grandbaby of mine doing?" Annabel asked.

"The trip was fine, and the baby's fine, too, Mum. He'll be here before we know it," Andreas said.

"I'm glad you two arrived first," Annabel said, looking up at her son. "It will be nice to have you with me when the others get here."

"Mum, you don't need to worry about Hugh and Rhisiart; they will be fine. It's Cadi you have to worry about," he replied, giving his mother a dark look.

"Please, no disparaging remarks," Annabel said in a scolding tone. But her expression softened and I knew she didn't hold Andreas's words against him because he was right.

Sian put her hand over her belly and asked Annabel, "Do you mind if I lie down for a bit? I'm so very tired."

"Not at all, Sian. If there's anything you need, just let someone know," Annabel replied. She nodded her head toward me. "Eilidh, can you show Sian which room will be theirs? I don't know where Brenda went."

"Sure," I said. I noticed the long look Andreas gave Sian. "Sian, follow me and I'll take you. It's on this floor, so you don't have to climb any steps."

"Thank you," she said with a small sigh. I hadn't realized women in the late stages of pregnancy could be so tired. I thought they had their old energy back after the first trimester. I had no personal experience, of course—and now probably wouldn't, thanks to my divorce—but I remembered Greer saying she had lots of energy toward the end of her pregnancy.

Sian moved slowly, so I waited for her at the door while she gathered up her purse and her jacket. I stood aside to let her out the door first, then followed her and closed the door quietly behind me. "This way," I said, nodding my head toward the hallway to the right of the front door.

She followed me down the long stone hallway that mirrored the hallway where my own room was located. She didn't bother to look up at any of the portraits that hung from the stone walls, Andreas's ancestors' eyes, also the ancestors of her unborn child, watching her as she walked.

"Have you heard from Hugh and Cadi?" she finally asked.

"Not yet. They shouldn't be too far behind you," I said.

She let out a loud sigh. "I guess we'll have to pretend to get along until this week is over," she said, her voice grim.

There was nothing I could say to that.

"What about Rhisiart?" she asked.

"He'll be here tonight, but not until quite late, I think," I said, turning my head to look at her as we walked. "He was coming up from London. I believe he had a meeting with his agent this afternoon."

We came to the door of the room she and Andreas would share for the week. Just like mine, and most of the other rooms in the castle, this room was large, dark, and cool, with a huge fireplace for warmth. The room was vaguely circular because it was set along the inside of one of the castle turrets. Stone walls lent the room a feeling of security, which was amplified by long heavy drapes hanging from each of the windows. All the bedroom chambers in the castle, much like the common rooms, were furnished with dark, heavy antiques and this room was no exception.

Adding to the heaviness of the furniture was dark, plush bedding piled on the four-poster bed. As Annabel's favorite son, Andreas was privileged to be a guest in the most sumptuous guest room in the castle.

I saw that Brenda had already placed the couple's luggage in the huge armoire. I looked around approvingly and asked Sian if there was anything I could get for her.

"No, I'm good," she said. The hearth was cold and dark now, but I told her I could ask Brenda to build a fire for her.

"Don't bother," she said. "I just want to be left alone. I'll get under the covers and I'll be warm enough."

I nodded and left the room, closing the huge door quietly behind me. Sian was not my favorite person and I was glad to leave her in her room. She and Andreas had visited Annabel a few times over the past two years and I had always found her to be a bit snooty and standoffish. I walked back to the sitting room, where I paused before pushing the door open and announcing my presence.

The door was slightly ajar and I could hear Andreas and Annabel speaking in low voices. "Mum, she's been a horror ever since she became pregnant," Andreas was saying.

Annabel clearly didn't think much of his opinion on the subject. "You have a lot to learn about pregnant women," she said. I could hear the faint smile in her voice. "They can be moody and they're almost certainly uncomfortable, so if they indulge in a little complaining, that's their prerogative."

"Were you like that when you were pregnant?" Andreas asked.

"I'd like to say I was pleasant and charming as ever, but I suppose your father might have had a different opinion."

Silence. The mention of Andreas's father had stalled the conversation. I knocked on the door as I pushed it open slowly and entered the room.

"Ah, here's Eilidh," Annabel said with a smile. "Andreas, I don't know what I would do without her."

I waved her words away with my hand. Her praise was flattering, but it always made me feel more essential than I really was. And Andreas apparently agreed. "You'd be just fine, Mum," he said. Did he say that because he was stroking her ego, as I frequently did, or did he say it because he really felt my presence in the castle was unnecessary? I couldn't be sure. I hoped it was the former.

Annabel reached her hand toward me and I walked forward to take it in mine. I didn't care what Andreas thought. As long as Annabel felt she needed me, I would stay with her.

Just then Brenda knocked on the door and came into the sitting room. "Yes, Brenda?" Annabel asked.

"Sian is asking for Andreas."

Andreas sighed and turned to his mother. "I'll go see what she wants. I'll come find you later after I unpack."

"Be good to her, dear. That's my grandchild she's carrying," Annabel said with a wink.

He followed Brenda out of the room. I could hear them talking, but their voices receded as they went down the hallway.

"What would you like me to do now?" I asked Annabel.

"I think I'd like some tea," she said. "Would you mind asking Maisie to bring some up for me?"

I left her alone in the sitting room while I went downstairs to the kitchen in search of Maisie. I found her wrestling with a large roast, trying to baste it without letting it slip around in the roasting pan.

"Maisie, let me help you with that," I said, hurrying over to the oven and grabbing oven mitts from the counter nearby.

"Thank you, Eilidh," she said with a grunt, sticking out her bottom lip and trying to blow hair out of her eyes.

I held the pan while she used a fancy-looking implement to scoop up the basting liquid. It was a deep, rich-looking brown broth.

"It smells wonderful," I said, breathing deeply and enjoying the scent of the beef and roasting vegetables.

"Annabel asked for the roast because her sons are the meat-and-potatoes type," she said, straightening up next to the oven. She reached around to rub the small of her back. "This gets harder every year," she said.

"What does?" I asked.

"Making the big, fancy meals. It's hard on my back."

"Do you want me to get you some aspirin?"

"No, thank you. I sent Brenda for some." She turned to look out the kitchen door, then spoke almost to herself. "Now where has she gotten to?"

"I saw her a few minutes ago. Sian was looking for Andreas, so Brenda came to the sitting room to get him."

Maisie gave me a look of disgust. "That girl of mine. Always hanging around Andreas whenever she gets the chance."

I smiled. I could see how a man with Andreas's good looks could be hard for a teenage girl to ignore. Or a grown woman, for that matter.

"Oh! I almost forgot why I came down," I said. "Annabel would like some tea. She sent me down to tell you, but why don't I take it up? You rest your back."

"Would you mind? It would be so nice if you could take the tea things upstairs for me. Or I could have Brenda do it, if she ever shows up again."

"I don't mind at all." I knew where the tea set was located, and Maisie put on the kettle to heat while I readied the tray to take it upstairs to Annabel. She always liked me to join her for tea, so I put out cups for two. The kettle was making the wheezing noise that came right before boiling, so Maisie hurried to pour the water into a silver pitcher to take upstairs. She had just set the kettle back on the stove when Brenda burst through the kitchen doorway, her eyes red-rimmed and teary.

She stopped short, then turned away hurriedly when she saw me, but Maisie wasn't about to let her go anywhere.

"Brenda, where have you been? I need help in here." She paused and got a good look at Brenda's face. "What's the matter now? Don't tell me you're crying over Andreas."

"It's none o' yer business," Brenda said, sniffing. She wiped her nose on the sleeve of her shirt. Maisie shook her head as I picked up the tea tray. I didn't want to be present when Maisie talked to her young daughter about older men. Older *married* men.

I returned to the sitting room, where Annabel was standing by the window overlooking the grounds behind the castle. The hilly fields, yellow-green at this time of year, stretched to the horizon, broken here and there by large stands of trees and a long stone wall that had been there for centuries. It had served to protect long-ago generations of the Tucker family, their castle, and the village from unwelcome English invaders at one time, but now it served merely to break up the property into different fields, most of which were used for horse riding. Annabel's late second husband, Brian, had been a gentleman farmer, as Annabel had explained to me, but those fields had lain fallow since his death.

She turned around and smiled at me when I set the tray down on a small table next to her armchair. "Thank you, Eilidh. I thought Maisie was going to do that."

"Maisie's back hurts, so I didn't want her carrying the tray up the stairs."

Annabel changed the subject. "I think it went well with Andreas and Sian, didn't you?"

"Mm-hmm," I answered noncommittally. I didn't really know how everything went with Andreas because I had left to take Sian to her room, but what I had heard sounded like Andreas was fed up with his wife. Annabel didn't know I had heard that part of the conversation. And as for Sian, she hadn't stayed in the sitting room long enough with Annabel to do anything but exchange courtesies. I thought Annabel was grasping for good omens.

"Poor Sian doesn't feel well," Annabel said, as if reading my thoughts. "I don't think my son is entirely sympathetic to her condition."

"Never having been pregnant, I guess I don't really understand it myself," I answered. "But my cousin Greer had a baby and she told me what it was like."

Annabel smiled at Greer's name. "I'll never forget how happy Margot was when her granddaughter was born. How is Ellie?"

"She's doing very well. Loves having James as her new dad, loves school, loves art."

"That's wonderful to hear."

* * * *

There was a knock on the sitting room door and Brenda stuck her head in. "Hugh and Cadi are here, Miss Annabel."

"Oh! I didn't expect them so early," Annabel fretted. As she set her teacup down on the table tea sloshed over the side. "Please show them in, Brenda."

She busied herself mopping up the tea with a napkin from the tray, but I took her hands gently and eased her into her armchair. "Annabel, I'll clean this up. You need to sit down and take a few deep breaths. You're shaking." I had never seen her like that.

She ran her hand across her brow and slumped back into her chair. "Thank you, Eilidh. I'm so nervous. It's been a long time since I saw Hugh and Cadi and I guess I'm a little overwhelmed."

"That's understandable. You'll settle down once you take a few deep breaths. In through your nose, out through your mouth. That'll slow your heart rate." She closed her eyes and did as I suggested. I could see her shoulders fall, as if she was already beginning to relax a bit. But then there was a quick knock on the door and she sat up in her chair, straight-backed and at attention.

Brenda pushed the door open without waiting for Annabel to say anything and stood aside to let Hugh and his wife, Cadi, enter the sitting room. In the two years I had worked for Annabel I had heard stories about Hugh and Cadi, but I hadn't met them yet. And from what I'd heard, I wasn't sure I wanted to meet them.

Chapter 2

Hugh looked nothing like Andreas. He was on the short side of medium height, with a thick middle and graying curly hair cropped close to his head. He stepped into the room and glanced around quickly, his eyes taking in every detail, then fixed his focus on his mother.

Annabel rose from her chair and walked toward him, her hands outstretched. He took her hands in his and kissed her lightly on both cheeks. I caught the briefest glimpse of hurt in Annabel's eyes when she glanced at me—I think she had hoped her son would embrace her and the years of physical and emotional distance would fall away.

Hugh disengaged himself from his mother's hands and looked behind him toward Cadi, who had been standing in the doorway watching her mother-in-law and her husband.

Cadi was, in all physical respects, the opposite of Sian. She was petite with elfin features and pixie-cut blonde hair. She teetered on high heels and wore a handsome powder blue wool coat with a wide collar and a matching plaid scarf.

"Cadi, come say hi to Mum," Hugh said. Cadi stepped forward lightly and kissed Annabel on each cheek, following her husband's lead.

"It's good to see you both," Annabel said, her voice a tiny bit shaky. "Please, come sit over here and have some tea." She looked at me and I understood the look in her eyes. It clearly said, *please help me.*

I stepped forward and extended my hand, first to Hugh and then to Cadi, introducing myself as Annabel's assistant. Annabel's eyes held a look of relief. "Yes, I'm sorry. I should have introduced you," she said, looking at me. Then she turned to Hugh and Cadi. "Eilidh is a huge help around here and if you need anything while you're here, she's the one to ask. She knows everything about what's been planned for your holiday."

Hugh and Cadi nodded at me with slight smiles, their faces unreadable masks. For a moment no one spoke. Then I broke the silence, saying, "Let me run downstairs and get more teacups and biscuits. I'll be right back." I know Annabel hated for me to leave her alone in the room with her son and his wife, but I thought Hugh and Cadi might be more likely to let down their guards and talk freely to Annabel if I weren't in the room.

I excused myself and went downstairs where I found Maisie leaning heavily against one of the wooden counters in the kitchen, drinking from a steaming cup.

"I thought you were going to sit down and take a break," I scolded her with a smile.

"I will. I just need to get a couple more things done for dinner and then it's just a matter of letting everything cook for a while. I'll rest then."

"I came down for more teacups and biscuits," I told her. "Hugh and Cadi are upstairs."

"I know," she said, pushing herself away from the counter. "Brenda came to tell me. How's it all going up there?"

"Okay, I suppose. It's a bit awkward."

"They haven't seen each other in a long time," Maisie said, shaking her head. "I imagine none of them knows what to say to each other."

"That's why I left to come down here, and it's why I should probably get back up there," I said. I took two teacups from the orderly cupboard where Maisie kept them and grabbed a plate of biscuits Maisie had prepared while we talked. "Thanks."

When I got back to the sitting room Annabel was pouring tea into her own cup and Hugh and Cadi were at the window where Annabel had been standing just moments earlier. He was talking in a low voice and pointing to something in the distance. Annabel took a deep breath when she saw me. Her relief was almost palpable.

"Here are teacups and more biscuits," I said brightly. "Cadi, Hugh, please come help yourselves."

Hugh and Cadi left their posts at the window and each of them reached for a cup and saucer. Hugh helped himself to several biscuits and poured a hefty amount of sugar into his cup. Cadi took just one biscuit and a cup of tea, which she drank black.

Annabel settled back into her armchair, seeming to relax a bit. She asked the couple questions about their trip from London and about their jobs. Hugh worked as an accountant and Cadi was a speech pathologist. She didn't seem to notice Annabel's glare when she mentioned that with her recent raise, she now made just a tad more than Hugh. Both Cadi and

Hugh perked up when they were talking about themselves, and I noticed they didn't ask Annabel how she spent her days.

When they had finished talking, silence settled over the room again. I set down my teacup and offered to take them to their room. Brenda had apparently taken their luggage because they had none with them. They both took leave of Annabel with a nod, then followed me down the hallway.

I walked them past the room where Andreas and Sian were, then at the next door I opened it and stood aside while they entered in front of me.

"It's cold in here," Cadi said, hugging herself and shivering dramatically.

"I'll ask Brenda to come in and set a fire for you," I offered.

"I'll do it," Hugh said. "I know what I'm doing."

"Can't we open the drapes?" Cadi asked. "It's awfully dark in here."

I walked over to the first window and pulled a long cord that hung down next to the drapes. I swept them open to reveal a beautiful view of the fields and the stone stables where Annabel kept her favorite horses. Then I did the same at the other window and turned to Cadi. "Is that better?" I asked.

"Much," she said. "Thank you."

I turned to leave the room and Hugh stopped me. "How long have you worked for Annabel?" he asked.

It always annoyed me when people referred to their parents by their first names. "Just over two years," I said with an icy edge to my voice.

"Oh." He turned back to the fireplace where he had been crumpling paper. I assumed he was done asking questions so I left, closing the door quietly behind me.

I returned to Annabel, who was standing at the window in the sitting room again, this time with a cup of tea. She smiled at me when I came in. I knew she kept a flask of whisky in a desk drawer, and I suspected she had added a tipple to her hot drink. Her eyelids were a bit lower than they had been when I left the room, and she seemed more relaxed. I raised my eyebrows at her. "How's your tea?" I asked pointedly

She giggled. "Better now," she said. "That Cadi is insufferable."

"She wasn't so bad," I said. "She just likes to talk about herself."

"It was the *way* she talked about herself," Annabel said. "And I'm just sure she was ticking off my shortcomings in her mind while she prattled on about her job."

I smiled at my boss. "This will all be over in less than a week. Don't forget that."

"I won't, believe me." She raised her teacup to me in a mock salute. I smiled, thinking she must have used a fairly heavy hand when she poured the whisky. "Has Maisie said when dinner will be?" she asked.

"I'll run down and ask her," I said.

I left the room, hoping Annabel would leave the rest of the whisky alone, and ran lightly down the stairs to the kitchen below. It was empty.

"Maisie?" I called.

"In here!" came the muffled response. "I'll just be a minute!"

I waited in the kitchen, closing my eyes and smelling the air, which was scented with beef, roasted vegetables, cinnamon, and apples.

Maisie came in a moment later, pushing hair back from her forehead. "Sorry, Eilidh. What do you need?" Her eyes held a worried look.

"Is everything all right?" I asked.

"Ach-y-fi. Eighteen-year-old girls are not easy to deal with," she said. I didn't pry. There was obviously something going on with Brenda and it was really none of my business.

"I remember being a teenager," I said. "As hard as it is for the parents, I think it's even harder for the girl."

"You're probably right about that," Maisie said. "You were one more recently than I. I can hardly remember."

"She'll be fine," I assured my friend. "You've done a good job with her."

"Thanks, but sometimes I wonder…"

Dinner was to be served in an hour. I went upstairs to report to Annabel and to suggest that she rest before the evening meal. When she went to her room, I went outdoors for some air. I felt sorry for Brenda. It was indeed difficult being a teenage girl, and I suspected she was sweet on Andreas, the handsome man forbidden to her.

It was brisk outside, and I walked quickly to stay warm and to clear my mind. I started down the long drive in front of the castle, content to be outdoors and alone with my thoughts. Fields stretched into the distance on both sides of the drive, and I gazed at their endless undulations, fading with the coming of winter. There was a soothing rhythm to the seasons here at the castle in Wales, just as there had been in the Highlands of Scotland. Autumn brought a slowing down, a dormancy of both people and growing, living things.

The sound of a motor from an approaching car startled me away from my thoughts. I instinctively stepped closer to the side of the drive to let the newcomer pass. A small blue car sidled up to me in the drive.

"Eilidh?" came the voice from the car.

I bent down slightly to peer into the driver's side. It was Rhisiart. "Rhisiart! We didn't expect you so early!"

"Can I give you a ride back to the house? Hop in," he said, reaching over to open the passenger door. I slid into the seat beside him and blew on my hands to warm them. "What are you doing outside without gloves?" he asked. "It's cold out here."

"I was just taking a quick walk before dinner," I explained. "I didn't realize it was this cold out."

He turned the heat up in the car, though we would be at the house in a couple minutes. "So how's everything at the house? How's my mother?" he asked. I looked sideways at him, wondering if there was a hidden meaning behind his words. He looked genuinely interested. I decided he was just being curious.

"As you'd expect," I said. "A bit tense, but otherwise fine." I didn't tell him Annabel had felt the need to add whisky to her afternoon tea.

Rhisiart hadn't been to visit his mother since the first month I was living at the castle, working as her assistant. His hair had grown longer and he wore different glasses, but otherwise he looked the same as he had the last time I had seen him—same long aristocratic nose, same dark brown eyes with the same long lashes, same fair skin.

He pulled up to the front of the castle and I got out. Then he drove the car round to the parking enclosure while I went inside to tell Annabel and Brenda of his arrival. Annabel was surprised that he had gotten out of London so early, and Brenda hurried to his assigned room to make sure everything was in order.

"I haven't seen Rhisiart in over a year," Annabel fretted, toying with the silk scarf around her neck.

"Everything will be fine. He seems happy to be here. He asked about you," I said, hoping this would help relax her. But I wasn't sure it worked. She seemed to retreat within herself.

"I made so many mistakes when the boys were children," she said quietly.

"But that is all in the past, and this is your chance to make a fresh start," I said gently. "Isn't that why everyone is here?"

"Yes, but I'm thinking I made another mistake," she said miserably.

"This was the right thing to do. It's not a mistake. Now perk up—Rhisiart will be here any minute."

Annabel smiled up at me from where she sat in her chair and reached up to pat my hand, which rested behind her head on the chair. We were silent for a few minutes, then there was a soft knock at the door.

Annabel gave me a quick glance as she stood up to greet her youngest son. He strode into the room, as if he had just been at the castle days earlier, and went to his mother. He held her at arm's length and looked her up and down.

"Mum, you're looking well," he said with a smile, then kissed her on both cheeks as Cadi had done.

"It's lovely to see you, my dear," Annabel said. Her voice was tinged with something—was it hurt?—when she replied to Rhisiart. I think she hoped he would give her the big hug she so longed for. But he clearly wasn't ready.

"Where are all the others?" he asked.

"In their rooms. Brenda will show you to your room—I gave you your favorite—and we'll all gather in the dining room for dinner."

Brenda must have been lingering outside the door waiting for her cue, because she appeared almost immediately and offered to take Rhisiart to his room. He smiled at her and declined. "I know the way," he said curtly. He lifted the leather satchel he had brought inside with him and left the room without a backward glance for his mother.

She turned to me after we had listened to his footsteps receding down the hallway opposite the one where Hugh, Cadi, Andreas, and Sian were staying. "The room where he's staying used to be the boys' playroom. He would spend hours in there as a child. He would rather be in there than on the horses or outdoors or playing with his mates from school. His favorite activity was to read. I suppose that's where he found his passion for writing, too." Rhisiart was a writer of thriller novels and he had found great success with his published works.

"Is he working on anything new?" I asked.

"I don't know. We'll have to ask him at dinner," she answered. "I email him every so often, but I haven't talked to him in a while."

I found it sad that she didn't have contact with her sons on a regular basis. I was on the phone with my mother at least once a week, and with both Greer and Sylvie, too. They had kept me from losing my mind when Callum and I divorced after the dreadful mistakes he made that landed him in prison, and I couldn't go more than a few days without talking to them. I tried to imagine how I would feel if I only communicated with them by email. But then, I had a different relationship with my family than Annabel did with hers.

Annabel went up to her room to change into her new dinner dress and came back down just a few minutes later. She looked lovely as usual, but her eyes betrayed her worry and insecurity.

Maisie rang a bell that indicated dinner would be served in five minutes. Annabel and I stood up to be the first ones in the dining room. I knew Annabel wanted to be in her seat when everyone came in for dinner. I hadn't wanted to join the family for their first meal together because it seemed somehow intrusive, but Annabel had insisted that I be there for her. She needed the moral support, she said.

The dining room was cream and gold with gilt furnishings and a long cherry table. Striped drapes matched the rest of the room and held some of the gloom from outdoors at bay, with the help of a magnificent crystal chandelier centered over the table and several lamps placed discreetly around the large room. The chairs were upholstered in the same fabric as the drapes and it gave the room an elegant, cultured look.

I stood behind my chair while Annabel took her seat at the head of the table. I was surprised to feel a bit nervous as we waited for Annabel's sons and the others to join us. There was an empty glass by my plate and I took it over to the sideboard where there was a heavy crystal decanter full of red wine. I poured myself a generous measure of it and took a long sip. Annabel watched me and giggled. "You're nervous, too, aren't you?" she asked in a low voice.

"I guess I am. I didn't think I was," I said. "Hopefully the wine will help with that." I smiled at her, then went to sit down.

Hugh and Cadi were the first ones to come in. Cadi preceded Hugh through the double doors. She was wearing a cabled gray sweater dress and sported another colorful silk scarf around her neck.

"Have you had a chance to get settled in?" Annabel asked, as Brenda showed Hugh and his wife to their chairs.

"Yes, although Hugh forgot our toiletry kit," Cadi answered with a withering glance at her husband.

"Not this again, Cadi," he replied with a scowl. "I told you I'd go out after dinner and find a shop that sells whatever you need."

"Humph," she said. "I've already made up my list."

He rolled his eyes and pulled out his chair, then sat while Cadi stood next to her chair, obviously waiting for him to pull her chair out for her. After a long moment it became clear he wasn't going to do it, so she pulled out her own chair and sat down with a heavy sigh.

Hugh had just opened his mouth to say something else when Andreas and Sian came into the room. Sian waddled a bit, but she looked more rested than she had earlier. "Sit here next to me," Annabel instructed Andreas. He pulled out Sian's chair for her and sat down between his wife and his mother. Hugh gave his brother a long look.

"How have you been, Hugh?" Andreas asked, turning his attention to the others at the table.

"Fine," Hugh answered in a clipped tone.

"And you, Cadi?"

She shrugged. "All right."

Andreas waited a beat before speaking to his brother again. "Sian and I are fine, too. Thanks for asking."

Hugh looked up from the napkin he was tracing with his finger and sneered at Andreas. It was quickly becoming clear that this meal might not be terribly pleasant.

Sian smiled brightly at Annabel then looked around the room. "Everything looks lovely, Annabel," she said.

"Thank you, dear," Annabel answered.

There were three quick taps on one of the open doors and Rhisiart came in. Andreas stood up and walked over to where his younger brother stood in the doorway and shook his hand, then Hugh rose and shook hands with Rhisiart, though he wore a stiff, almost pained, expression.

Rhisiart came over to the table where all the women were still seated, and he bent down to kiss Sian, then Cadi, on the cheek. "What lovely ladies you are! Sian, you're simply glowing!" She blushed in response.

Rhisiart seated himself on Annabel's other side, opposite Andreas, and opened his napkin. "I'm sure you have something wonderful planned for dinner, Mum," he said.

As if on cue, Maisie appeared with Brenda at her side. Each woman carried a large tray. On Maisie's tray was the roast of beef with all the vegetables. On Brenda's tray were assorted serving vessels, one with gravy, one with green salad, one with dressing for the salad, and one a basket of delicious-looking rolls.

"Can I help you two with those?" I asked, rising and beginning to push my chair back.

"No, no. Have a seat," Maisie insisted. Brenda placed her tray on the sideboard and set each item on the table. Maisie put the large platter with the meat and vegetables in the center, smiling as Annabel's sons looked on with expressions of "ooh" and "looks delicious."

And then it happened. Brenda was placing the gravy next to Sian when her hand slipped and the gravy spilled over the table and into Sian's lap. Sian let out a cry and Brenda stepped back in surprise, her hand over her mouth and a look of horror in her eyes.

"Are you all right?" Andreas asked Sian, standing up and pulling Sian's chair out. Annabel hurried over to where Sian was standing up before grabbing a napkin from the table and wiping Sian's sleeve where the gravy had spilled.

Maisie had looked up from arranging the platter in the middle of the table and was giving Brenda a look of fury. "What's the matter with you, Brenda?" she cried.

"Are you burned?" Annabel asked anxiously.

Sian was angry. "No, but just look at this sweater! That gravy will ruin it," she said, glaring at Brenda.

"I'm so sorry. I didn't mean it. Honest, I didn't," Brenda sputtered. She backed away from the table, then turned and fled from the room.

"I'm sorry, ma'am," Maisie said. She held her hands out toward Annabel in a pleading gesture, as if begging forgiveness for her daughter. "I just don't know what's gotten into Brenda lately. She's not been herself."

"We can talk about this later," Annabel said to her. "For now, let's worry about getting the gravy off Sian and off the table and the floor."

Maisie bustled out of the room and was back in just a few minutes with rags and a bucket of soapy water. In the meantime, Sian left to change her clothes and get cleaned up.

We all settled back into our chairs and waited for Maisie to finish cleaning Brenda's mess. When she had left to return to the kitchen, we all sat in silence for a few moments. Then Annabel spoke. "Brenda has been a bit off lately. She hasn't seemed herself."

Only I was able to corroborate that statement, since the rest of the diners hadn't been in the castle for a long time, and it was true. Privately, I was a bit worried about Brenda. She had been clumsy and irritable lately. She had always seemed like a nice girl, but I had to admit to myself that she had a secretive side I didn't know much about.

Conversation turned away from the household employees and to the weather, local happenings, and old acquaintances. Annabel was happy to be able to share news of the boys' old friends and their families. In many cases, the friends had moved to other parts of the United Kingdom or even farther afield, but the families remained in the village, as so often happened in old Welsh communities.

When Sian returned to the table, she looked flushed. "Is everything all right, Sian?" Annabel asked, concern in her eyes.

"I'm fine, thank you," Sian answered with a thin smile. As she sat down she glanced at Andreas, who held her eyes for a moment. I don't know who else noticed—probably no one. But the look they shared piqued my curiosity. What was going on? It had to have something to do with Brenda, I was sure of it. Perhaps Sian was jealous of the feelings the girl obviously held for her husband.

Annabel tried to keep the conversation light for the remainder of the meal. Brenda did not come into the dining room again, though Maisie came in several times to clear dishes away and to serve dessert.

After dinner we all moved to the vast salon across the hall from the dining room. It was warm in there, though, thanks to a fire roaring in the huge fireplace, and we sat facing each other uneasily

The silence had grown a bit too long when Annabel spoke up. "Sian, are you sure you're all right? I'm dreadfully sorry Brenda was so clumsy. I'll have to speak to her tonight or first thing tomorrow."

"I'm really fine," Sian assured her mother-in-law. "The girl is obviously love-struck."

"Sian, please," Andreas said, a warning note in his tone.

"By whom?" Cadi asked.

Sian raised her eyebrows pointedly. "By Andreas, of course. Brenda can barely hide her feelings for him. She acts this way every time we visit."

"Sian sees things that aren't there," Andreas said lightly.

"How long has it been since you were last here at the castle?" Hugh asked her.

Sian looked at Annabel. "What would you say? About four months?"

Annabel nodded. "That sounds about right."

"I remember because the last time we visited I was just getting over my morning sickness," Sian told Hugh.

Cadi looked away, her eyes having glazed over while Sian was talking. It seemed she wasn't interested in the details of Sian's pregnancy.

"Do you have any fruit tea, Annabel?" Cadi asked. "I really prefer it to this chamomile."

"Yes, I think so," Annabel said. "I'll ring Maisie for it." She shifted so the toe of her shoe hovered over a button on the floor. The button was connected to an old bell system that had been in use in the castle for hundreds of years. It was the antique version of an intercom system.

I stopped her before she could depress the button with her foot. "I'll get the tea," I offered. "Maisie's back is bothering her, and I hate to see her going up and down the stairs so often. I'll be back in just a minute."

I left the room without waiting to see if anyone would insist that Maisie bring the tea. Cadi, especially, liked the idea of having a servant to bring whatever she wanted, so I suspected she might try to stop me so Maisie could perform her duties. But maybe Cadi thought I was enough of a servant to suffice in this situation.

Below-stairs I heard the wracking sobs before I saw their source. A pitiful sight met my eyes when I reached the doorway of the kitchen. Neither mother nor daughter had heard my approach, and the sight of Brenda on her knees on the cold stone floor stopped me where I stood.

Chapter 3

She was in full wail when I saw her. Her body was shaking with the force of her cries. It was a wonder she couldn't be heard from the sitting room upstairs. Maisie knelt on the floor next to Brenda, her arm around her daughter's shoulders.

I should have turned around and left quietly, but Cadi would no doubt wonder where the tea was and it clearly wasn't the best time to ask Maisie to bring anything up to the sitting room. I cleared my throat and stepped into the room.

"Maisie? Brenda?" I asked softly. "Is everything all right? Are you hurt, Brenda?" I knew she wasn't, that this had something to do with her earlier mishap in the dining room, but it felt like the right thing to say.

She looked up at me, startled. Her eyes were bloodshot and puffy, and her flushed face was streaked with tears. Maisie looked at me, too, and closed her eyes almost as if she were embarrassed.

I knelt down with them. "Can I do anything for either of you?" I asked. I was concerned that something was seriously wrong with Brenda and I wanted to help. "Can I get you a glass of water, Brenda?"

She shook her head and choked back another sob, then put her hands over her face. I looked at Maisie and she gazed at me with a helpless look, her eyes pleading and her mouth pinched and drawn. Tears shone in the corners of her eyes and I could almost feel the pain she was feeling, though I didn't know the cause of it.

"We're having a rough time of it, Eilidh," she said softly. That much I knew.

"I don't want to intrude or interfere," I said. "I actually just came down for tea for Cadi, but I don't have to go upstairs if you need me down here for anything."

Brenda continued to cry while Maisie shook her head. "Thank you, Eilidh, but this is something Brenda and I have to deal with ourselves."

I pushed myself to my feet and walked softly to the cupboard where the fruity herbal teas were stored. I took what I needed from the cupboard and went to the kitchen door. Before I left the room, I turned to Maisie and Brenda. "Please don't hesitate to ask me for anything you need," I urged them. "I'll be happy to help."

Brenda's crying had slowed since I entered the room, but she didn't look up from the floor. She just gave a slight nod. Maisie looked up at me again and mouthed the words "thank you." I returned to the sitting room with a feeling of overwhelming sadness for Brenda. Whether her outburst had something to do with Andreas or with her embarrassment over spilling an entire gravy boat earlier or something else entirely, my heart broke for her.

Back in the salon we talked for a bit about Sian's pregnancy, but Annabel was the only other person in the room who could relate to Sian's experiences. Cadi rolled her eyes and sighed dramatically more than once, and each time Annabel shot her a look of dark disapproval. Cadi didn't seem to care. Andreas looked thoroughly bored, Hugh examined his fingernails with great intensity, and Rhisiart thumbed through a novel that had been sitting on the coffee table. Even Annabel's questions to Sian seemed forced, as if she were reading from a script. I got the feeling she would rather have been spending time alone with her sons and I couldn't blame her—they were really the ones she wanted most to see. Not that I didn't enjoy talking about nesting, cravings, and baby names, but I barely knew Sian and found that her pregnancy details were really more information than I needed or wanted.

After a half hour Sian announced that she was ready for bed. Cadi quickly agreed, saying that the "extraordinarily long day" had left her "practically lifeless." I was glad to see her leave and I know Annabel was, too.

When Sian and Cadi had left, Annabel moved to sit closer to Andreas. She patted his knee, finally wearing a smile. She obviously preferred the company of her boys to that of their wives. Andreas was her favorite—she had said as much several times since I'd started working for her—and I knew why. He was the only one who bothered to visit her.

I sometimes wondered what was behind his visits—was it really love for his mother? Was it a sense of familial duty? Was it to curry favoritism? I didn't know, and I suppose it didn't matter. As long as Annabel was happy, that was the important thing, wasn't it?

After chatting about the weather and other mundane topics for several long minutes during which her sons' expressions turned from dutiful attention to glazed boredom, Annabel stood up and walked over to the hearth. I knew what was coming.

She stood up a little straighter and cleared her throat.

"I'm sure you've all figured out why you're here, but we haven't actually said it out loud. I've been waiting for a long time to talk to you boys, but I just haven't been able to bring myself to do it until now. I guess it's really the new grandbaby coming that spurred me to want to do it." Andreas was watching his mother intently. Annabel was twisting a handkerchief she held and laughed nervously. She looked at me and I nodded to encourage her to keep talking. This was obviously very hard for her.

"Well, here goes." She took a deep breath and continued. "I know that things weren't easy while you boys were growing up, and I want to say that I'm sorry." She paused for a moment.

Andreas spoke. "Mum, you don't…"

Annabel shook her head and held up her hand. "Let me finish or else I won't be able to. I'm sorry for the things I didn't do, the things I didn't say, to save you from your own father. I'm sorry that I didn't protect you when you needed protecting and that I didn't stand up for you. I was young and not very bright, and I thought the brutality would stop by itself. But it didn't, and you boys paid as high a price as I did."

She stopped speaking, and the room fell silent.

"Thank you, Mum," Rhisiart mumbled, looking down at his hands. His brothers nodded their agreement.

I shifted uncomfortably in my chair. Now that Annabel had gotten through this conversation, the hardest part of the boys' visit, she didn't need my support any longer. This was a subject they needed to discuss as a family, and I was an outsider. After a long moment I stood up. "If you'll all excuse me, I think I'll go to bed." Amid a murmured chorus of "goodnight," I closed the door to the salon quietly and walked quickly toward my room on the opposite wing of the castle. I paused when I reached the steps leading down to the kitchen, wondering if I should go down to see if everything was all right, but I decided I was an outsider in the drama playing out between Maisie and Brenda, too, and that what I needed most was a good night's sleep.

My room was cold when I went inside. I built a fire in the fireplace and sat in front of it for a while, reading a book I had taken from the library on the second floor of the castle. It was one of Rhisiart's books. The name "Rhisiart Tucker" was prominent above the title on the cover. It featured a man running down a darkened rainy street with the lights of the Eiffel Tower twinkling in the background. Though thrillers weren't my favorite books to read, I found that Rhisiart's writing drew me into the story unfolding in the Fourth Arrondissement and I was enjoying the fast-paced tale.

When I started yawning I closed the book and crawled under the covers of the big bed. Though the fire had made me toasty and comfortable while I sat reading, my sheets were still shockingly cold when I touched them. The first few minutes in bed I shivered and hugged my knees to my chest until I finally felt warmth seeping through my bones and could stretch out. Annabel would be happy, I knew, to have the short speech to her sons out of the way. I didn't know how the three men felt about it, but at least it hadn't been greeted with anger and blame, which I knew she had feared. Knowing she would go to bed relieved tonight was a relief to me, too.

The only little prick of worry I had as I drifted off to sleep was Brenda— both the incident in the dining room and the resulting episode I had witnessed in the kitchen. My heart went out to the young girl, and I knew her mother was worried about her, too.

When a loud bang startled me out of a deep sleep in the middle of the night, I sat up straight in bed and cocked my head, listening for other noises. I didn't hear anything. I probably dreamed it, I thought.

I snuggled down under the covers again and was soon dozing, but through the fog in my sleep-addled brain I was sure I heard faint crying. I sat up again. The room was deliciously warm from the fire that still burned low in the grate, but I still hated to get out from under the comfort of the blankets. Reluctantly I tucked my feet into the slippers I kept at the side of the bed and went to the door. After opening it cautiously, I peered into the long hallway. The gas-lit sconces provided quivering candlelight at regular intervals, making the spaces between them eerily dark.

Even in the dim light, though, there was no mistaking the shadow that flitted across the hall down toward the main door to the castle. I hesitated, not knowing who the shadow belonged to or whether I should try to figure it out. The crying continued, now a little louder because my door was open. My mind told me to shut the door, get back into bed, and ignore the nighttime goings-on. My heart told me to find out who was crying and whose shadow I had seen from the safety of my bedroom doorway.

I followed my heart, as usual.

It was very cold in the hallway, so I ducked back into my room for my thick robe. Then, pulling the sash tight around my waist, I slipped into the hallway and closed the bedroom door behind me.

I instinctively stayed close to the wall as I followed the flickering sconces to the castle's great hall. In daylight, this entrance to the home was a magnificent gallery of antique furniture, a polished stone floor, stained glass windows, an enormous, colorfully-painted wooden coat of arms, and even an ancient suit of armor, posed with a lance. In the dim light of night, however, the main hall was a frightening place. The furniture gave way to dark, shapeless forms, the suit of armor took on a more sinister stance, and the stained glass, which depicted pastoral scenes in daylight, seemed to glow with an evil darkness.

When I reached the huge front door, the iron bolt that kept the door locked from the inside had been slid to one side. Someone had left the castle. That must have been the bang I heard. The person I had seen stealing along the corridor was nowhere to be found. Maybe the bang was a person coming in, not going out. Perhaps the person I had seen had just come in from outdoors. I hadn't heard anyone as I made my way to the great hall, and I didn't see or hear anyone now that I was standing by the front door.

I was perplexed. I hadn't dreamed it. There had been a person in the hallway and I had come quickly to the main entrance to the castle. How could I have missed him—or her? But I had gone back into my room to pull on my robe. Had the person disappeared in such a short time? Had he or she gone upstairs? Downstairs? Had the person perhaps ducked into one of the rooms on the main floor and was waiting, listening, until I left to return to my bedroom? The thought sent chills up to the nape of my neck.

Was I just being silly? Maybe Hugh had gone out for Cadi's toiletries, though it was quite late for that. Maybe someone had gone down to the kitchen to get a snack. That was a far more likely explanation. There were a million reasons someone in the castle might be about during the night, *so stop making up sinister reasons,* I told myself with a grimace.

But that didn't explain the crying I had heard so plainly. Was the person in the hallway the one who had been crying? And what had he—or more likely, she—been crying about? I didn't know Andreas or Hugh or Rhisiart very well, but none of them seemed to be the emotional type.

I was spooking myself and it was getting very cold standing still in the great hall, so I turned on the lights and peeked into the sitting room and the dining room. I didn't see anyone in either room so I hurried back to the safety and warmth of my own room and my own bed.

It was still dark out when I awoke, but my room faced the east and I could see a tinge of pink in the sky in the distance. I showered and dressed quickly so I could greet everyone as they filed into the dining room for breakfast. Annabel was an early riser, so I liked to be available when she woke up just in case she needed me for something. I sat down at the dining room table by myself. The newspaper was already there, so I read that until I heard the stirrings of guests. Maisie and Brenda came in and out of the dining room several times to leave chafing dishes, a teapot, and a small samovar of coffee. I helped myself to a cup of tea, then another, while I waited for Annabel to join me. As I expected, she came into the dining room before any of her sons or their wives.

"How'd everything go after I went to bed last night?" I asked as she sat down next to me.

She thought for a moment before answering. "I think it went quite well. I asked them to forgive me for not helping them when I was the only one who could, and they told me they forgive me for my mistakes. I hope that Sian and Cadi can forgive me if their husbands can."

"You couldn't have hoped for a better outcome," I said, taking a sip of tea.

Annabel sighed. "If I had never gotten myself into that mess, nothing bad would have happened to the boys."

"But as you said, you were young. You got yourself into a situation that you weren't prepared to handle. You did the best you could."

"But did I, really? Or was I just as afraid as they were?" She shook her head. "I don't like to think too deeply about it or I might not like the truth I discover."

"Annabel, what's done is done. You can't change it now, so it's best to move forward. And that's exactly what you're doing now. You may not have been able to help the boys in the past, but you're doing the right thing now. And they seem to have forgiven you for it. They love you. You know that."

"Sometimes I wonder. It's too bad we can't go back and change the things we did wrong, isn't it?"

My mind went back to Cauld Loch when I heard her words. I thought of my marriage to Callum, his mistakes, and our divorce. Would I have changed anything? I didn't think so—at least, I wouldn't have changed anything about myself or my actions. I would have changed Callum's actions, that was sure, but I didn't have that power. What I had said to Annabel applied to me, too—the past was in the past, and all I could do was to move forward. Which is exactly what I was doing.

Just then Cadi came in. Her eyes were bright and they darted around the room when she saw Annabel and me.

"Good morning, Cadi," Annabel said. "I hope you slept well last night."

"I did. Thank you. I expected the room to be cold, but we lit a fire in the fireplace and it was nice and warm. Almost too warm, really."

"Speaking of warm, I think I need a sweater," Annabel said, standing up.

Cadi helped herself to a cup of tea then came and sat down next to me.

"What did you think about what happened last night?" she asked. I was startled for a moment, thinking she meant the sounds I had heard in the hallway, but I realized she was probably talking about Annabel's apology to her sons. Hugh must have discussed it with her.

"You mean Annabel's apology?" I asked. "I know how nervous she was to talk to everyone about it, and I know she was afraid the boys wouldn't accept her apology or allow her or themselves to move on from it, so I think it went quite well."

Cadi waved her hand. "Oh, that. Yes, I suppose that went fine. God knows Hugh has been waiting for an apology for years. I meant what happened afterward."

I shook my head warily, not wanting her to know I had heard the crying and the banging. "I don't know what you're talking about. What happened?"

Her eyes widened. "Didn't you hear the fight?"

"No. What fight?"

"Between Andreas and Sian."

"I must have missed it."

"I don't know how you could have missed it," Cadi said, taking a long swig of her tea. "They were loud enough to wake the dead."

"Where?"

"In their bedroom. It was after midnight when Hugh came to bed. Andreas and Sian and Hugh and I are on the same wing. He had just gotten into bed when we heard shouting." She paused, probably for dramatic effect. "Hugh has these earplugs he uses at night because he doesn't sleep well. So he put the earplugs in and fell asleep after about fifteen minutes. The fight kept raging and I swear I heard Sian crying. Then about an hour later one of them left. I'm surprised you didn't hear the front door slam."

"I had no idea," I lied.

"That's shocking," Cadi said, tossing her short hair. "Whoever slammed the door needs to be much quieter. It even woke Hugh up, despite his earplugs."

It was against my better judgment to ask what the fight was about, but I had a feeling Cadi would volunteer the information if I waited long enough.

"Hopefully the fight was just a short-lived one and they'll be fine this morning," I said.

"Don't count on it," Cadi answered. "Fights like that one tend to repeat themselves over and over, if you know what I mean."

I stared at her blankly. I really didn't know what she meant, but I knew my response would nudge her to reveal the cause of the fight.

"Money," she said, speaking as if I were simple.

"Money?" I repeated. I had been under the impression money was not an issue for Andreas and Sian.

"That's right," Cadi answered smugly. "You'd think a couple with everything wouldn't fight about money, but they were furious."

"How could you tell?"

"I heard them throwing around words like 'mortgage' and 'credit cards' and 'bills.' When you think about it, those are the financial things couples fight about. They're no different from the rest of us, I guess." She sounded almost gleeful.

Cadi had a point—Andreas and Sian *did* seem to have everything. They drove an expensive car, they wore designer, albeit casual, clothes, Sian carried a very expensive handbag, they had a posh address in London, and I had seen pictures of the baby's nursery—it was breathtaking and definitely the room of a privileged child. Why should they be fighting about money?

Annabel came back into the dining room wrapped in a warm sweater. "This is much better," she said. "Both of you girls help yourselves to breakfast. I'll wait for the others."

I went to the sideboard and prepared a plate of eggs, beans, and mushrooms. I had a feeling I would need some fortification to get through the day, so I took more food than usual. I sat at the dining room table while Annabel read the paper and Cadi simply sat looking out the window, sipping her tea now and then. Surely it had gotten cold.

Hugh came in next, followed quickly by Rhisiart. Each of them greeted Annabel with a peck on the cheek and Hugh sat down next to his wife. "Where are Andreas and Sian?" he asked.

"Not here yet," she replied tersely.

"Did you say something about their fight last night?" Hugh asked her.

"Not yet," she said, her gaze darting toward Annabel. Annabel looked over the top of the paper.

"What? Did Andreas and Sian have a fight last night? Oh, dear."

"I'm sure it's nothing, Mum," Hugh said, walking over to the sideboard to load a plate with potatoes, eggs, sausage, and mushrooms. He plunked the plate down on the table and helped himself to a cup of tea with a shocking amount of sugar. Cadi watched him and grimaced.

"Well, I don't like to think that they're unhappy about something, especially with the baby coming," Annabel fretted.

"Mum," Hugh said with a sigh. "Every couple fights. It's normal. Now eat breakfast and stop worrying, for pity's sake."

"I'll wait for them," his mother answered. "I want to make sure everything is all right. You are all scheduled to go hiking this afternoon, right, Eilidh?"

she asked, turning to me. "I want everyone to enjoy the day." Hugh shook his head and started eating. Cadi asked Annabel for a section of the newspaper and leafed through it, scanning the headlines while Hugh and I ate breakfast.

I had just finished my last sip of tea and was pushing by my chair back to go get another cup when Sian came into the room. Her eyebrows were knit together and her face looked stormy.

"Has anyone seen Andreas?" she asked.

We all looked at each other and shook our heads. "Where is he?" Cadi asked.

"If I knew that I wouldn't have asked," Sian answered with a sneer.

"I haven't seen him yet this morning," Annabel said, ignoring the glares that passed between her daughters-in-law. "Why don't you sit down and have some breakfast? You look a little peaked."

Sian gave Annabel a look of frustration, but she did as her mother-in-law suggested. She didn't eat much, though, opting for just a piece of bread and a cup of herbal tea.

"Sian, are you sure you're eating enough?" Annabel fretted. "I don't want to meddle, but I want to make sure you're getting plenty to eat. I want to make sure that grandbaby of mine is growing. Should I ask Maisie to prepare something else?"

"No, no," Sian hastened to assure Annabel. "I'm fine. Just not very hungry, I guess. I'll eat more later, I promise."

"Anything wrong, Sian?" Cadi asked, her voice all innocence.

Sian cocked her head and stared at Cadi through narrowed eyes. "As if you have no idea what's going on."

"I don't know what you're talking about," Cadi said, a slight smile touching her lips.

Sian rolled her eyes. "Cadi, you're positively flushed with excitement over what you must have heard last night. Stop pretending."

"Well, you two *were* a little loud. And I don't know who left through the front door and slammed it, but that shook the building to its very rafters."

"It could have been Andreas. I don't know," Sian answered.

"I'm sure it was Andreas," Cadi said.

"Cadi, let it go. It's none of our business," Hugh admonished her, then continued, ignoring his own advice. "Sian, what's Andreas up to that's causing money problems?"

"Our financial matters are none of your business, Hugh," Sian said.

"You made them our business when you shouted them at the tops of your lungs last night," Cadi said.

Sian stood up and threw her napkin down on the table. "Annabel, I'm afraid I've lost my appetite. I'm going for a walk." She turned on her heel and stalked out of the room as best a pregnant woman could do.

Annabel stood up, too. "Oh, no. Now what'll we do? Andreas must be around here somewhere. He should really be the one to talk to Sian. I don't know what's going on between the two of them. I'm sure Sian doesn't want to talk to me about their problems."

"I'll ask Maisie to make up a plate for Sian to eat later," I offered. It gave me an excuse to leave the dining room, where it was becoming increasingly tense. I went downstairs to the relative calm of the kitchen and found Maisie in there.

"Maisie, could you fix a plate so Sian can have her breakfast later? She's not herself this morning and I don't think she feels like eating right now."

"What's the matter?" Maisie asked.

"She and Andreas had an argument last night and I think she's still a bit upset," I said.

"Sure," Maisie said. She wiped her hands on a dish towel hanging next to her and hurried up the stairs. I lingered in the kitchen, wondering how long I could stay down there without Annabel starting to wonder where I had gone. I loved the peace and quiet of below-stairs and wasn't ready to return to the family.

But the peace and quiet didn't last long.

Chapter 4

Maisie came back downstairs after just a few minutes and informed me with a sympathetic smile that Annabel was looking for me.

I found my boss in the sitting room, twisting her scarf in her hands, a familiar gesture when she was upset or anxious about something.

"Maisie told me you're looking for me, Annabel. What's wrong?"

"I'm afraid this argument between Andreas and Sian is serious. Andreas won't answer my texts and I haven't seen him anywhere this morning."

"He may be your son, but don't forget he's a grown man," I told her. "Maybe he just needs some time to himself. I'm sure he'll answer your texts when he's ready."

"Did you hear the door in the great hall slam last night?" she asked me.

I nodded. "It woke me up. Did you hear it?"

"No," she answered, shaking her head sadly. "I'm sure it was him. He must have been terribly angry to leave like that, especially with Sian so close to having the baby. That's not like him."

I wondered how well Annabel actually knew Andreas—he and Sian hadn't exactly been frequent visitors since I had come to the castle. They had only visited four or five times over the months I had lived in Annabel's home and never overnight; to me, their relationship with Annabel had never seemed especially close.

"Would you like me to look for him?" I asked. "This place is huge. Do you think it's possible he's lying low on one of the upper floors, maybe in a storage room or one of the bedrooms that isn't used?"

Annabel pursed her lips. "I doubt it. He's not a child, and that's the sort of thing he and his brothers used to do when they were very young."

"It couldn't hurt to try," I said gently.

"All right," Annabel agreed. "I'm going out to see if Sian's all right."
I went to my bedroom to fetch my mobile phone in case I needed a light.

Mobile phone in hand, I went to the main staircase. At the first landing there was a window overlooking the fields and the drive in front of the castle. I half expected to see Andreas walking toward the house, but the only people I saw were Sian and Annabel. I continued up the stairs to the top floor, where the hallway sconces were burning and the doors, like soldiers at attention, all stood closed to visitors. Once the sound of my footsteps died down, the silence was complete.

It was positively spooky.

I opened the door nearest me, then peered around the edge of the door, shaking my head vigorously as if to shake off any doubt or fear. I reached for the light switch on the wall and a single lamp came to life, giving a meager light to the room. I was in a storage room, so I looked around and under a few large pieces of furniture that were lined up neatly against the walls and I checked in the adjoining dressing room, but there was no one in there but me. I turned off the light and repeated the same actions in every room until I reached the end of the hallway without seeing any sign of Andreas.

I methodically searched the lower floors but after a few hours I was forced to admit that Andreas was not in the castle. It must have been him leaving when I heard the door slam during the night. As I descended the main staircase I looked out the windows and saw Sian and Annabel emerge from the English cottage garden. Of all the gardens surrounding the castle, including a wildflower garden and a Christmas garden, the English cottage garden was Annabel's favorite. She loved to show people the plants she spent so much time tending. She and Sian were both worrying about Andreas, I was sure, so it was a good thing for them to have some time together.

Finally I went downstairs. Hugh, Cadi, and Rhisiart were already finishing lunch in the dining room.

"Annabel tells us you've planned some sort of hike for us this afternoon," Hugh said, pointing at his hiking boots. "We don't need to be entertained, you know."

"I know, but Annabel didn't want you to feel cooped up indoors. She thought this would be fun for you."

"How much is the guide?" Cadi asked.

"Annabel had already paid the guide, including the gratuity. It won't cost you anything," I answered with just a hint of annoyance.

"Good," Cadi muttered.

"The guide should be here soon," I said. "Would you like to wait out front? He'll arrive in a van so you don't have to drive anywhere."

"Good lord, we're not children," Rhisiart said in disgust.

"Annabel knows that," I answered lightly. "She just wants you to have a worry-free holiday."

Rhisiart made a "hmm" sound and shrugged his arms into the coat he carried. I walked the three of them to the front door. The trail guide happened to be parked outside already, so he bundled his guests into the van. I wasn't sorry to see them drive away.

As I was turning to go back inside I noticed movement out of the corner of my eye. Griff, the man who managed Annabel's stables, was coming around the nearest turret toward the front of the castle. I waited for him. He was of medium height with a stocky build and sandy-colored hair. He was dressed in a heavy jacket and muddy work boots. He looked down at his feet once he was inside. "Should I take these off?" he asked me.

"If you don't mind," I said. "I don't want to make more work for Brenda." He bent down to unlace the boots and then stood there in his sock feet.

"What brings you up to the house?" I asked.

"Annabel called me. She asked if I'd come up here. She wants to talk about building onto the stables." I nodded. Annabel had spoken to me about the possibility of taking on more horses and creating a park where old horses could come and live out their "retirement" in happiness. Apparently she had decided to take the next step and discuss the issue with her stable manager. Talking to him would help take her mind off Andreas, too. I suggested that Griff have some lunch while he waited for Annabel. He accepted and we sat across from each other in the dining room as we enjoyed Maisie's hearty meal of ham sandwiches with potato salad.

Griff was quiet and easy to talk to. I told him what had been going on.

"Andreas'll be back when he's good and ready," Griff said.

"I hope that's soon," I answered. "It's rather selfish of him, considering he's going to be a father very soon. I'm sure Sian is worried about him and she has enough to think about right now."

He nodded in agreement and just then Annabel appeared in the doorway. "I apologize for being late," she said. "I was showing Sian the English garden." She greeted Griff warmly and sat down at the table after helping herself to a small lunch. I got up to leave, but she asked me to stay and talk about the planned horse retirement park with her and Griff.

Griff was enthusiastic about the plan. He said he would come up with some rough sketches for enlarging the current stable and adding on a new tack room. Eventually he stood up to leave.

I walked to the front door with him and stood waiting while he put his boots back on. When he left he hurried in the direction of the stables, turning around once to wave in my direction. I waved back and shut the door to find Annabel standing behind me.

"What a nice man," she said, giving me a sly look. This wasn't the first time Annabel had pointed out Griff's fine personality or his rugged-outdoorsman looks, but I was in no mood for matchmaking, so I talked about something else.

"I searched the rooms on the upper floors and didn't find Andreas, obviously. As Griff said earlier, I'm sure Andreas will come back when he's good and ready."

"I know that. Sometimes I wish my son would think of someone other than himself." She turned around and walked toward her sitting room. "I have some things to do for my club," she said, referring to the local ladies' club she presided over. "Why don't you take some time for yourself? When is Sylvie getting here?"

I had almost forgotten about Sylvie in the stress of looking for Andreas. I glanced at my watch. "She should be here in time for dinner," I replied.

"You should send Brenda out to the coach house to make sure everything is ready for her," Annabel said. The coach house was the guesthouse. In days gone by it had been used to store carriages, but as the castle made its way through the twentieth century the coach house fell into shambles from disuse. One of the pet projects of Annabel's second husband had been to restore the building and turn it into a beautiful place for guests to stay. Annabel had wanted all her boys and Sian and Cadi to stay in the main house with her, so my guest would have the coach house all to herself.

I left Annabel in the sitting room and went in search of Brenda. When she had brought breakfast into the dining room earlier she had seemed subdued and I wondered how she was doing today. I found her talking to Maisie downstairs. Again, her eyes were red-rimmed and she was sniffling.

"Have I come at a bad time?" I asked.

Maisie crossed her arms over her chest. "You've come at a perfect time. I was just telling Brenda to get back to work." She looked pointedly at her daughter, who looked away. A red flush made its way up the back of her neck under her ponytail and I could tell how embarrassed she was.

"Brenda, I was hoping you could run out to the coach house to make sure everything is ready for my cousin. She's going to be here tonight around dinnertime."

Brenda nodded and left the room quickly. I looked at Maisie, wondering if she would tell me what was going on. I suspected Brenda was upset because Andreas was nowhere to be found, but I couldn't be sure.

Maisie grimaced and started wiping down one of the kitchen counters. "That girl of mine. She doesn't know enough to come in out of the cold. Can't she see the problems Andreas brings?" This was the first time I had heard Maisie mention Andreas's name in connection with Brenda, and I was surprised to hear her say it.

"Poor girl," I murmured.

"Poor girl nothing," she retorted. "She needs to pick herself up and get on with her life." She snorted. "How she can think Andreas can solve all her problems, I don't know. Seems to me he's the cause of most of 'em."

"Maybe once she grows up a little she'll realize the folly of chasing after Andreas."

"Humph," was all Maisie said.

I was in my room on the computer when Brenda knocked on my door. "The coach house is ready, Eilidh," she said. "I put the pretty soaps and the best towels in the powder room."

"Thank you, Brenda. I'm sure everything is perfect. You'll like my cousin. She's lots of fun."

Brenda smiled in reply and closed the door. I had wanted to question her about Andreas, but there was really no way I could without seeming nosy.

I closed my laptop and sat in front of the cold fireplace to read a book for a little while. Working for Annabel was rewarding in many ways, and I liked that the job gave me some downtime to do things I enjoyed, like reading. Annabel was also slowly teaching me to ride, which I loved.

After a while I got up to get some tea. When I opened my door I could hear the hikers coming inside from their afternoon on the trail. I went to greet them.

"How was the hike?" I asked.

"Cold," Cadi said. Her cheeks were ruddy. "Unbearably cold, actually. I wished I had taken gloves."

Hugh came up behind her. "Did you have fun, Hugh?" I asked.

"It was better than I expected," he said. "Cadi here didn't like it as much as I thought she would, but that's normal, isn't it, Cadi?" He jabbed her in the ribs and she scowled at him.

"I liked it fine," she said. "I just wished it was a bit warmer, that's all." Her complaining was becoming tiresome to me, and I'd only been around her a wee bit since her arrival the day before. I didn't know how Hugh could stand it on a daily basis.

"Rhisiart enjoyed it," Hugh said. "If you're looking for praise, perhaps you'll get it from him."

I turned away and went down to the kitchen, annoyed that he would assume I had been "looking for praise" for setting up the hike. I was merely asking if they had fun to be polite. And to make sure they didn't have a miserable time. I was beginning to realize that Cadi often had a miserable time and actually preferred things that way.

Maisie had announced that dinner would be served at six o'clock, so we all gathered in the dining room a few minutes before six. Annabel was late, which was unusual for her. Right at six o'clock, Maisie brought a platter of salmon into the dining room and set it on the table. "This will be getting cold quickly," she said, attempting to nudge us to the table.

But Annabel wasn't there yet. Hugh looked at me for guidance. "Do we wait for Mum or can we sit down and eat before the fish gets cold?"

"I think she would want us to eat without her, but I'm going to see where she is. She's usually punctual." Hugh and Cadi, Rhisiart, and Sian all sat down at the table. I was turning around to leave the room when Annabel appeared in the doorway.

Her hair, normally neat and pretty, was spiky and disheveled. It looked like she had run her hands through it. Her eyes were wild and her hands, one of which held a mobile phone, were trembling.

"Somebody help me," she said hoarsely. We all hurried toward her at once.

"What's wrong, Mum?" Rhisiart asked, his eyes wide and concerned. He held one arm while Hugh took the other and together the two men helped her to the table, where she sat down heavily. The mobile phone she had been holding dropped to the floor. I bent down to pick it up and saw that the line had gone dead.

"Annabel, what happened?" I asked, kneeling down next to her. Cadi and Sian stood next to me.

"I just rang off with a friend of mine in the village. The police found a body in the river." Annabel's skin was dry and a ghostly shade of white. "It's Andreas. I just know it."

Sian gasped and we turned to look at her. Hugh took one step and was at her side in an instant to ease her into a chair. Annabel watched with a grim expression.

"How do you know it was Andreas?" Cadi asked as we all turned our attention back to Annabel.

"I just know. I just have this feeling," Annabel answered.

"You can't know, Mum," Hugh said in an irritated voice. "You aren't a soothsayer."

"But I'm a mother," she told him, her eyes finally losing the dead look and blazing at him. "I have a mother's intuition. I know it was him." She turned to Sian with a sad look. "I'm sorry, Sian. I just had to come down here and tell everyone."

Sian swallowed and took a deep breath. "Can someone please ring the police? We don't *know* any of this is true."

As if it had become a living thing that could hear and understand us, Annabel's mobile phone rang in my hand. We all looked at each other. "Eilidh, would you please answer that?" Annabel asked.

I pushed the "talk" button. A male voice asked to speak to Annabel. "Just a moment, please," I said. I covered the speaker with my hand and held the phone out to Annabel. "He wants to speak to you."

"Who is it?" Hugh asked. Annabel silenced him with a look.

"Who is this, please?" I asked the man.

"Fred Straither."

I covered the speaker again and repeated his name to Annabel in a low voice. She looked up at me with scared eyes. "He's the one who told me about the body," she said.

"Do you want to talk to him?" I asked. She held out her hand and I placed the phone in it.

"Hello, Fred." She listened for a moment, her breathing becoming shallower and the last of the color draining from her face. She gave me the phone and pointed to it. "You talk to him," she said, burying her face in her hands. "I just can't!" she cried.

Sian had begun to stand up, but Hugh put his hand on her shoulder, gently pushing her back into the chair. "Fred, this is Eilidh, Annabel's assistant. She's asked me to talk to you."

His voice seemed louder than it had before, probably because of the complete silence in the dining room where we all stood. "I've just talked to one of the constables in the village. They're saying the body is Andreas, Annabel's son. Why would they be saying such a thing?"

"Andreas has been missing today, Fred. I hope the constable was wrong. I'm going to ring up the police now and try to find out what's going on. Thanks for calling."

I ended the call and dialed the police immediately, without waiting for anyone to ask questions or demand an explanation.

Once a constable was on the phone, I explained who I was and repeated the rumor Fred had shared with me and Annabel. The officer said he couldn't talk to me and needed to speak with a family member. I glanced at Annabel, who looked as if she were about to faint, and Sian, whose gray pallor concerned me. I handed the phone to Rhisiart.

"This is Rhisiart Tucker," he said, his voice sounding authoritative and strong. "What's going on here?"

He listened attentively for a moment, his countenance growing graver. Finally he said, "Thank you. Someone will be there soon."

He rang off and knelt down next to his mother. "The constable says the body found in the river does look like Andreas. He would like you or Sian to go down to the village to have a look at it."

Annabel looked at her son with something akin to horror in her face. She shook her head vehemently. "I can't. I can't do that."

Rhisiart looked at Sian. "Sian," he said gently, "do you think you could go down to the village? Hugh or I will drive you."

Sian had been staring straight ahead, not saying a word, while Rhisiart was on the phone and talking to Annabel. "Yes," she said after a long pause.

Hugh held out his hand to her and she allowed him to help her to stand up. She looked down at Annabel. "I'll be back soon."

Annabel stood up and hugged Sian, the tears starting to fall.

Sian pried herself away from Annabel and said to her, "Not yet, Annabel. It might not be him. Let's hope it's someone else." Cadi wore a shocked look. Suddenly she ran from the room, saying over her shoulder that she would get Sian's coat for her. She was back in just a minute, then she stood behind her sister-in-law and helped her with the coat. She was gentle and kind, wisely shedding her abrasiveness for a few moments. Hugh ran outside to get his car before speeding away toward the village with Rhisiart and Sian. Cadi and Annabel and I were left in the sitting room, silent, wondering what news the trio would bring back with them.

Though we drank quite a lot of tea that evening, none of us felt like eating. Maisie came to clear away the fish and the unused dishes and to fill the teapot with hot water frequently. It seemed forever before the big front door creaked open and Sian, accompanied on either side by Hugh and Rhisiart, appeared in the doorway to the dining room, her face red and swollen, her nose puffy.

"It's him," she said with a sob, sitting down in the empty chair next to Annabel. Annabel looked like someone had punched her. Stunned, she reached for Sian's hand.

"You're absolutely sure?" she asked. Sian lifted her head to stare at her mother-in-law.

"Of course I'm sure. I'd know my own husband!" Her cries became louder and more wretched. Annabel was crying now, too, making a moaning noise that I never want to hear again as long as I live. It was a keening animal sound, the sound of a mother who has just learned of the death of her son.

"I don't believe it," she repeated again and again. "He was just here last night!"

Sian was having a hard time catching her breath. Hugh and Rhisiart looked at each other, clearly not knowing what to do next. Cadi stepped in and put her hand on Sian's back.

"You need to take slow, deep breaths, Sian. There, that's it. Slow down. Make the exhale longer than the inhale. That's it." With Cadi's coaching, Sian was finally able to calm down enough to breathe normally.

Annabel appeared to be in shock. She shook her head as if to clear it of some unpleasant thought and walked over to the window, where she looked out over the fields that were hidden by the darkness. Hugh and Rhisiart again exchanged glances. Rhisiart joined his mother at the window, putting his arm around her thin shoulders and pulling her close to him. She leaned against him and I could see her shoulders shaking from her sobs. She looked up at him, her face streaked with tears. "What was he doing in the river? He couldn't have drowned. He was a strong swimmer. I don't know why he would have gone down to the river at all." Rhisiart could only shake his head.

"I don't know, Mum," he replied.

I felt like I shouldn't be there, like I was intruding on the family's grief. But I didn't want to leave and have them think I didn't care or didn't want to be around them.

I didn't want to go to Annabel yet—her son was comforting her and I wasn't entirely sure any comfort from me would be welcome. Annabel and I had become close during my time in the castle, but as close as we might be, I wasn't family. She needed her family.

It was this macabre scene that greeted Sylvie when she arrived at the castle just a short while later. In all the sadness and shock, I had forgotten she was coming. The great doorbell sounded through the halls and running feet, no doubt Brenda, could be heard heading toward the front door. A moment later Brenda stood in the dining room doorway, looking bewildered by the silence punctuated by cries.

"Uh, your guest is in the great hall, Eilidh. Do you want her to come in here?" Annabel turned away from the window and spoke to me.

"This is probably not the best place for her right now. Maybe you could show her to the coach house and I'll see her tomorrow."

"Of course," I replied, glad of an excuse to leave the family to their grief.

I left the dining room with Brenda and pulled the doors closed behind me. "What's the matter?" she whispered, her eyes wide.

"They just found out Andreas passed away." The words were out before I remembered Brenda's relationship to Andreas. She stopped as if she had hit an invisible wall and put her hands to her mouth.

"No!" she cried out.

"Brenda, pull yourself together. I probably was out of line by telling you. I just blurted it out without thinking. The family needs us to be strong right now because they're in shock. If we fall apart it won't help anyone and it will definitely make the family more upset."

She nodded, unable to speak. Then I watched as she turned on her heel and ran toward the stairs leading down to the kitchen. Maisie would have her hands full tonight.

My breath caught in my throat when I saw Sylvie waiting for me in the great hall, dressed in her customary jeans and boots, her hair pulled back in a ponytail. It had been a long time since our last visit and it never ceased to amaze me how much she looked like her sister, Greer, with shoulder-length brown hair and slim features. I held my finger to my lips and gave her a big hug, then led her quickly outside the front door.

"What's going on?" Sylvie asked.

"You'll never believe it. Andreas, Annabel's son, died. He's been missing since this morning."

"What?" she cried. "What happened?"

"We don't know. His body was found in the river that winds through the village. I don't know any more than that."

"I shouldn't be here," she said.

"Oh, please stay," I said, almost begging. "I don't want to intrude on the family and I need someone to keep my mind off things. You being here is perfect."

"But Annabel won't want me to stay."

"I really don't think she'll mind. She's putting you in the coach house. It's been renovated and you'll love it. She did say she isn't ready to see you tonight, but she'll see you tomorrow. She wants you to stay."

Sylvie looked dubious. "If you're sure," she said with a note of uncertainty.

"I'm sure. Let me show you where the coach house is."

She followed me around the front of the castle to a long stone pathway that led from the left side of the castle to the coach house, which was at least a tenth of a mile away. She pulled a suitcase behind her.

I unlocked the door to the coach house and my cousin stepped into the salon with a gasp of delight. The soaring ceilings, with their original rafters, were dotted with hanging pendant lights giving the salon a soft glow. A massive fireplace at one end of the room, cold and dark now, would be providing comfort and warmth in just a few minutes. In contrast to the inside of the castle, which was decorated and furnished with a heavy nod to its ancient history, the coach house had been renovated with a view toward comfort and modernity. Ivory and beige furniture was placed around the salon in groupings designed to foster intimate conversation. Occasional tables were thoughtfully placed within reach of every seat in the room so guests always had a place to set their beverages and snacks. Three low tables covered with coffee table books and Welsh-themed bric-a-brac were placed strategically around the huge room. The effect was airy and light, even though darkness cloaked the floor-to-ceiling windows circling the salon.

I showed Sylvie to her room and her bathroom. She was just as impressed with the private areas of the coach house. The rooms were generously and thoughtfully appointed with every amenity a guest could need or want, and I knew she was thrilled with the sleeping arrangements. She could visit the castle anytime she wished, but she could always return to the homey comfort of the coach house.

The kitchen, though modern and sleek, wouldn't get much use while my cousin visited. Annabel had already made clear that she wished her to take her meals with me and the rest of the family in the castle dining room and Sylvie liked that idea. Sylvie was not the cook in her household—her husband, Seamus, was the gourmet.

While I started a fire in the salon, Sylvie deposited her bags in the bedroom. I went in search of a bottle of wine and found one in a small wine refrigerator built into the kitchen cabinets. When I had located two wineglasses and some fresh cheese and crackers, Sylvie joined me by the fireplace.

She wanted to know all about the day's events. When I had told her everything, she finally sat back against the sofa cushions to take it all in.

"How did he die?" she asked.

"No one knows yet. I assume we'll find out more from the police in the morning."

"How's his wife taking it?"

"It's hard to say. I think she's so shocked that she hasn't had a chance to let it sink in yet."

"When's the baby due?"

"In a few weeks," I replied. "Annabel has been so excited about the prospect of a grandchild, but I don't know how this will affect her feelings."

"She'll still love the baby."

"Of course, but I wonder whether she'll even want to see the baby at first. It will be such a painful reminder of Andreas."

"But it's a baby," Sylvie said, as if the issue were as clear as glass. "Who wouldn't want to see their first grandchild?"

"Someone who's devastated by the death of the baby's father and doesn't want to look at a face that will remind her of her son."

Sylvie nodded thoughtfully. "I see what you mean now. I hope that doesn't happen."

"I'm sure Sian does, too," I said. "I don't know anything about Sian's family, but I do know she was counting on Annabel's help when the baby was born."

"Was the baby going to be born here?"

"No, though that might happen now, depending on whether Sian stays here or goes back to London."

"Does she have a job?"

"Yes, but I guess it's an arrangement where she can work anywhere. She doesn't have to go into an office. Marketing or something like that. So she could stay here and work if she chose to."

We sat in front of the fire for a while longer, not saying anything, just enjoying each other's company, but I felt I should get back to the main house and check on Annabel to see if she needed anything from me.

I bid Sylvie goodnight, told her to have a long lie-in the next morning, and returned to the castle via the stone pathway leading away from the coach house. The night had grown colder and the sliver of moon had disappeared behind clouds that promised to bring rain before morning. The scent of pine needles was heavy on the air and I hurried along the path, anxious to get to a place where I could be around other people. I didn't mind being about in the daylight, but nighttime outside the castle was eerie.

Chapter 5

I entered the castle through the front door and stood in the great hall, listening for any sound. It was silent. I peeked into the dining room, which was empty and dark except for one dim lamp burning on the sideboard. Likewise, no one was in the sitting room or the drawing room. I assumed everyone had gone to their own rooms.

I hesitated before going upstairs to check on Annabel, but I was worried about her and I wanted to make sure there was nothing she needed. I knocked quietly on her door and heard a feeble, "Come in."

When I peered around the edge of the door, I was not surprised to find Annabel sitting in one of the armchairs in her room, the lights off and the fire burned down to meager flames in the fireplace. She liked to have a roaring fire when she went to sleep at night, but she hadn't bothered to stoke it on this night.

I touched her shoulder tentatively. "Annabel? Is there anything I can do for you?"

She sniffled and put her hand over mine on her shoulder. "No, Eilidh. I'm afraid there's nothing. I don't know how we're going to get through this."

"We'll get through it by taking one day, one hour, one minute at a time," I told her, pulling up another chair and sitting across from her. The flickering firelight cast long dancing shadows in the dark of the room and by that faint light I could see Annabel's face, drawn and pained.

"There's no other way, is there?" she asked.

I shook my head. We sat in silence for a long time, just thinking, until I sensed Annabel had fallen asleep. It was getting chilly in her room, too. I added more logs to her fire, which had burned out, helped her up, and made sure she got ready for bed. She was often a light sleeper, but I fervently hoped she would be able to sleep through the night. She would need as much rest as she could get to withstand the stress and emotions over the next several days.

After I left her room I returned downstairs and crept past Sian's room. I could hear muffled sobbing coming from the other side of her door, but I was unsure whether I should intrude to see if she needed anything. I decided to leave her alone and let her cry herself out. When I went past Hugh and Cadi's room, there were no sounds from within.

I crawled into bed, exhausted and finally feeling hunger pangs from having missed dinner. I briefly considered trekking down to the kitchen for a snack, but once I was burrowed under the covers I couldn't bear the thought of the damp air and the cold stone floor on my feet. I fell into a deep sleep and didn't wake up until the sun was high in the sky the next morning.

I went first in search of Annabel, who had also slept uncharacteristically late. I knocked on her bedroom door and waited a moment before I heard a quiet "Come in."

She was sitting up in bed. She looked at me with an overwhelming sadness that told me how she had slept during the night. "I can't cry anymore," she said. "I feel empty. I just can't understand how he could have died."

I didn't know what to say. She probably didn't need me to say anything—what she needed was someone to be with her and simply to listen to her.

"Want to join me for some breakfast? We both slept late this morning," I told her.

"I'll be down in a little while," she said. "Eat without me if you're hungry." Annabel didn't leave her room without looking impeccable. She showered, dressed, and applied make-up before making an appearance in the dining room each morning. I told her I would wait for her and went downstairs to read the newspaper.

I was the first one in the dining room. Apparently the rest of the family had slept late, too. I opened the paper and the first story above the fold was about Andreas's death. I let out a groan. That was the last thing Annabel or anyone else, especially Sian, needed to see first thing this morning. I skimmed the article.

A body found on Friday by fishermen in the River Bowen has been identified as that of Andreas Tucker, formerly of Thistlecross and currently a resident of London. Mr. Tucker is survived by his wife, Sian Tucker, and their unborn child, his mother, Annabel Baines, brother Hugh Tucker and his wife Cadi, and brother Rhisiart Tucker.

Police are not commenting on the circumstances of Mr. Tucker's death.

Footsteps sounded outside the dining room and I debated whether to hide the paper. But I knew that would be useless—the family would eventually read the brief newspaper account and it wasn't my place to be hiding it from them.

Sian appeared in the dining room doorway. Like Annabel, she looked as if she hadn't slept at all. There were gray bags under her eyes and her shoulders were slumped with the weight of despair.

"How are you doing this morning, Sian?" I asked her. I stood up to pull out a chair for her, but she shook her head.

"Have a seat; I can do that," she said, giving me a slight smile. "I didn't sleep very well last night. I can't drink caffeine, but I wish I could. I have a feeling I'll need it today."

She was probably right. The circumstances under which Andreas's body had been found would no doubt require a police investigation which, I was sure, had already started. I hadn't given much thought to the police coming to the castle to ask questions, but I supposed it was to be expected.

"We're all here to help, so don't hesitate to take a break and get away from everyone anytime you need to," I told Sian.

"Have the police been here yet?"

"Not that I know of. We all slept late this morning—you, me, Annabel. I was the first one in here this morning, so I assume Rhisiart and Hugh and Cadi slept late, too."

"What about your cousin?"

To my surprise, I realized I hadn't even thought about Sylvie. "I don't know. I'll run over to the coach house and see if she's up yet."

I excused myself while Sian halfheartedly picked at a plate of eggs and toast. As much as I wanted to help her, I didn't know her well and I didn't know what to say. I couldn't imagine how she must be feeling; there was no way I could put myself in her shoes. She must have so many questions. I went outdoors and jogged round to the stone path that took me to the coach house. I had raised my hand to knock on the door when it opened and Sylvie stood there smiling. I was suddenly struck with a feeling of nostalgia that was so strong I stopped short.

"What's the matter?" she asked.

"Nothing. Seeing you just reminded me of Cauld Loch, that's all. It hit me hard all of a sudden."

She gave me a quick hug and drew me inside. "Have you seen the article about Andreas?" she asked.

"Yes. I didn't know whether to hide it from the family or not," I answered.

"I wouldn't hide it," Sylvie put in. "It's not as if they don't know what happened."

"That's true."

"Will you be helping Annabel with funeral preparations today?" she asked.

"Probably. I've only seen Annabel this morning long enough to encourage her to go down to the dining room for something to eat, but I'm sure there'll be funeral and burial details to discuss."

"What would you like me to do?" Sylvie asked.

"You can come over for breakfast and meet the rest of the family, then I guess you can do what I had planned for them today—horse riding."

"That sounds fun, though it would be better if you could go with me. I feel strange being on holiday and enjoying myself when Annabel is going through such a hard time," she said.

"Annabel really wants you to be here and she wants you to have fun," I assured her. "She's very gracious and she knows this is a holiday for you. You didn't even know Andreas except through whatever your mum said about him, so there's no reason for you to be in mourning."

"Do the police really not know what happened to him?" Sylvie asked, lowering her voice as if someone from the main house might overhear.

"Nobody knows," I said. "I imagine they'll start questioning people today."

"I don't want to be around for that," Sylvie said with a shudder. No doubt she was thinking about the events back in Cauld Loch two years previously, when Florian McDermott, a client of her husband, had been killed. Florian's death and the violent events that followed required Sylvie and her husband to deal with the police on many occasions.

"You probably won't have to be around for most of it, but they may want to talk to you just because you arrived on the same day Andreas died."

"I can handle that," she said.

"Let's go over to the castle so you can see Annabel and the rest of the family and eat breakfast," I suggested. "Then I'll introduce you to Griff, who manages the stables for Annabel."

Sylvie bundled up in a coat and scarf and followed me back to the castle through the morning fog and chill. Annabel was in the dining room talking quietly to Sian when I entered with Sylvie in tow.

"Annabel, you probably remember my cousin, Sylvie Carmichael," I said. "Sylvie, you remember Annabel Baines."

Sylvie shook hands with Annabel and expressed her condolences. Then I introduced her to Sian, and she repeated her sorrowful greeting. Sian acknowledged her graciously, then excused herself to go back to her room.

"Sian, we're going to have to start planning the funeral arrangements today," Annabel said in a gentle voice. "If there's anything I can do to help, just ask." Her eyes glistened with unshed tears and Sian looked back.

"If you'd like to make the arrangements, Annabel, that would be fine with me. Or maybe we could do it together. I'm not sure I'm up to doing something like that all by myself."

"Of course, Sian. Let me know when you're ready to talk about it," Annabel answered. If I knew Annabel, she would consider it her duty as Andreas's mother to participate in the funeral arrangements.

As Sian walked into the hallway, she paused for a moment, her voice quiet as she spoke to someone. Shortly after, Hugh and Cadi came into the room. They must have been talking to Sian. Their faces were drawn, as if they hadn't gotten any sleep, either. They went directly to Annabel and kissed her cheeks. Rhisiart followed them into the room, walking briskly but his eyes downcast, as if he didn't want to look at anyone directly. He poured himself a cup of tea before he noticed Sylvie, then he walked over to her and introduced himself. Hugh and Cadi followed suit.

The six of us sat down for breakfast after helping ourselves to some of the food Maisie had laid out much earlier that morning. Brenda came into the room once to see if the teapot or coffeepot needed refreshing, and I watched her closely to see if there was any emotion written on her face. Indeed, she had a stricken look about her and had been crying. She stared straight ahead with red-rimmed eyes, focused on her task rather than on the people in the room. When she asked Annabel if she needed anything for herself or for her guests, I noticed she didn't look directly at Annabel. Instead she looked over Annabel's shoulder, where she didn't have to make eye contact with anyone.

"No, Brenda, that'll be all for now. Thank you, dear," Annabel answered. Brenda left the room hastily, her sniffling echoing down the hallway. I knew her routine—she would head to Annabel's room to make up the bed and tidy up in there, then she would begin the rounds in the guests' bedrooms. I wondered how she would react when she got to Sian's room. I felt sorry for her for losing someone she obviously cared so much about, but I worried that her demeanor would further upset Sian.

I wondered if I should tell Brenda to skip Sian's room. I looked at Annabel, who was talking to Rhisiart about his next book. It seemed both understood their conversation was solely to keep everyone's mind off their suffering and grief, so he was animated and talkative in discussing his next project.

I leaned down and whispered into Annabel's ear. "Do you think Sian would appreciate being left alone this morning? I could tell Brenda not to bother cleaning her room."

Annabel looked up at me in confusion. "I would think Sian would appreciate some order and tidiness in there. Having someone else to do that for her might be very helpful." I was surprised. Didn't Annabel see what I saw every time Brenda was near Andreas? Did she miss the signs of puppy love? Maybe I was missing something. But I didn't think so. I abandoned the idea of telling Brenda to skip Sian's room.

I should have followed my own instincts.

After breakfast I took Sylvie out to the stables in the glen behind the castle and introduced her to Griff. Since she knew how to ride, all Griff had to do was saddle up the horse and tell her where she would most enjoy riding. Griff and I waved her off, then Griff turned to me. "I read the paper this morning. How is everyone taking the news up at the house?"

"Not well, as you can imagine. I wish I could just ride off with Sylvie, but I need to be up there today." Griff returned to his work and I went back to the main house. I found Annabel in her sitting room, where she asked me to ring up the vicar in the village and find out when the church would be available to hold Andreas's funeral service. There were several times available, so I wrote them down and set them aside to discuss with Annabel and Sian in a little while. Annabel was busy answering calls and accepting condolences from friends in the village and the surrounding county. I was happy to be of help to her and Sian, though it might have been nice to get away from everything and go horse riding with my cousin, too.

I had rung off with the vicar when Annabel and I were startled by shouting in the hallway. It was coming from the direction of Sian's room. I was the first one out the door, but Annabel wasn't far behind me.

We ran toward the yelling and stopped short when we found Sian in the doorway of her room, giving Brenda a dressing down at the top of her lungs. Brenda was standing before Sian, her shoulders slumped, her hands limply at her sides, her tears silently falling onto the stone floor.

"Sian, what's the matter?" Annabel called, hurrying up to them.

"I found her trying to take something from our room!" Sian shouted, jabbing her finger toward Brenda as she spoke.

"What was it?" Annabel asked.

"Nothing, I swear," Brenda insisted.

Annabel turned to Sian. "What was it?" she asked again.

"I don't know," Sian replied angrily, crossing her arms over her chest and resting them on her belly. "She was rifling through one of our drawers when I came into the room."

"I told you, I was putting away a pair of socks that had been in the laundry," Brenda said.

"Fat chance of that," Sian sneered, then she started crying, too. "I don't know how I'm going to survive this, losing my husband and being eight months pregnant! Do I have to deal with a thief in our midst, too?" she shrieked.

Annabel took her by the elbow and led her into the room, murmuring to her in a soft, low voice. The door closed behind them and Brenda and I were left standing in the darkened hallway. The stone walls and the dim sconces belied the light that was shining bright and cold outside.

I turned to Brenda with questioning eyes. "I didn't steal anything, I promise," she said, reading my mind. "I was putting socks away."

Her eyes pleaded with me to believe her, and I did. I felt sorry for the young woman, being berated in front of us like that. I was surprised that Sian would lose control. Even with all she was trying to endure, she seemed the type of person who would try to maintain a veneer of civility.

"Let's chalk this up to grief and suffering for now," I told Brenda. "You'd better hurry down to the kitchen to help your mum with luncheon. She'll need help carrying the trays."

Brenda nodded and scurried down the hallway toward the stairs leading down to the kitchen. I shook my head, mostly out of sorrow for everyone involved in this tragedy, and returned to the sitting room to wait for Annabel.

When she returned she looked exhausted. She ran the palm of her hand over her forehead wearily. "Poor Sian. To accuse Brenda like that. Her suffering is almost too much for her to bear. I'm going to call the doctor you lined up and see if he can give her something to help her rest." I found the number and she rang up the doctor. Once she explained the problem, he said he would come out to the castle to see Sian before prescribing something to help her calm down and get a little sleep.

As we had expected, it wasn't long before the police arrived. Brenda admitted two constables to the main hall and came to find Annabel and me in the sitting room, where I was listening as Annabel spoke to her barrister on the phone. He had promised to come out to the castle as soon as possible, but when he heard Brenda announce the arrival of the police, he advised Annabel not to speak to them until he arrived, but she hung up after telling him she would talk to them because she had nothing to hide.

Annabel greeted the constables in the main hall and invited them into the sitting room to answer their questions about Andreas. They asked me to leave the room while they spoke to Annabel. I wondered if she had made the right choice in answering their questions before her barrister arrived.

I waited impatiently in my room for the constables to call for me. I tried reading more of Rhisiart's novel, but I couldn't concentrate on the words and kept reading the same paragraph until I put the book aside in frustration. I thought about going outside for a walk, but I wasn't sure I was allowed to leave the house while they questioned the others. I tried checking email and social media, but I found nothing could hold my interest. Finally I went downstairs in search of Maisie and Brenda to see if they had heard anything as they went about their chores in the house. Brenda had seen the other family members go into the dining room one-by-one, first Sian, then Hugh, then Rhisiart, and finally Cadi, but she hadn't heard anything about the questions or the constables' theories on Andreas's death. Brenda was still upset at having been yelled at by Sian.

When the constables called me into the sitting room I sat down and wiped my clammy hands on my trouser leg. *There's no reason to be nervous*, I chided myself. *They're just gathering information.* But there's something about the police being in one's home and place of employment that makes one jumpy.

The police questioned me about how I came to be working for Annabel and why I had left Cauld Loch. They asked about Aunt Margot's relationship with Annabel and my relationship with Annabel's family.

Finally, when they had exhausted all the possible lines of questioning about my past, my ex-husband's past, the reasons behind his current imprisonment, and my present employment, they turned to their questions about Andreas's disappearance and his death. I recalled for them the bang I had heard the night Andreas went missing, then the soft crying I had heard afterward. I told them I had gone looking for the source of the crying and hadn't found it.

When they asked how much I knew about the fight between Andreas and Sian, I had no firsthand knowledge to share with them. I had heard about the fight from Cadi and told them so. I knew Sian had confirmed their argument, but I was not certain about its cause, its outcome, or the words that were spoken in anger.

The police seemed satisfied with my answers, but took all my contact information in case they needed to talk to me again. They also noted that Sylvie would have to be questioned, too, since she arrived at the castle shortly after Andreas's body had been discovered.

When I had been dismissed, I went in search of Annabel while Maisie took my place in the sitting room. I found my boss in her room, nursing a headache.

"Would you like to lie down for a little while?" I asked her. "I can make calls or do whatever you need me to do while you rest."

"I would love to do that," she answered, "but I don't think I should. I'd like to get all the arrangements in place myself so I can feel like I've done everything I can for Andreas and Sian. And if I rest now, I might not be able to sleep tonight, and the thought terrifies me."

I nodded with perfect understanding. I had suffered so many sleepless nights during that time in Cauld Loch. Daytime stress had sent me straight to my bed to escape the feelings of hurt and anger in sleep, and I paid for it night after night by lying awake, staring at the ceiling and wondering what the future held. I didn't want Annabel to experience those same feelings.

"What's next, then?" I asked.

"I'd like you to ring up the village newspaper and the London papers and ask them for the details about submitting an obituary. His London colleagues will need to know what's happened, and I'm afraid Sian is in no shape to make the necessary arrangements."

I returned to the sitting room and placed one call. The village newspaper still didn't have a user-friendly website, so I had to talk to one of the staff members there. She was aware of Andreas's death and had been expecting my call, she said. She expressed her condolences and I promised to pass the message along to Annabel and the rest of the family. When I rang off I checked the websites of the London papers and gathered the information necessary for the family to submit an obituary. I wondered who was going to write it. Probably Sian was the most logical choice, since she lived with Andreas every day and knew of his hobbies, his business particulars, and his passions. She could incorporate all those things into a lovely tribute to her husband. But I wondered if Annabel would want a hand in writing the obituary, too.

When we all gathered in the dining room later that evening for dinner, Sian surprised everyone by asking Rhisiart to write the obituary.

"Why me?" he asked. Then he added hastily, "Not that I don't want to. I'd be happy to do it. I just thought it might be something you'd like to write yourself."

"But you're the writer. It'll sound so much better if you write it," Sian insisted. "And I really can't bring myself to do it." Sian looked around the table and for the first time I noticed how thin and haggard her face looked, how much her appearance had changed in just the past two days.

"That's fine," he answered. "I'll do it tonight." I saw the look of hurt that flickered across Annabel's face, but she covered it up so quickly that I don't think anyone else noticed it.

Sylvie had joined us for dinner and told us all about her afternoon spent horse riding. Her story was a welcome respite from the constant talk of Andreas and his death. From the looks she gave during the discussion, Sian didn't seem pleased that my cousin had been outdoors enjoying the countryside when the rest of us were in mourning, but she didn't say anything.

I stopped over at the coach house after dinner for a glass of wine. I didn't want to hear another word about Andreas; Sylvie obliged by telling me all the news about the family and all my old friends and acquaintances back in Cauld Loch. We enjoyed a quiet evening during which I apologized profusely for not joining her on the afternoon's excursion.

"That Griff is something," Sylvie said with a wink. "Is he single?"

"Why? Are you looking?" I asked with a laugh.

"Of course not. But there *is* one single person here," she said, eyeing me over the top of her wineglass.

"Don't be ridiculous," I scolded. "I'm not looking for anyone. I've sworn off men."

"You're most likely to find a good one when you're not looking," she said slyly.

"Sylvie, you're impossible," I said, draining my glass. "I should get back to the house. I'm exhausted. Hopefully we'll all sleep well tonight." I bid her goodnight and returned to the castle, where the only light came from the small lamp burning in the great hall and the wall sconces flickering in the semi-darkness down the hallways to the bedrooms.

All was quiet, probably because none of us had slept the previous night. I didn't hear crying or banging or even talking. I woke up well-rested and ready to face whatever challenges the day might bring.

Chapter 6

The first challenge presented itself quite early. The two constables who had interviewed everyone the previous day were back the next morning while the family and I ate breakfast together in the dining room. The doorbell echoed through the downstairs and I could hear Brenda hurrying to answer its ring. Presently she came into the dining room, her gaze darting around the table, with the two constables behind her.

"The two constables are here again to see you," she said to no one in particular. Annabel stood to greet them.

"How can we help you this morning?" she asked, a worried look on her face.

One of the constables cleared his throat. "Can we speak to Sian Tucker in private, please?"

Annabel turned in surprise to Sian, whose face had drained of its color when she heard her name spoken. She stood up, wobbling a bit, and walked forward. "We can go into the drawing room," she said, her voice sounding stronger than she looked.

The two constables followed her through the door and into the adjoining drawing room, then one of them pulled the door shut so they had some privacy. The rest of us sat silently at the table, looking down at our plates, casting sidelong glances to see what everyone else was doing and, possibly, thinking.

No sound issued from the drawing room, but only two people returned to the dining room—the constables. Sian wasn't with them.

Annabel gave the officers a questioning look, then they asked her to accompany them into the drawing room, too. It was only a moment before we heard a wail coming from the room behind the closed door. Hugh jumped up, ran to the drawing room door, and flung it open. Annabel was slumped in a chair, sobbing, holding onto the arm of one of the constables.

"Mum, what's going on?" he demanded.

It was hard to understand her through her cries, but Annabel raised her head to look at him. The rest of us could see the goings-on from where we sat at the table.

"Andreas was pushed into the river and he drowned. He was murdered!" And she cried harder, her shoulders heaving with the effort of crying and trying to catch her breath. Everyone looked at her in shock.

"But that doesn't make sense," Rhisiart said, standing up and walking toward Annabel. "Andreas was a good swimmer. How is that possible? And who pushed him?"

Hugh took charge of the scene in short order. He asked the officers to leave the drawing room and called for me to help Annabel to her room. He asked Cadi to pour tea or coffee for the constables and asked Rhisiart to get the necessary information from them.

But the constables had other ideas. They informed us that Sian had gone to her room through the other exit in the drawing room, rather than facing the rest of us. They said they would need to question everyone again, beginning with Hugh and Rhisiart and continuing with Annabel and Sian when they had composed themselves sufficiently. They also demanded to see Sylvie immediately. One of the officers accompanied me to the coach house to get her and escort her back to the castle. Once inside the officer commandeered the sitting room and the other used the drawing room.

Sylvie waited a long time for the officers to finish talking to Hugh, Rhisiart, and Cadi before being called in to answer questions. She obviously had nothing to say to the police since she didn't know Andreas or any of the family members or staff at the castle, but the constables nevertheless kept her for almost an hour.

"They were certainly thorough," Sylvie whispered to me after she had been released from questioning. The constables appeared together in the dining room and asked each of us to go into the village to the police station to give a formal statement. We all agreed to do so, then they asked that Annabel and Sian be brought out of their rooms to answer questions about the night Andreas went missing.

Hugh went to fetch Sian and I went upstairs to Annabel's room, where I found her reading a book and dabbing her eyes with a tissue.

"How are you feeling?" I asked her.

"Horrible. To think that my favorite son's last hours were spent in dreadful fear," she said, tears coursing down her cheeks, "I just can't bear it."

"The police need to talk to you," I said gently.

"Again?" she asked. "Must they intrude now? Haven't I been through enough?"

"You have," I agreed, "but they're just doing their jobs. The quicker we answer all their questions, the quicker they'll leave and get working to find out who killed Andreas."

I shouldn't have phrased my answer that way, because she started crying harder. "Annabel, you just need to pull yourself together for a little while and then you can come back and take all the time you need without any interruptions."

She nodded, gulping, and said, "Very well. I'll go answer their questions, but I want them out of here as soon as possible. Are they questioning Sian, too?" I nodded. "Have they no respect?" she asked in disgust.

"They're just doing their jobs," I reminded her.

"Bah," she answered, waving her hand toward me. By this time I knew Annabel well enough to know she wasn't angry with me, just frustrated by the situation.

One of the constables talked to Annabel in the drawing room while the other questioned Sian in the sitting room. Annabel had asked to be in the sitting room because it was her favorite room in the castle and she felt most comfortable in there, but her request was denied. I wondered why—was it to keep her out of her comfort zone, or was it because the officer in the drawing room had been assigned to speak to her? Probably a combination of the two.

The questioning didn't end until afternoon. We all convened in the sitting room after the police left to compare notes about what they had asked and to whom. Maisie and Brenda came in to set up a large tea service for everyone. "Did the constables talk to both of you, too?" Annabel asked. Both women nodded, but offered no further information and didn't seem inclined to gossip about the questions.

I wondered how Brenda was handling all the questions and speculation about Andreas's death. I hadn't spoken to her privately in a couple of days. She was looking wan and tired, a signal that she wasn't sleeping, that the entire situation had taken hold of her imagination and propelled her into a state of despair, but I felt it would be inappropriate of me to ask her. It was none of my business.

I was struck by a sudden and unwelcome thought. *Is it possible Brenda knew Andreas better than she was letting on? Is it possible they were romantically involved before Andreas's death? In that case, it's no wonder she seems so weepy and fragile.* It was an ugly thought, and I kept it to myself, knowing that giving voice to it would create a tension and a level of stress within the family that none of them would handle well. But I made a mental note to discuss the possibility with Sylvie later that evening.

Annabel had asked Maisie to prepare a light meal for dinner, since no one in the household seemed hungry. Our utensils clinked against the plates in the cold silence of the dining room. The funeral was scheduled for the following afternoon and everyone was lost in their own thoughts.

After dinner I went over to the coach house to spend some time with Sylvie. We sat before a roaring fire in the salon, curled up on the sofas in the warm lamplight.

"What do you think?" I asked her after I had presented my thought that perhaps Brenda and Andreas had been having an affair.

Sylvie looked doubtful. "I don't know. It couldn't have been much of an affair, if there really was one. Andreas didn't spend that much time at the castle, did he?"

"An affair is an affair," I said, "regardless of how often they saw each other."

But the more she thought about it the more sense the idea made. "You know, not seeing him often would give her all the more reason to pine after him," she said thoughtfully. "Maybe that's the reason she's so distraught, Eilidh. She's been having an affair with Andreas and she can't tell the world how much she loved him because he was married. And now he's gone," she said.

"You didn't like the idea a minute ago and now you sound a little too excited about it," I said with a grimace.

"I don't mean to. I just think we've figured out why a housekeeper is so despairing over the death of someone she allegedly didn't know very well."

"You might be right," I said, pointing at her with my glass.

"So what do you do about it now that you've got it figured out?"

"That's the problem, I suppose. There's nothing that can be done."

"What about telling Annabel?"

"I don't think I could do that," I said. "She would fire Brenda in an instant. And if Brenda leaves, then Maisie would be sure to leave, too, either on her own or because Annabel might fire her, too. And then we're left without a housekeeper and without a cook. Besides, what if it's not true?"

"Are you going to tell the police your theory?"

I thought for a moment. "I don't think there's any reason to tell them. After all, it's just speculation, though I think it makes a lot of sense. Let them figure it out. I'm not in the business of creating more problems for the household."

As the fire died down and I began to feel comfortably drowsy, I went back to the castle through the moonlit night. Sylvie was already on her way to bed and I was looking forward to a good night's sleep before the stress of Andreas's funeral the following afternoon.

As I reached for the giant handle on the castle's front door, I was startled when the door swung open. Stepping backward, I almost stumbled on the top stone step. Rhisiart stood in the doorway, looking concerned.

"Eilidh! You startled me. Are you all right?" he added, almost as an afterthought.

"I'm fine," I assured him. "You didn't hurt me—just scared me."

"Sorry about that," he said, opening the door wider so I could step into the great hall. "Where are you coming from?"

"The coach house. I feel bad that Sylvie is here on holiday and I haven't really been able to spend much time with her, so I've tried to go over there in the evenings and chat."

"I'm headed out to the pub in the village. There wasn't nearly enough food for dinner and I'm ravenous. Care to join me?" he asked.

"Have you looked in the kitchen downstairs?"

He shook his head. "The only thing that will satisfy me right now is a shepherd's pie. I hope the pub's serving food this late."

"I'm sure you can get something there, even if it's not shepherd's pie," I said.

"Are you coming?" he asked with a hint of impatience.

"All right. I'll go." I was feeling a bit peckish, too, and the wine would keep me up all night if I didn't have food in my stomach to counteract its effects.

We went around to the parking enclosure and got in his little runabout. He drove fast, like someone from the city who didn't get to the countryside very often. We were in the village in no time, and pulled into a spot across the road from the pub. There were still a number of cars parked outside, so I knew it would be crowded.

We found two spots at the bar and ordered food and two pints. He got his shepherd's pie and I ordered a Thai green vegetable curry. Once we had ordered, Rhisiart leaned back on his stool and gazed around the room, taking it all in slowly. "Sometimes I miss being in a little village," he said wistfully.

"It's funny how people sometimes long for the things they don't have. I think it would be thrilling to live in London."

"It can be thrilling, but there's just something about a Welsh village that brings back fond memories and makes me feel nostalgic," he said.

I nodded, but wondered how he could feel nostalgic in the village where his brother was murdered. He must have sensed what I was thinking, because he gave a slight smile. "I guess I should rephrase that. I generally feel nostalgic. Maybe not so much at the moment, knowing how Andreas died."

"What do you think happened?" I blurted out. I hadn't meant to ask him, but the wine and a few sips of beer had loosened my tongue. He looked surprised.

"I don't know. I haven't seen Andreas in a long time. I hate to say it, but I really didn't know him very well. I don't know if it was a random act of violence or if he was deliberately targeted."

"How are you going to write his obituary if you didn't know him?"

"I'm a writer. That's what I do. I'll write something that's appropriately mournful and respectful. Don't worry. It'll sound fine."

Through the fog in my mind it took me a moment to understand what he was saying. It seemed callous. Coming from a close-knit family, I found it unfathomable that one sibling wouldn't know another well enough to compose a thoughtful, heartfelt tribute. But my family was nothing like Annabel's—that much I already knew.

I had heard rumblings of the problems in Annabel's household when the boys were young, when Annabel was married to her first husband, who died under unusual circumstances many years ago. They were usually in the form of *sotto voce* conversations between my Aunt Margot and her late husband, my Uncle Mack. I had spent untold hours at their house playing with Greer and Sylvie. I always lent an ear when I heard them discussing Annabel because I remember thinking "Annabel" was the most beautiful name I had ever heard and I loved to hear it spoken.

Aunt Margot and Uncle Mack would have their heads together and I would hear words and phrases like "Annabel's boys" and "poor things" and "monster." Sometimes I was scared by the things they said, but that only made me listen harder. When they realized I was nearby, they always stopped their whispering and put smiles on their faces. I always wondered what they were saying and hoped they weren't calling Annabel a monster. I hated to think she wasn't as wonderful as her name.

I didn't hear those conversations very often, but I do remember clearly the few times I heard them. And I remember distinctly the day I realized what they were discussing.

Annabel's first husband, Arthur, was a wealthy man with a hot temper. Annabel had no need to work outside the home in the years they were married because he provided very well for the family. According to what I overheard from my aunt and uncle, he provided well for them because he felt it to be his duty. He also loved impressing the people of the small village where they lived and the best way to do it was to show everyone how well the Tucker family lived.

But things inside the castle were not as rosy as they seemed. Arthur drank heavily and was brutally beating his sons and his wife. Because the boys did not attend school with the other children in the village and because the family had a governess who would only come to the castle on the days she was summoned, their bruises would remain hidden and no one would speak of them. No one knew what compelled Arthur to beat his family. Aunt Margot would visit Annabel and glimpse the welts and bruises on her and her sons. Annabel would try to hide the raw marks, but Aunt Margot spotted them.

The worst part, as I heard Aunt Margot express it, was that Annabel did not protect her boys from their father. This, I assumed, was the reason the boys rarely, if ever, visited their mother after they had grown up and moved away. Then there was the confusion surrounding the death of Arthur Tucker. Someone had called the ambulance after finding Arthur dead one night, but no one ever admitted to having been the caller. There was never much of an investigation into Arthur's death because his blood alcohol level was so high that night; it was assumed he fell, sustained a head wound, and bled to death. But the mystery of who summoned the ambulance to the castle was never solved.

After Arthur's death Annabel had married Brian Baines, a man who, by all accounts, was kind, generous, and loving to Annabel and her sons. But still, Hugh and Rhisiart didn't return.

But Andreas did. He didn't come often, but he came and that meant the world to Annabel. That's why Andreas was her favorite, and though it pained me to think that any mother would choose a favorite among her children, I understood why. I believe Annabel feared that since Andreas was gone now, she would never see any of her family again, including the grandchild she so longed to meet.

"Are you all right, Eilidh?" Rhisiart asked. His words jolted me out of my thoughts and brought me back to the tiny village pub.

"Yes, sorry about that. I guess I let my mind wander a bit."

"That's all right. Ready to go back?" he asked.

I nodded. He paid the bill for our food and drinks and I was pulling my coat on when I caught a glimpse of someone I recognized. Griff was standing with a small group of men, all dressed in work clothes and boots, over in the corner at a high table. I didn't know if he had seen me, but I raised my hand in greeting. He raised his glass in return. So he had seen me. I glanced once over my shoulder as I walked through the pub door into the cold darkness; he was still watching me.

Rhisiart drove more slowly on the way back to the castle, for which I was grateful. I was afraid he wouldn't remember the roads in the area as well as he thought and would run us off the road or worse, run us straight into the river. But we arrived at the castle safely and he pulled round to the parking enclosure. We entered through one of the back doors of the castle and I thanked him for dinner.

"You're quite welcome," he replied. "And thank you for the company. Maybe we can do it again sometime." I wasn't sure what he meant by that, so I didn't answer, but gave him a quick wave and turned down my hallway. I was ready for bed and I hoped that the food would do its job and help me get to sleep and stay asleep all night.

I woke up the next morning refreshed, but with a slight feeling of dread, knowing Andreas's funeral service was just hours away. I wondered how Annabel and Sian would handle the emotion of saying goodbye to him.

After breakfast Sylvie raided my closet for clothes that would be suitable for the funeral. Since we were about the same size, I had told her not to bother buying anything new for the service. There was no reason to spend a lot of money in one of the village dress shops for something she hadn't intended to buy. It was fun helping her pick out the clothes she would wear, because we treated it like a fashion show. It would be, I knew, the only lighthearted time either of us would enjoy all day. Once she had decided what to wear, she left the house to go for a walk and I went to see if there was anything Annabel wanted me to do before the funeral.

She was crying softly in her bedroom when I found her. Wiping her eyes at the sight of me, she smiled tremulously and asked if I was ready for the service. "I'm ready," I answered. "Do you think you'll be all right this afternoon?"

"I think so," she said, straightening up a bit. She knew all eyes would be on her and Sian this day, and she wanted to put on a brave front.

Sian was in the dining room when I went in for a cup of tea. She looked worn and tired, but I was glad to see she was trying to eat something. She couldn't afford to add to her grief by not eating enough for her child. "How are you doing today, Sian?" I asked her.

She looked at me sadly. "All right, I suppose, all things considered. I just want it all to be over."

I nodded, remembering the day of Uncle Mack's funeral. The sadness was palpable, but the predominant feeling was of wanting everything to be over so people would go home and leave the family alone. I could understand Sian's sentiments.

When it came time to leave for the funeral, I piled into Sylvie's car with Maisie and Brenda. It was a wonder we fit four grown people into Sylvie's tiny auto. We drove slowly to the church in the village, the last in a line of cars from the castle. Annabel and Sian were already seated in the front pew of the church when my companions and I walked in. We had spent several minutes looking for a parking spot. The street had already been lined with funeral attendees. I wondered if they were all people who had known Andreas or if they knew Annabel or if they simply came out of respect for the family. Probably a combination, I supposed.

I sat several rows behind the rest of the family. Annabel craned her neck and I gave her a little wave when she saw me. She had probably been wondering what had taken us so long. Her eyes were dry and her mouth had a determined shape to it, as though she refused to allow herself to cry yet.

I sat with Sylvie on one side of me and Maisie and Brenda on the other. I tried to ignore Brenda's sniffles and noises, but I found it difficult. As sorry as I felt for her, she was behaving inappropriately for the funeral of someone else's husband. Maisie whispered something sharply in Brenda's ear and most of the noises stopped.

The funeral service was not long, as the family had requested that mourners not be invited to share personal stories about Andreas. Annabel and Sian had agreed from the start that hearing such stories would only make a difficult day much harder to bear.

When the service was over we all stood in the cemetery in back of the church and watched as Andreas's burnished walnut casket was lowered into the earth. The family members each threw a handful of dirt onto the casket before turning around to resume their positions around the grave. Rhisiart held one of Annabel's arms to give her the support she seemed to need, and Hugh and Cadi did the same for Sian. I stood aside with the other mourners; Sylvie, Maisie, Brenda, Griff, and the other two men who worked with Griff stayed with me. When the burial ceremony ended, we all returned to our cars and drove back to the castle, where a light meal awaited all the mourners, as was the custom in the small village.

I had hastily arranged the meal earlier, knowing Maisie and Brenda would be at the funeral service and unable to prepare food. They had set out chairs and small tables around the dining room of the castle during the morning, expecting a large crowd of mourners. The caterer, a friend of Annabel who had kindly offered her services, had arrived early in the day and set up all the food, which was kept warm in silver chafing dishes.

As people began to arrive after the burial, Brenda ushered them into the dining room where they could help themselves to food. Annabel and Sian accepted mourners in the drawing room, where a fire in the large fireplace warded off the chill of the day.

I was at a bit of a loss during the afternoon. Sylvie went back to the coach house after she had expressed her condolences to Annabel and Sian, but I felt I should stay in the castle in case I was needed by someone. There were quite a few people milling about; I didn't know most of them and most of them had never seen me. I introduced myself to a few people as they departed the castle having paid their respects to Annabel and Sian, but in general I kept to myself and simply made sure there was enough food and drink for all the guests.

As often happens after a funeral, particularly a funeral for someone of Andreas's age, talk turned to whispered speculation as to the cause of death.

In particular, as I sidled over toward a group of young men of Andreas's approximate age—probably old friends from the village—I heard them talking about possible reasons for the tragedy.

"Poor bloke. And with a baby on the way," one said softly.

"Who do you suppose did it?" another asked.

"It could have been any number of people, really, given the business he was in," the first one said. All his comrades nodded.

"Someone from around here?" the second man asked.

"Who knows?" the first man answered. "Someone easily could have followed him up from London."

"I wonder how the coppers'll narrow it down," one of the men said with a smirk. "So many suspects."

Just then one of the men looked over his shoulder and realized I had been lingering near the group. He nodded his head ever so slightly in my direction and the group changed the subject to the latest sports news. I moved away, trying to remember what I had heard about Andreas's work.

Was he in advertising? Some kind of high-pressure business? Banking, perhaps? I couldn't recall. I would have to ask someone. But the family wasn't ready to answer questions like that, especially from me. I may have been good friends with Annabel, but I was still her employee.

But they would have to answer such questions soon enough from the police.

Chapter 7

Indeed, the police arrived at the castle first thing the next morning. I had just gotten to the dining room when the front doorbell sounded and I could hear Brenda hurrying through the great hall. When she entered the dining room with two officers in tow, she looked scared. She announced in a quivery voice that the officers wanted to speak to Sian. I told her to wait with the officers while I went to find Sian.

She was in her room, trying to fit into a sweater that was clearly too small for her growing frame. She turned to me with tears in her eyes and threw the sweater on the floor.

"Damn this thing!" she yelled, then took a steadying breath and made an effort to calm herself. "What do you need, Eilidh?"

"There are two police officers in the dining room to see you." I reached down to pick up the sweater from the floor. I folded it and laid it on her bed. "What about that one?" I asked, pointing to a sweater that lay over the back of the armchair next to the fireplace.

"I feel so fat in that one," she said miserably.

"It brings out the green in your eyes."

She smiled and reached for the sweater. "Thank you. I don't suppose it really matters how fat I feel, does it? It just means the baby's getting bigger." She rubbed her hand on her belly slowly, a faraway look in her eyes. I didn't have to ask what she was thinking about—that Andreas would never see the baby.

She sighed. "I suppose the sooner I answer their questions the sooner they'll leave and the sooner we'll have an answer about how Andreas died."

I could tell from the look in her eyes that she had had enough of the questions, enough of the speculation, and probably enough of the castle and its inhabitants. "Will you tell them I'll be there in a minute?" she asked.

I returned to the dining room, relayed the message, and left to find Annabel. She needed to know the police were back and asking more questions. I was surprised to find her outside, wandering in the English garden.

It was early for her to be outside. I debated whether to disturb her, but she heard my footsteps and beckoned me to join her.

"I already know the police are here," she began, bending down to deadhead a flower. "Have they asked for me?"

"They've only asked to talk to Sian so far."

"It's only a matter of time, I'm sure."

I nodded. "Is there anything you'd like me to do today?"

"I'd like to go riding. That would be good for me, I think. Can you get hold of Griff and ask him to have Miss Muffet ready after lunch?"

Miss Muffet was Annabel's favorite horse. She was gentle, sweet, and obedient. Many times she and Annabel would disappear across the fields and be gone for hours, simply enjoying the outdoors and each other's company.

I left Annabel in the garden and returned to the castle, where I rang up Griff. He answered his mobile phone as I walked into the sitting room, and I was shocked to see him in there, standing by the mantel looking uncomfortable.

"Griff!" I said in surprise, laughing. I put away my phone. "I didn't know you were in the house."

"I came up because Mr. Rhisiart called for me," he answered.

"Have you talked to him yet?"

"No. He asked me to wait in here."

"Do you want me to go get him?" I asked.

"No, thank you. I'll just wait."

"I was just calling you to let you know that Annabel wants to ride this afternoon. Can you have Miss Muffet ready after lunch?"

"Sure," he said, shuffling his feet, his hands in his pockets. He looked decidedly nervous.

"Is everything all right?" I asked.

"I don't quite understand why Mr. Rhisiart called me up here. I hope nothing is wrong," he said in a worried voice. It bothered me to hear Griff refer to Rhisiart as "Mr. Rhisiart." It had an odious sound to it, as if there was an implied suggestion that Griff wasn't as worthy a person as Rhisiart.

"Why don't you just call him 'Rhisiart'?" I asked.

"He asked me to call him 'Mr. Rhisiart.'" I must have raised my eyebrows. "Isn't that what you call him?"

"No. And I wouldn't even if he asked me to. I am not his servant, and you aren't either. You should either call him by his first name or tell him to call you 'Mr. Griff.' Does he refer to you that way?"

Griff grinned. "He doesn't, but it doesn't bother me as much as it bothers you, apparently."

"It makes my blood boil."

"You should spend more time around horses. You might not get upset about things as easily."

I was taken aback. "I don't get upset easily, do I?" I asked him.

"I don't know, but you're upset about how I talk to Mr. Rhisiart. I mean, Rhisiart. I hadn't given it a thought."

"Maybe you're right. I probably *should* get out and ride more often."

"Let me know anytime you want and I'll have a horse ready for you."

I had been riding a few times since living at the castle, but I was by no means the expert rider Annabel was. Riding horses cost money, and when Callum and I were married there was never enough money to indulge in hobbies like riding. Annabel had insisted that I learn to ride when I first started working for her, "just in case" she had said, so she had taught me the basics. I could see what all the hype was about—there was something quite mysterious, quite powerful, about being on a horse. Perhaps it was the added height it gave me, or perhaps the feeling of a huge, muscular beast under me, or perhaps it was just the feeling of being outside, alone except for the animal, exploring at my own pace. I loved feeling the wind on my face and I loved the smell of horses. Griff was right. I *did* need to spend more time riding.

Rhisiart came into the sitting room just then. "Ah, Griff, I'm glad you're here," he said. Griff shot me a glance and a small smile.

"Did I miss something?" Rhisiart asked.

"Not at all, sir," Griff answered.

"Good. I thought not. I asked you up here to talk about possibly renovating the stables."

If Griff had expected to discuss any particular topic with Rhisiart, this wasn't it. His eyes widened, then narrowed. "If I may say, sir, I've already discussed the renovations with Annabel."

"I'm thinking more for racing horses."

Griff gasped and started coughing. "Annabel does not wish to keep horses for racing, sir."

"I'll talk to her. Things may be changing around here a bit."

Griff eyed Rhisiart suspiciously. He didn't like the sound of what he had just heard. Then he looked at me. I shrugged. Rhisiart had already seated himself in Annabel's favorite chair and seemed to take no notice of our exchanged glances.

I didn't want to eavesdrop on their conversation, so I left the room and went down to the kitchen for a snack. Maisie was sitting down, wiping her eyes when I walked into the room; her face was puffy and pink.

"Is everything all right, Maisie?" I asked.

I had startled her. She looked up, blinking tears away, and then looked away quickly. "Oh, Eilidh, I'm sorry you had to see me like this. I'm fine. Just being silly. What brings you down here?"

"A snack. No, don't bother," I said as she stood up and bustled toward the cupboard. "I'll find something." She sat down again and watched me with a slight smile as I rummaged through the cupboard looking for something that struck my fancy. I found a box of crackers and went to the refrigerator. "Any good cheese in here?" I asked over my shoulder.

"We have some wonderful cheese I bought in the village," she said, coming over to where I stood perusing the contents of the refrigerator. "It's smoked English cheddar. I had a bit of it. You'll love it."

She pulled down a small wooden cutting board while I unwrapped the cheese, then opened the box of crackers. I cut two thin slices of cheese and put them each on a cracker and handed one to Maisie.

"Don't mind if I do," she said. "I could use a little snack."

"Everything all right?" I asked again.

"Eilidh, children are the most wonderful thing that will ever happen to you. They're also the hardest."

"Brenda giving you a hard time?"

She nodded. "She gives me trouble sometimes, that girl. I feel like I'm walking on eggshells around her."

"I suppose teenage girls are like that. I probably gave my mum a run for her money when I was Brenda's age. Heck, I probably still give her a run for her money!" I said with a laugh.

Maisie smiled. "I hope you're right and that it's just her age. If she doesn't grow out of this behavior, I'll lose years off my life."

"Hang in there," I said, slicing off more cheese for each of us. "She's bound to change as she gets older." *Easy for me to say,* I thought. *I don't have any children. I don't even have the prospect of having them.* The thought made me suddenly sad.

Maisie seemed to sense my melancholy. "If Brenda doesn't change, maybe you'd like to adopt her." Her remark made me laugh and I returned upstairs with a smile on my face. Poor Maisie would just have to wait for Brenda on the other side of her teenage years. Luckily for her, that was only a couple years away. I hoped her situation would become easier as Brenda matured.

As if hearing my thoughts, Brenda descended the steps to below-stairs as I was going up. "How are you doing, Brenda?" I asked.

She averted her eyes and answered in a small voice, "All right, I suppose."

"Be good to your mum," I cautioned with a smile. She didn't seem to hear me.

I had been gone just long enough for Rhisiart and Griff to finish their conversation. Rhisiart was coming out of the sitting room as I passed the doorway. "Eilidh, just the person I wanted to see," he said.

"What can I do for you, Rhisiart?" I asked.

"I was wondering if you'd care to go to the pub with me again tonight," he answered. "I enjoyed your company last time."

"I probably shouldn't. I haven't seen much of my cousin since she's been here. I was hoping to go with her to the pub. Perhaps we'll see you there."

"Sure. That makes sense. Maybe I'll see you there." He turned and walked away hurriedly. Griff came out of the sitting room next.

"I can't believe the nerve of him," Griff said. "He wants to add more stables for race horses. Annabel will hate the idea of having race horses in the stables."

"I wonder why he's so keen to have race horses here," I mused. "I wonder if it means he'll be spending more time at the castle."

"Who knows?" Griff grumbled. "I hope not."

I smiled. "Griff, you sound like you don't like Rhisiart."

"I don't mind telling you that he gets under my skin, Eilidh. I'll bet you he has plans to take over this whole place now that the favored son is gone. I'll bet he's trying to get Annabel to change her will."

I laid my hand lightly on Griff's arm. "Let's not get ahead of ourselves," I cautioned. "We don't know anything about Annabel's will or Rhisiart's plans for the future. Maybe it's all completely innocent."

Griff gave me a look that told me I ought to know better. "I could be right," I said, trying to convince myself as much as Griff. "Besides, Annabel is very much alive and doesn't show any signs of needing a will anytime soon."

"Thank God for that," Griff muttered. "I couldn't stand it if Rhisiart moved in." I wondered what Griff would think of Rhisiart's invitation for me to join him at the pub later. It didn't really matter.

After Griff left I walked over to the coach house to see Sylvie. She was getting ready to go hiking. "Why don't you join me?" she asked. "You could use a few hours away from that family."

She was right. "I'll go on one condition," I said.

"What's that?"

"That you go with me this afternoon to a cooking class. I scheduled one for the family, but I don't know if they're going and it's too late to cancel. Might as well get Annabel's money's worth. I had a whole slate of activities planned, and I have a feeling I'll have to cancel the rest of them."

Sylvie grinned. "That would be fun. I could go home and surprise Seamus with my new skills. It's not fair that he has all the fun in the kitchen. What are we going to learn?"

"I'm not sure, except it's a French dinner party theme."

"Ooh, that sounds *magnifique*," Sylvie said with a laugh.

When I returned to the castle I went in search of Hugh and Cadi. I found them in their room, arguing about when they were going to return home. The bedroom door was thick, so they must have had their voices raised quite high. I knocked on the door and the voices stopped.

"Who is it?" Hugh asked.

"Eilidh," I called.

The door opened and he stepped aside to admit me. "What is it, Eilidh?"

"I have a cooking class scheduled for the family this afternoon. I'm trying to get a head count of who might like to go."

"I'll go," Cadi said. She had been sitting on the edge of the bed and she stood up to walk toward the door. She shot Hugh a dark look. "I'll do anything to get away from this stifling house."

"Watch it, Cadi," Hugh warned.

"We're leaving before dinner," I told her. "The theme is a French dinner party, so we'll make dinner and eat it there."

"Good," Cadi said.

"Hugh, do you want to go with us?" I asked.

"Who else is going?"

"Besides Cadi and me, my cousin Sylvie is going. I haven't asked Rhisiart yet."

"I'll go if he goes. I don't want to be the only bloke."

I smiled at him, then noticed that Cadi wasn't smiling. "I think you should stay here," she told him. "You and I need a few hours apart."

The look Hugh turned on his wife was one of pure anger. "Is nothing private?" he snarled.

"Take it easy, Hugh. It's not as if everyone in this old place doesn't hear us fighting."

He brushed past me and stalked down the hallway. I turned to Cadi and she laughed lightly when she saw the look of surprise on my face. "He'll be fine. Needs to cool off, that's all. God, this place gets under my skin!" she said in a loud voice, raking her hands through her hair. "I'll be glad to get away for a while this evening."

I left her in her room to go in search of Rhisiart, whom I found in the drawing room reading a newspaper. "Does anything interesting ever happen in this village? I don't remember it being this boring when I was growing up," he said in frustration when I came into the room. I didn't feel the need to remind him his brother had been murdered just a few days ago. *That should be excitement enough for anyone,* I thought.

"Rhisiart, do you want to join us for a cooking class this evening?" I asked.

"I thought you were going to the pub," he answered.

"I might go with Sylvie, but that'll be later on. The cooking class takes place around the dinner hour and we eat there."

"Is Hugh going?"

"No."

"Then I'll go."

I hadn't realized there was such animosity between the brothers, but Rhisiart's comment made me wonder. How well did he get along with Hugh? How about Cadi?

"Cadi's going," I said.

"I'll go anyway. I just don't want to get stuck spending the evening with my dear brother."

I gave Rhisiart the details of the cooking class and he said he would meet the rest of us there. I found as I went looking for Sian I was not looking forward to his presence at the class. He would be the only man and a girls' night out, even if it had to include Cadi, sounded fun. Sian was reading a magazine in her room when I found her. As I had suspected, she had no interest in a cooking class. I tried cajoling her into going, but she seemed content to stay at the castle.

I changed into clothes suitable for hiking and joined Sylvie in the coach house before we struck out together across the fields behind the castle. I led her directly to the forest that bordered the fields and we spent the next several hours following one of the trails that Griff had marked through the dense trees.

Sylvie asked me all about Rhisiart while we walked. "He asked me to go to the pub tonight with him," I told her.

"Are you going?" she asked with a grin.

"Take it easy," I chuckled. "No. I mean, I told him maybe he could meet us there after the cooking class, but I said I'd be with you."

"I don't want to interfere with your date," she said.

"You don't seem to understand," I said, rolling my eyes. "I don't want to have a drink with him alone. There's something about him that makes me uncomfortable. I can't put my finger on it, but it's just this feeling I get."

"Haven't you been to the pub once with him?"

"I have," I admitted. "But that was kind of a special circumstance. We were both starving and he caught me off guard when he asked me to go get something to eat. I didn't think of it as a date."

"He might have thought of it like that," Sylvie pointed out. "Men can be so thick that way." She changed the subject. "Do you ever hear from Callum?"

"No. And I don't want to, either." Her question had suddenly put a damper on my spirits and all I wanted to do was return to the castle. "We should turn around and head back so we have time to get ready for the cooking class. I want to shower and change," I said.

Sylvie looked a bit taken aback. "I didn't mean to upset you," she said. "I mean, by mentioning Callum. I was just surprised to hear talk about dating, that's all."

"Who's talking about dating?" I asked crossly. "I'm not dating anyone. And least of all Rhisiart!"

I could tell she shared my hurry to get home. The pleasant mood had darkened and I felt guilty. It was my fault for reacting the way I did to talk of Callum, but she should have known better.

When we returned to the castle Sylvie went back to the coach house to shower and change and I did the same in my room. By the time we got in the car to drive to the cooking class, I was feeling much better. The first thing I did was apologize to her for my earlier behavior.

"I just want you to have a wonderful holiday," I said. "And all of a sudden we were talking about Callum and he's the last person on earth I wanted to think about today. And we were talking about Rhisiart, and I don't like to think that he wants anything more than friendship with me, and then we were talking about dating, and the thought of it absolutely scares me to death."

"I should have known better than to bring up Callum. I'm sorry about that."

I gave her a quick smile. "That's okay. Now, enough about men and let's go learn how to cook French food."

The mood in the car was lighthearted the rest of the way to the cooking class, which was held in an old Norman-style home several villages away.

I was glad we could drive there in the soft sunshine of the afternoon—I wanted Sylvie to see some of the gorgeous scenery surrounding the county where Thistlecross Castle was located.

It was a beautiful afternoon for a drive, and somewhere behind us I knew Rhisiart was driving Cadi to the class. Indeed, they arrived at the old home where the class was to take place just a few minutes later than we did and we all walked in together.

Our instructor introduced herself as Jacqueline. She explained that she was a former cook at the Canadian embassy in London. I had read a bit about her online before booking the class and I had chosen this particular class because I was so impressed with her credentials.

The menu was elegant yet, Jacqueline promised, easy for novice chefs. We were going to prepare Muscovy duck with crispy skin, a bouillabaisse with garlic aioli, spiced pears, a salad with a pomegranate vinaigrette, and an apple jalousie for dessert. The kitchen was a huge room with heavy wooden workstations arrayed in two rows. Cadi and Rhisiart shared one table and Sylvie and I shared another. We tied on aprons and examined our knives and got to work under Jacqueline's expert tutelage. As she explained, each workstation had a different part of the meal, and we rotated so each of us could experience the entire meal process. We sliced pears and apples, steamed clams, tested the fragrant soup before and after we added the saffron, and learned how to use puff pastry.

Jacqueline kept everything moving so we could eat dinner at the appointed hour. At the back of the kitchen was a long wooden farmhouse-style table set with rustic place settings and centerpiece. Fall flowers, fruits, and vegetables made up the décor, and the table runner was made of old flour bags sewn together. Jacqueline poured wine for everyone and passed a baguette. Each of us tore off the amount of bread we wanted and Jacqueline came around with the bouillabaisse and aioli. I put a dollop of the aioli on my bouillabaisse and ate my first bite with a sigh of contentment. It was perfect, and as I looked around the table at my fellow diners, I could tell how much they were enjoying the experience, too.

We insisted that Jacqueline join us for dinner, so she ate with us and regaled us with stories of her years managing the embassy kitchen. We enjoyed a long, leisurely meal. Everything was divine—that is, until Jacqueline excused herself to take a phone call and talk turned, as I should have expected, to Andreas and his cause of death.

"Do we have to talk about this now?" I asked in a voice that hinted of my annoyance. "We've been having such a good time. Why ruin it?"

"I think we should talk about it," Cadi insisted. "After all, it's the most important thing going on right now in any of our lives, isn't it?"

"It may be the most important thing in my life right now, and in yours and Rhisiart's, but it is not the most important thing in Sylvie's life," I said, waving my hand toward my cousin, who sat across from me. I was sure she didn't care to discuss the murder of someone she barely knew in gruesome detail at dinner.

Sylvie shook her head almost imperceptibly at me, which I took as an indication that she didn't mind Cadi talking about Andreas. Cadi looked around conspiratorially. "I don't want Jacqueline to come back and hear this," she said in a loud whisper.

"Hear what?" I asked.

"What I learned about Andreas."

Now she had my attention, as much as I hated to admit it. Did she know something about Andreas that the rest of us didn't know?

Rhisiart made an impatient motion with his hand. "Well, are you going to tell us or do you want us to guess at it all night?"

Cadi gave him a smirk and looked over her shoulder. "I heard that Andreas had more than one job, if you know what I mean."

"We have no idea what you mean. Quit talking in riddles and out with it." Rhisiart sounded cross.

"I mean that his income didn't come just from his job at the London firm."

"And?"

"You didn't hear this from me," Cadi whispered as we all leaned in a bit closer, "but I have it on good authority that he's been dealing."

"Dealing what?" Sylvie asked in what seemed like an unusually loud voice.

Cadi stared at her. "Drugs. Cocaine, to be precise. What rock have you been living under?"

Sylvie glared at Cadi and I held up my hand. "Cadi, please. That's not necessary. You could have meant lots of things."

"Like what, for example?"

"Girls, enough," Rhisiart said. "Cadi, how do you know this?"

She gave him a coy look. "I have my sources," she said.

He snorted. "Give, Cadi. How'd you find out?"

I glanced at Rhisiart. Had he already known the information Cadi shared? I couldn't tell from his expression. She ignored him.

"Cadi, I don't believe it," I said. "What makes you think it's true?"

"You're more naïve than most, Eilidh," she said, her voice low. "Ever noticed Brenda's eyes? Ever noticed her sniffling constantly? Why do you think she does that?"

Her words hit me hard. I was quiet for a moment. Should I reveal my own suspicions? It was probably time to say something.

"I think Brenda was distraught over Andreas's death because she was in love with him."

"That's rot," Cadi said. The words sounded cruel coming from her lips.

"It's as good an explanation for her physical symptoms as the rubbish you're accusing her of," I said. My skin was hot and I could feel the anger rising in my chest.

"Just think about it for a moment," Cadi said. "Brenda always has red runny eyes, her nostrils are red and raw, and she's come emotionally unglued. Of course she's one of his clients."

"She could just as easily be crying over his death, as so many other people have. Red eyes and nostrils are signs of someone who's been upset and blowing her nose a lot," I argued.

"Well, if I can't convince you any other way," Cadi said, "I have seen them together in the drawing room when they think they're alone. She was passing something to him and he was passing something to her in return."

"That doesn't prove anything," I insisted. "I think it's possible they were having an affair. That's what people do when they're having an affair—pass things to each other when they think no one is looking."

Cadi shook her head. "I don't know why you can't see past the end of your nose," she said. "It's very clear to me what's been going on."

"I think you're being very unkind," I said. The evening was ruined. Rhisiart shifted in his chair and Sylvie was visibly relieved when Jacqueline came back into the room and served the jalousie to all of us at the table.

But I couldn't eat. The dessert looked beautiful, with a perfectly golden and crispy crust and syrupy apples layered on its surface, but I simply could not bring myself to take even one bite. Cadi's words had turned my stomach. I thanked Jacqueline and pushed my plate away, explaining that I was much too full from the delicious dinner to eat any more.

Jacqueline put my jalousie in a cardboard box so I could take it home with me to eat later. I accepted the box with thanks, but I had a feeling I wouldn't want the food any time soon. Perhaps Annabel would like it.

When we had left the class with promises to make arrangements to return someday for another cooking lesson with Jacqueline, Cadi and Rhisiart drove off first while I sat in the car with Sylvie.

"Do you think she's right?" I asked. She knew what I was talking about without me having to elaborate.

"I hate to say it and I don't want it to be true, but it makes sense," she said. "It's possible." Somehow I didn't mind as much when my cousin spoke about Brenda and Andreas that way. It seemed a much kinder way to speculate, rather than the gossipy suggestions Cadi was making.

"I just hate to think Brenda is doing that to herself and that Andreas might have been helping her," I said.

"We don't know for sure that was going on," Sylvie said. "It's just one plausible possibility."

I was becoming more miserable by the minute. "I wish Cadi could keep her mouth shut," I said angrily. "She rarely has a kind thing to say about anyone."

"I noticed that," Sylvie said dryly.

"Maybe I should just ask Brenda what's going on," I said.

"I don't know if you should do that," Sylvie replied. "It's really not anyone's business, is it? I mean, if she was having an affair with Andreas, she's certainly not going to want to discuss it with anyone in the family or even anyone in the castle. And if it's drug use, then maybe it's something you should discuss with her mother rather than her."

The thought of having to talk to Maisie about either Brenda's possible drug use or a possible affair with Andreas was dreadful. I couldn't imagine approaching her. What if she didn't know? It would be a terrible shock to her. But what if she did know? I was sure she wanted her family's personal business kept private. She wouldn't appreciate meddling by me or anyone else.

Maybe Sylvie was right. Perhaps I shouldn't mention it to anyone. It wasn't my business or anyone else's, including Cadi. But then a thought struck me—what if Brenda's behavior was tied in somehow with Andreas's death?

The questions were getting too hard, too complicated, too heart wrenching. "Do you think I should say something to Annabel?" I asked.

"I don't see why you need to," Sylvie answered. "At least until there's something definite about either the drug use or the affair."

"What I don't understand is why Andreas would have an affair with anyone. Sian is beautiful, there's a baby on the way, and it seemed like he had everything going for him," I said.

"We don't know for sure that he was having an affair, even though I agree that it's another plausible explanation for the way Brenda's been behaving. We can't accuse him without more information. Besides, just because a marriage is happy on the outside doesn't mean anyone knows what's going on behind closed doors."

She was right. I thought back to the fight Cadi and Hugh had been having when I interrupted them to ask about the cooking class. Though they didn't seem to care who heard them or who knew what was going on behind their closed door, who knew what other fights they had had since arriving at the castle?

Chapter 8

I groaned as I pulled the car into my parking spot. "I hope I don't run into anyone inside," I said. "I want to go straight to my room and be ignored by everyone." Sylvie invited me to return to the coach house with her for a glass of wine, but I couldn't even muster the interest to do that.

But I didn't get to my room before being assailed by Rhisiart. His car had already been in the enclosure when I parked, so I knew he would be inside.

"Eilidh!" he called, running up behind me as I approached my bedroom. I flinched and turned around.

"What is it?" I asked. I didn't care how cross I sounded.

"What did you think of the cooking class?" I fixed him with a gaze through my narrowed eyes. I couldn't believe he really wanted to discuss French cooking techniques right now.

"I enjoyed it, at least until Cadi opened her mouth at dinner," I retorted.

"Indeed. What did you think of all that?"

"I think it's a disgrace to dishonor Andreas's memory with talk like that, and I believe Brenda is nothing more than a lovesick teenager who feels like her world is ending now that the subject of her affection has passed away."

"You seem quite sure of that," Rhisiart said.

"It's entirely possible and it's what I choose to believe," I said flatly.

"Do you want to go to the pub with me and we can talk about it some more?"

"No. I'm sorry, Rhisiart. I'm very upset by all we talked about at dinner and all I want to do right now is be alone."

He nodded, a look of disappointment—or was it anger?—crossing his face. "Sure. Whatever."

"Goodnight, Rhisiart." I closed the door behind me and waited, listening for his retreating footsteps. I didn't hear them right away, but after several moments I could hear him walking down the corridor.

I wasn't ready for bed, so I added more logs to the fire and sat in my armchair to read a book. But I was too restless for that, too, so I got up for my laptop and settled back down to do some research.

I spent the next two hours perusing different sites devoted to cocaine use, its symptoms, its effects, and treatments. Sure enough, Brenda *did* have some of the symptoms of cocaine use described by the websites I read. Runny nose, red-rimmed eyes, sniffling. But my reeling brain kept reminding me that those same symptoms were common among people grieving. I finally closed the laptop, my eyes tired from reading the screen for so long. I vowed as I got into bed that I would pay much closer attention to Brenda in the coming days to see if she exhibited any other signs of cocaine use. If she did…Well, I didn't know what I would do. I had no choice but to wait and see.

In the morning Annabel wanted to hear all about the cooking class. She seemed to be in good spirits for the first time since we heard the news of Andreas's death, so I went into great detail for her.

I had walked her through every step of the cooking class for several minutes when she gave me a funny look. "What's wrong?" I asked.

"I don't know," she answered. "Quite suddenly I'm not feeling very well. A bit of a sour stomach. Can you tell me the rest of your story later? I'm not sure I want to talk about food any longer."

"Of course. Can I get anything for you?" She shook her head. "Let's get you to your room." I took her by the arm and walked beside her up the stairs, noticing that her face looked ashen.

I helped Annabel into a thick robe and then texted Maisie, asking her to bring tea to Annabel's room. I waited in her room for Maisie to bring the tea service, then poured the tea and helped her lie back against her pillows. She closed her thin eyelids and gave a long, tired sigh. When I offered the cup of tea to her, she shook her head and held up a limp hand. "No, thank you. Not right now. I'll drink it when I wake up, dear."

I waited for a few moments in the chair near the bed until Annabel's breathing was slower and regular, then went back downstairs in search of Hugh or Rhisiart. I found Hugh in the drawing room and told him that his mother wasn't feeling well.

"Really? What's the problem?" he asked from behind his newspaper.

"She's quite pale and her stomach is bothering her. She wouldn't take the tea Maisie brought up to her room."

"Probably a bit of indigestion. I'm sure it'll pass. Do you know where Cadi is?"

"No." I didn't care where Cadi was, either. I was still angry from her malicious gossip of the previous evening.

"Would you send her in here if you see her?"

Hugh didn't see the look I gave him because he hadn't looked up from his reading. I wasn't his servant. If he wanted to talk to Cadi he could find her himself.

I left and went downstairs to the kitchen. "Maisie, what are you planning for lunch?" I asked.

"Sandwiches and fruit salad," she answered. "At least that's what I was planning. Do you want something special?"

"Not for me," I replied. "I think chicken soup might be nice for Annabel. She's not feeling well."

"Certainly. Just let me know when she would like it in her room and Brenda or I can take it right up to her."

I thanked Maisie and went back upstairs, where Rhisiart was coming in the massive front door.

"Where's Mum?" he asked.

"She's up in her room. She's not feeling well," I replied.

"What's the matter?"

"She complained of a sour stomach, but she was awfully pale, too. She's sleeping now."

"I have to ask her a question about the horses. I'll talk to her when she wakes up."

I wondered what that was all about. No doubt something that would upset Griff. Since I wouldn't be needed by Annabel right away, I set off toward the coach house to see what Sylvie was up to. As I rounded the corner of the front of the castle, I almost ran into Griff, who was stalking toward the main door. His face was flushed.

"Griff, what's wrong?"

"I'll tell you what's wrong. Rhisiart has just paid me a visit in the stables. He's talking about trading most of our horses for race horses! Can you believe it? I need to discuss this right away with Annabel. I can't continue working here if my authority in the stable is going to be constantly undermined by Rhisiart."

"I'm afraid you can't talk to Annabel right now. She's sick."

He looked surprised. "What's the matter with her? She never gets sick."

"Her stomach is bothering her. I thought her skin looked very white, too. Hopefully a good long nap will set her to rights."

"I hope so. I can't go on serving two masters. Rhisiart seems to think I answer to him, but his ideas are in direct conflict with those of his mother, and she's the one who signs my paychecks. I don't know what to do anymore." He shook his head in disgust.

"I'll let her know you're looking for her as soon as she wakes up," I promised. "I'm sorry Rhisiart is giving you such a hard time. He can be rather pushy, can't he?"

"That's a very nice way of putting it," he said, smiling. He turned to walk back toward the stables, then looked over his shoulder at me. "When are you ever going to get out for a ride?"

I thought for a moment. Why not now? Sylvie was quite capable of amusing herself for a couple hours, so she didn't really need me to suggest activities for the day. And a ride might be just the thing I needed to clear my head after the events of the previous evening. "You know something? I think I'll go right now. That may be just what the doctor ordered."

"Great! Come back to the stables in a few minutes and I'll have Penelope saddled up and ready to go."

I returned to the castle and changed my clothes, then went out to the stables in search of Griff and Penelope. I found them leaving her stall, one in a long line of warm, sweet-smelling stalls that housed Annabel's pets, the horses from her second husband's polo-playing days. I stroked Penelope's long brown muzzle and accepted a carrot from Griff to offer to Penelope while she sniffed at me and studied me with her huge dark eyes.

"You know what you're doing, right?" Griff asked.

"Mostly, but it's been a while. Can you just wait here while I get up on Penelope and remind me of the basics?"

"Sure," he said with a smile. We led Penelope to the entrance of the stable, then I got up on her back once we were outside. She whinnied a bit, but it only took her a few moments to accept my presence and agree to be my partner for the ride. I sat atop her, looking down at Griff while he quickly reminded me of the basic rein motions. The things I had learned in my riding lessons returned as soon as he started talking, and I found that I hadn't forgotten as much as I thought I had.

"Do you know where you're going?" Griff asked as I turned Penelope around in a circle.

"I thought I would just head toward the woods and see where Penelope leads," I answered.

"I wouldn't," Griff cautioned. "You want to be in control at all times. That way Penny here will feel secure and reassured that you know what you're doing. It'll make her nervous if she thinks you're not in charge."

"All right, then. Which way should we go?"

He pointed in the direction of the woods, then explained where his favorite trail began. "If you head down that trail, you'll find yourself by a stream where you can give Penny a drink. Then keep going and you'll head round by the entrance to the castle property. You'll come out of the woods there, so just head up the road and the castle will be straight ahead. You can't go wrong."

I thanked him for the advice and started off at a slow canter in the direction of the woods. Or at least I tried to. Penelope had other ideas. Though I tried to show her I was in charge, she didn't seem to be listening. She rather stubbornly headed in the direction to the right of where I was trying to go, and I suddenly wondered if I remembered my lessons as well as I thought I had.

Griff was watching Penelope take me in a direction I didn't want to go. He came jogging up to us. "Penny," he began sternly, "you listen to Eilidh. She's the boss." He handed me a carrot that I could use to bribe the horse, but as I reached down to grasp it I began to teeter to one side of the saddle. Flailing out one arm and grasping for Penelope's mane with the other hand, I knew I was going to fall off the horse. I let out a cry and closed my eyes, bracing for the impact with the ground many feet below me.

But I heard an "oof" and opened my eyes to see I had landed on Griff, knocking him to the ground. He must have tried to stop my fall and gotten tangled under my body. I rolled off him with an embarrassed gasp and scrambled to my feet.

"Griff! I'm so sorry! Are you hurt?"

I could hear him wheezing, but he was facing away from me. Running around to the other side of Penelope, who was standing still as a statue, I knelt down on the ground so I could look into Griff's face. I was shocked when I saw that he was laughing.

"Griff! What's so funny?" I demanded. "Stop laughing!"

"I shouldn't laugh," he gasped, "but you should have seen yourself atop Penny! You're not hurt, are you?"

"My pride is hurt," I said with a grimace, "but otherwise I'm okay."

He pushed himself to a seated position and wiped his eyes with the sleeve of his coat. "I was trying to catch you. Sorry I missed!"

I laughed. "I'm sorry I landed on you. I'm not very graceful, am I?"

He chuckled. "No less than anyone else who falls off a horse. Can I help you get back on Penny?"

I looked askance at the horse. "Maybe I shouldn't ride today. I don't want to spook the poor girl."

"She's fine," Griff said, stroking Penelope's muzzle. "She stood still when you fell, didn't she? She knew it was an accident."

"Maybe I can give it another try."

"How about I go with you? I'm not sure you're quite the rider I thought you were. That way if you have any issues, I can be there to help you out. Or up, whichever the case may be." He gave me a broad smile.

I grinned. "All right. Hopefully there won't be any problems, though. I didn't mean to imply that I'm a better rider than I really am."

"I don't think you implied anything. I just assumed. Annabel likes to make sure the people she hires can ride so that she always has someone to go with her if she wants."

"Then I'm afraid she got less than she bargained for when she hired me," I said with a grin.

"Oh, I don't think so." Griff winked at me and I could feel the color rising from my neck to my ears. He helped me up on the horse, then tied Penelope to a post while he went back to the stable to saddle another horse for himself. He walked the horse out to where I sat on top of Penelope, then untied Penelope and swung up onto his own horse, Caesar.

"Ready?" Griff asked over his shoulder.

"Lead on!"

The horses clopped along, Penelope following Caesar closely, across the field behind the stables. My nerves quieted and I concentrated on nothing more than the scenery around me. There was a fine mist in the air and it formed a foggy shroud between us and the wood at the far side of the field. "We'll head right into those trees," Griff said. "Caesar can practically walk this trail blindfolded. I take him out there at least once or twice a week. We might stay a little drier in the trees, too. It looks like we might be in for a bit of rain."

"Should we go back?" I fretted.

"Not unless you want to. The trail is flat and easy, so the horses won't have a problem with it. If you want to go back, we can go. But if you want some peace and quiet, I would suggest staying out here for a little while."

He must have known the words "peace and quiet" would work like a salve on my soul. I nodded to him to lead the way, and he turned around and lifted the reins to nudge Caesar forward. Caesar was a huge black beast with a white streak down his muzzle, but he was as gentle as could be. He looked positively spooky in the misty woods in front of me and Penelope. The forest was almost silent except for the rhythmic clopping of the horses' feet. A light wind stirred among the treetops, but I barely noticed the gentle whispering of the branches as they moved. Neither Griff nor I spoke for many long minutes, until I thought I heard the sound of water running. "Do you hear that?" I asked in a quiet voice. I didn't want to break the spell the wood had cast on me, but I wanted to make sure I wasn't hearing things.

"Yes. There's a stream right over there," Griff answered, pointing to his right. "Shall we ride alongside it?"

"I'd love that," I replied. There was no sound I loved as much as that of water burbling. It was gentle, relaxing, and gave me a feeling of being far away from workaday cares. I followed Griff toward the sound of the water and before long I saw it ahead in the mist, tripping and dancing over stones in a winding path through the dense trees.

We stopped next to the stream and Griff swung off Caesar. Tying the reins to a tree growing right next to the water, he let Caesar drink his fill, which looked cold and refreshing. I was struggling to dismount from Penelope and Griff came over and held out his arms. I slid into them as gracefully as I could, which was decidedly inelegant, then hurried to tie Penelope's reins to a tree near Caesar. Penelope didn't need to be told what to do—she went directly to the stream and ducked her head to drink her fill noisily.

Griff had brought two oilcloths for us, so we were able to sit on the damp ground without getting wet. We sat cross-legged, Griff leaning against a boulder and I against a tree, and watched the horses drink. Caesar tossed his head and snorted.

"Easy, boy," Griff said softly. The wood was so quiet that the horse could hear the soothing tone of his voice. Griff turned to me. "I don't know what's spooked him. He's usually quite calm."

"Maybe he's feeling out of his element because there's another horse with him. Is it usually just the two of you when you come this way?"

Griff nodded. "Yes, but I don't think having an extra person and another horse around should bother him. He's used to Penny, and you're obviously not a threat." He smiled at me.

"I know, but maybe he senses the stress I'm under."

"You seem less tense to me, but I suppose Caesar is more sensitive to those things than most people are."

"You might be right. I *am* less tense. A ride was exactly what I needed, I guess." He nodded as if to say "I told you so." We lapsed into silence as we listened to the gurgling water.

But Caesar wouldn't stop whinnying, and Penelope eventually joined him, forming a duet of unease. Griff looked up in surprise when Penelope began making noises, then stood up and turned slowly in a circle, watching the trees closely. He squinted, then looked down at me.

"Looks like we're not alone," he said quietly. "The horses knew it. There's someone over there among the trees." He pointed in the direction from which we'd come.

"Who is it?"

"I don't know." Then he raised his voice. "Hallo?"

"Hello there," came the reply. Rhisiart. I would have recognized his voice anywhere. But apparently Griff didn't, for he looked at me in confusion.

"Who is that?" he whispered.

"Rhisiart."

He rolled his eyes. "I should have known. A lovely ride through the wood and he can't even leave me alone for that."

I chuckled. "Maybe he's not stalking you. Maybe he's just going for a walk."

"Mark my words—he's following me. Or you. He's not here by accident. I can tell by the way Caesar and Penny are acting. They smell his pheromones. They know he's up to no good."

His words unnerved me. What could Rhisiart possibly want with either of us out here in the woods?

Presently Rhisiart came into view. It was no wonder we hadn't seen him earlier; he was dressed in dark green trousers, a light brown jumper, and a brown jacket. He was riding Ghee, the tan horse from Annabel's stables. Ghee was moving slowly, picking his way across the forest floor with great care.

"What is it?" Griff asked Rhisiart, a trace of annoyance in his voice.

Rhisiart didn't answer at once, but waited until he had stopped next to us and slid from Ghee's back to respond. "How cozy, finding the two of you here like this. I do hope I'm not interrupting anything." His eyes gleamed.

Griff swept his hand around the area where we were sitting. "Does it look like you're interrupting anything?"

"Not really. Too bad for you, old bloke," Rhisiart said to him.

I could sense Griff getting angrier with each passing moment. "What is it that you wanted, Rhisiart?" he asked, his fists clenching and unclenching.

"I'm just out for a ride. The damp weather makes me restless. I'm particularly fond of this trail."

"Rhisiart, did Annabel wake up before you left?" I asked.

"No. I'll talk to her when I get back." Griff looked suspiciously from me to Rhisiart. He seemed to know that Rhisiart wanted to talk to Annabel about the horses and possibly more changes in the stables.

"You should probably turn around and head back to the castle," Griff cautioned him. "Ghee hates to be out in the rain and it looks like the rain's coming."

"Don't want me out here with you, huh?" asked Rhisiart with a chuckle. "Well, I'm leaving. Good luck, old man," he added with a wink. I felt my face growing hot from embarrassment.

Griff and I waited in silence until Rhisiart had walked far enough away that we could speak without him overhearing us. Even then, we spoke in low tones.

"I don't know how anyone stands the man," Griff said, his earlier good mood vanished. "He's ruined my afternoon. We should probably head back."

"I don't mind riding in the rain if you don't," I said. I was hoping to restore some of his good humor. It worked.

"You wouldn't mind? I like riding in the rain and Caesar certainly doesn't mind. Let's give it a go and if Penny shows signs of wanting to go back, we'll turn around. Otherwise we can press on," he said with a smile.

We both stood up and I flailed about for a moment trying to get on top of Penelope while Griff folded the oilcloths. Then he gave me a boost and swung up on Caesar's back once I was settled in my saddle. We hadn't ridden far when the rain began to fall, but because we were sheltered from the worst of it we didn't get soaked. I mostly noticed the rain because of the sound of the raindrops plopping on the leaves.

We rode beside the stream for several more minutes, then turned away from it and headed in the direction of the castle, invisible in the foggy, rainy distance. I was riding behind Griff and I found myself turning around every few moments to see if Rhisiart was anywhere nearby. I didn't feel nervous, just curious. He seemed the type to enjoy his creature comforts and I wondered what would possess him to go for a ride when the weather promised rain. Was he meeting someone?

Griff said something that startled me out of my own thoughts. "Pardon me?" I asked.

"Are you lost in thought back there?" he asked, turning around in his saddle and grinning at me.

"I suppose so. I was just thinking about Rhisiart and wondering why he was out in the weather."

"I've a feeling that Rhisiart does not wish to be figured out," he said.

We had been riding for quite some time, and as we made our way back to the castle, I began feeling tense again. Our encounter with Rhisiart had me inexplicably rattled, and I was worrying about Annabel again. I hoped she would be feeling better by the time I got back to check on her.

Griff insisted upon brushing down Caesar and Penelope when we returned to the stables, and I thanked him for a lovely ride. "Anytime," he

said. He opened his mouth to say something more, but must have changed
his mind because he said nothing.

I gave him a little wave and hurried back to the castle. I took off my
coat and gloves in the main hall and listened for any sounds coming from
within the castle, but it was silent. Eerily so. I had a sudden hunch that all
was not well with Annabel. I don't know what gave me that uncomfortable
feeling—probably the utter quiet.

Taking the steps two at a time, I hurried up to Annabel's room. I gave a
perfunctory knock and opened the door. "Annabel?" I called in a soft voice.

"Mmmm." I heaved a sigh of relief upon hearing her voice, as weak and
low as it was. I had never been so glad to have a wrong hunch.

"How are you feeling?" I asked, walking closer to her bed.

She lolled her head from side to side, eyes closed. She looked horrible
in the dim gray light sneaking in around the drapes.

"What can I get for you? Tea?" I asked. I didn't expect her to want
anything, and she didn't surprise me.

"Nothing," she croaked, trying to moisten her lips. I went to her vanity
for a tin of lip balm. Annabel's vanity was almost sacred to her and it
was the only place she allowed herself to be messy and disorganized. I
rooted among all the potions and vials until I found something that would
soothe her chapped skin. I used a soft sponge to rub some onto her lips
and she grimaced.

"I'm sure nothing tastes good while you're not feeling well," I said.
"Let me get some hot tea up here and we'll see if you can drink it. Does
that sound all right?"

She nodded briefly, but still didn't open her eyes.

I left the door open a crack while I hurried down two flights to the
kitchen, where I found Maisie chopping vegetables next to the sink.

"Maisie, is there any hot tea water ready? Annabel is just barely awake
and I think something hot to drink would do her good."

"Should we call a doctor?" Maisie fretted. "She's never sick."

"I can ask her, but I'm sure she'll say no. Besides, it's really for Hugh
or Rhisiart to decide whether to call a doctor, I think, as long as they're
here in the castle."

Maisie nodded. "I suppose you're right. The tea water is hot. I'll make
up a cup for her and take it to her if you'd like."

"Don't bother. I'm heading back up to her room so I can take it to her."

Maisie poured the water over a tea infuser filled with chamomile leaves
and the mellow floral scent began to waft through the air in the kitchen.
I let the tea steep for a few minutes, then added a bit of sugar, some milk,

and a slice of lemon. Before I took the teacup to Annabel, I grabbed a biscuit from the cupboard, thinking she might be interested in a bit to eat.

"Let me know if she needs anything else," Maisie called after me as I went up the steps. I passed Brenda on her way downstairs and I smiled at her.

"How are you doing today, Brenda?" I asked.

"Okay, I suppose." She ducked her head and hurried away when she reached the bottom of the stairs, probably to avoid talking to me anymore. I was conscious of having paid a bit too much attention to her face as I passed her, worried as I was about whether she was really using drugs as Cadi had suggested. I couldn't get a good look at her eyes to see if she had been crying. Or something else.

But all thoughts of Brenda flew from my mind when I went into Annabel's room. As I came around the door I had left ajar, the first thing I saw was a white hand on the floor. Tea sloshed all over Annabel's night table as I set it down quickly, calling loudly for Hugh, Cadi, Rhisiart, Sian, anyone who could come help.

Annabel was lying face-down on the floor. A big bump had formed on her forehead and her eyes were open and glassy.

Chapter 9

"Annabel!" The urgency in my voice scared even me. I picked up her hand and held it in mine, trying to feel for a pulse. But I couldn't feel anything, and I only wound up frustrating myself because I didn't know where to properly look for it.

I dimly recall hearing footsteps running toward Annabel's room while I tried to turn her over. Hugh appeared in the doorway.

"What happened?" His words were rushed. "What's the matter with her?"

"I don't know. I went downstairs to get some tea for her and when I came back up I found her like this."

"Cadi!" he yelled. Only a moment later we heard more footsteps, this time from more than one person. Cadi and Rhisiart came into the room just then, followed a minute later by Sian, whose size hampered quick movement.

"Oh, no! What happened?" Cadi asked. Rhisiart stood behind her, his mouth set in a grim line. Sian gasped upon seeing her mother-in-law on the floor.

Hugh knelt down next to me and looked over his shoulder. "Call her doctor," he ordered. He felt his mother's wrist and his eyes narrowed as the room fell silent. I knew I should call the doctor immediately, but I felt rooted to the spot.

"I can't feel anything. Can you?" he asked me. I shook my head. Rhisiart shouldered his way between us and grabbed his mother's hand.

"There's no pulse," he said. He put two fingers on Annabel's throat, then shook his head. "Someone get me a mirror," he said. I leapt to my feet and ran to the vanity, where there was a handheld mirror. I grabbed it and handed it to him. Leaning over his mother's chest, he held the mirror close to her mouth. After several long moments he shook his head again. "She's gone. There's no sign of any breath on the mirror."

Cadi covered her mouth with her hands and Sian sat down heavily on Annabel's bed, her eyes closed and a look of pain on her face. I couldn't believe this was happening. Annabel had been perfectly healthy just a day ago. I could feel my breath coming faster and my legs turned to jelly. I sat down quickly next to Sian.

Hugh quickly took charge of the situation. "Eilidh, please tell Maisie to show the doctor upstairs as soon as he gets here. Cadi, please call the police."

"What for?" his wife asked.

"Because she's been found dead in her own home and showed no signs of being sick. That's why."

Cadi gave her husband a look full of scorn and left the room. My stomach lurched as I stood up to follow her, and I ran into Annabel's bathroom, hoping I wouldn't be sick to my stomach. I splashed cold water on my face and was able to collect myself before heading downstairs in search of Maisie. Cadi was waiting for me in the great hall.

"What do you think happened?" she asked in a whisper.

"I don't know." I didn't know what to think, what to say. I was simultaneously horrified and shocked and confused. I missed Annabel already. What could have happened to her? She had been weak, yes, but she was able to speak. Had she suffered a heart attack or a stroke? Was it something she ate? It had all started with a stomachache. I thought back to the meals she had eaten, then realized I hadn't been with her the previous night at dinner. I made a mental note to speak with Maisie about Annabel's last dinner. She had refused breakfast, so food from earlier in the morning hadn't made her sick. We had all eaten the same things for breakfast and lunch the previous day, and as long as the rest of us stayed healthy it probably ruled out those foods as a cause of Annabel's illness. I hurriedly dialed the doctor and asked that he come out to the castle as soon as possible, then went looking for Maisie. I finally found her standing in the doorway of Annabel's room, crying openly. I put my arm around her plump shoulders.

"What if something I cooked caused this?" she asked in a worried voice. "I'd never be able to live with myself. Dear, sweet Annabel."

"Let's not jump to conclusions about what caused this," I suggested. "The doctor should be here soon. Could you show him up here as soon as he arrives? Cadi called the police. I'm sure they'll be here first."

Maisie wrung the handkerchief she was holding. "And this so soon after Andreas's death." I could do nothing but shake my head slowly. It was inexplicable.

The police arrived in only a few minutes. Even through the thick walls of the castle I could hear their sirens approaching. I wondered why they had their sirens on. It was too late for Annabel.

Maisie was already holding the door open for them when they came up to the front of the castle. Two officers walked briskly into the main hall and waited for Maisie to close the door and show them to Annabel's room. I was watching them from the stairway and I spoke to them as Maisie escorted them upstairs.

"I found her," I told them. "I had gone down to the kitchen for a cup of tea for her and when I came back she was on the floor."

The police officers both nodded, and one whipped out a small book and began to make notations with a stubby pencil. "What is your name?" he asked.

"Eilidh Stewart." He wrote that down.

Maisie stopped outside Annabel's bedroom door and didn't seem to want to step inside. I ushered the officers into the room and stood aside while they made everyone move out of the way, examined the body, made notes, and took photos. They turned to Hugh.

"Are you a relative of the deceased?" the younger officer asked. I cringed at the impersonality of the question. He must be relatively new, since Annabel was well-known in the community.

Hugh nodded. "I'm her son."

The other officer chimed in. "He's the younger brother of Andreas Tucker, who died last week." The first officer nodded, looking slightly embarrassed.

The police then took the names and home addresses of everyone in the room, including Maisie, who was still standing in the doorway, obviously reluctant to come in.

"Come in, please, ma'am," one of the officers said to her. He wrote down her name and asked who else worked for Annabel.

Maisie said she would go look for Brenda and I told him that Griff was probably out in the stables. "Do you want me to go get him?" I asked.

"No. We'll go out and find him," the officer answered. "Anyone else in the house?"

"Not in the house, but we have a visitor staying in the coach house. It's my cousin—she's here on holiday."

"We'll need to talk to her, too. Can you show me where this coach house is?" I nodded. He left his partner in charge of Annabel's bedroom and I walked with him out to the coach house. There were countless questions

I wanted to ask him while we walked, but I remained silent. I wondered what was going through his mind. Did Annabel die from natural causes? Did something else cause her death? Even though I knew calling the police had been the proper thing to do, merely having them at the scene of Annabel's death lent a suspicious note to the situation.

I knocked on the door to the coach house and Sylvie answered just a moment later. Her eyes widened in surprise when she saw the officer standing next to me.

"What's going on?" Then, recovering herself, she said, "Come in." She stood aside so the officer and I could enter.

"Annabel passed away," I said simply. Sylvie gasped. "I found her on the floor of her bedroom after I had come in from my ride this morning."

"How did she die?"

"We don't know. That's why we called the police. The doctor's on his way."

"Mum will be crushed," Sylvie said softly. She turned to me with sad eyes. "I'm so sorry, Eilidh. I know how much you cared for Annabel. Are you all right?"

I swallowed hard. "Not really."

The police officer gave my cousin a questioning look. "How did you know Annabel Baines?"

"She was one of my mum's best friends."

The officer sat down on one of the sofas in the salon and Sylvie sat opposite him. There appeared to be no need for me to stay, so I returned to the castle, where the doctor had just driven up.

"Doctor, thank you for coming," I said in greeting as I met him at the front door.

"Tell me what happened," he said, wasting no time in getting to the bottom of his patient's condition.

I related everything that had happened since the previous evening, and he nodded gravely. "I wish she had called me," he said.

"There really didn't seem to be any need to," I explained. "It appeared to be nothing more than a sour stomach."

"She's getting up there in years," he said, giving me a dark look. "Things can be more complicated as a patient ages." I didn't want to discuss it. The last thing I needed was to be told I might have prevented Annabel's death if I had recognized that this had been a case for the doctor.

He knew where Annabel's room was, so he led the way once we reached the top of the stairs. He went in before me and suggested to Cadi and Sian, both of whom were standing outside Annabel's door, that they return to their rooms for a while. I could hear them whispering as they walked away.

The doctor hadn't asked me to leave, so I stayed to watch him. Hugh and Rhisiart looked on from where they stood near one of the windows. The other police officer stood quietly in the corner of the room.

The doctor knelt down next to Annabel's body. He felt her wrist for a pulse, then her neck. He reached into the black leather bag he had brought with him and drew out a stethoscope. He listened to her chest for several moments, then folded the stethoscope and placed it slowly back into the bag. "She was a lovely lady," he said in a quiet voice. "I'm sorry I wasn't able to help."

"It happened so fast," I said, half to myself.

"Tell me what she's been doing the past few days," he said.

"Physically, there's been nothing out of the ordinary," I said. "But you know, of course, that her son passed away and she's been mourning him. He left behind a wife who's staying here with us, and she's pregnant, about to give birth very soon. Annabel was worried about everyone visiting because she wanted their holiday to be perfect, so that caused her some stress before their visit, then when Andreas died she lost her compass for a while. Just yesterday, though, she asked me to have the groom ready her favorite horse so she could go riding. She didn't end up going, but she had the desire."

"What has she been eating and drinking?" the doctor asked.

"She's eaten the same things as the rest of us, except I'm not sure what she had for dinner last night. I went to a cooking class with her son Rhisiart, her daughter-in-law Cadi, and my cousin, who's here on holiday. Annabel had dinner here at home, as far as I know."

"Can you ask Maisie what she served for dinner last night?" he asked. He knew Maisie from many years of being Annabel's personal doctor.

"I'll do that right now," I offered.

I hurried down to the kitchen, where Maisie and Brenda were talking together. "I'm sorry to interrupt," I said, stepping over the threshold. "But the doctor is asking what Annabel had for dinner last night."

"And so it begins," Maisie said, nodding at Brenda. "What did I tell you? They're already looking at my cooking as something that could have killed Annabel." Two tears made their way slowly down her cheeks and dropped from her chin onto the floor.

"Maisie, I don't think they believe anything you cooked made Annabel ill. The doctor is just asking questions at this point, gathering information about Annabel's last hours."

"How long do you think it'll be before he knows how Annabel died?" Brenda asked.

I shook my head. "I wish I knew. Hopefully very soon. So Maisie, what did Annabel have for dinner last night?"

I could see Maisie was beside herself with anxiety. Her right eye was twitching ever so slightly and her hands shook. "I can't even think," she said.

"Don't you keep a list somewhere of the meals you cook?"

"Yes. I'll look at that." She pulled a tattered notebook from a drawer and flipped to a page near the back.

"Ham and bean soup, bread and butter, and a pear. She had tea to drink." Maisie snapped her fingers. "I remember she said she didn't want much to eat because Hugh was going to the pub for dinner and it would just be her and Sian in the dining room. Sian isn't eating very much at this point because she's so uncomfortable after she eats."

"I'm glad you wrote it all down. That makes an easy record for the doctor. Anything else in the notebook from yesterday?"

"Just that lunch was ham sandwiches. Breakfast was the usual." Meaning there were a variety of foods available on the sideboard in the dining room, including porridge, eggs, toast, mushrooms, tomatoes, and breakfast meats. I couldn't recall exactly what Annabel had eaten, though I was sure it had been nothing out of the ordinary.

I squeezed Maisie's hand before returning to Annabel's bedroom. "Don't worry, Maisie. We'll get this straightened out. Nobody thinks you would do anything to hurt Annabel." She nodded and gave me a worried look.

"Thank you."

I reported everything Maisie had told me when I found the doctor in Annabel's room. He stroked his chin. "That doesn't sound unusual. Probably not food or drink. We'll have to see what the medical examination shows."

"Is that going to happen here?" I asked, a sudden and unreasonable fear taking hold in my chest.

"No. We're going to have to take her to the medical examiner's office for that."

I knew Annabel wouldn't want that and I told Hugh as much when he came back into the room. I told him I was apprehensive about letting her body leave the castle for an autopsy. My fears, however, were ignored. "By all means you should take her to the proper office to determine what caused her death," he said in an authoritative voice. It was then I realized that Hugh was probably in charge now, as her likely heir. It wouldn't be known for sure until Annabel's will was read, but I think we all assumed Hugh would be making all the necessary arrangements.

The doctor made a call on his mobile phone and requested that an ambulance be sent to the castle to pick up Annabel's body for transport to the medical examiner's office. When he rang off he turned to me. "I'd like to speak to the police officer. Would you please excuse us?" I nodded and closed the door firmly behind me when I went out into the hallway. Sian and Cadi had disappeared and I didn't care where they had gone. I only wanted to go to my room to think.

It was cold in my bedroom, but I had a fire crackling and roaring in just a few minutes. I sat in front of the hearth in my armchair and stared into the flames leaping and dancing. I missed Annabel already. Talking to my cousin would probably have been good, but I didn't want to be around other people just then. Besides, if the police had any more questions for me, they would want me nearby.

Tears didn't come as I had expected them to. I wanted to cry, but I couldn't. It didn't seem real that Annabel was gone. I wondered idly what would happen to the castle, who would own it, who would move in after the rest of us had gone our separate ways. I wondered what I would do for a job, but I didn't feel a sense of anxiety or worry—only a heaviness in my heart.

I wondered about Maisie and Brenda. What would they do? Maisie had worked for Annabel for many years and if I knew Maisie, she would already be beside herself with worry about what she would do for a new job. Brenda, being much younger, would probably find something in short order, but it might not be with her mother. I knew they liked working together, even if some frustration with each other crept into their work at times.

Eventually, warmed by the fire and weary of all that had happened, I fell asleep in my chair. I awoke to a knock at my door. "Eilidh?" a voice called. It was Brenda. "The police are looking for you."

"Thanks, Brenda," I called. I tried to disguise the sleepiness in my voice. "I'll be right out."

The officers were waiting for me in the sitting room. I was glad to see neither had chosen to sit in Annabel's favorite chair. "How can I help you?" I asked.

"We're told you were Annabel's right hand."

"I don't know that I would describe myself that way, but I did manage most of her affairs."

"Do you know if she had a will?"

"I'm sure she did, but I don't know where it is or what it says. I suppose her barrister would know the answer to that."

"Can you give us the name of her barrister?"

"I can. She used Mr. Hadley from Cardiff," I added, implying that a quick visit to see Annabel's barrister wouldn't be likely. Cardiff was over an hour away.

"Thank you. We'll have someone get in touch with him."

I went to my desk and rifled through a file that held recent correspondence from Annabel. I knew I had posted a note to the barrister and that he had responded in kind. He shared Annabel's aversion to technology. In just a moment I had located his address and telephone number. I wrote down the information the officers had requested and handed them the paper. "Do you have any idea how Annabel died?" I asked tentatively. I wasn't sure it was my place to be asking such questions.

It didn't matter. "We don't have anything yet. We need to wait for the medical examiner's report before we know what we're dealing with here."

"So what happens now?" I asked.

"We're still waiting for the ambulance to retrieve the body for transport." I winced at his words. The ambulance wasn't transporting just a body—it was transporting Annabel.

I was suddenly ravenous. "Would you excuse me, please?" I asked. I should have used my manners and asked if the officers wanted anything from the kitchen, but I was tiring of the way they kept referring to Annabel and I wanted to get away from them for a little while. Both officers nodded and I left.

When I went downstairs, I could hear someone crying. Maisie was sitting at the small kitchen table, weeping as though her heart would break. I sat down across from her. I didn't say anything—I didn't have to. I knew what was going through her mind and heart. They were the same feelings going through my mind and heart. We mourned Annabel, we wondered about our jobs, and we felt guilty for worrying about our jobs at such a sad time. Maisie had the added concern that something she cooked could be blamed for causing Annabel's death. We sat quietly at the table until Maisie was able to compose herself. She wiped her eyes and said with an embarrassed laugh, "Sorry you had to see that. Not too pretty, is it?"

"There's nothing to be sorry for," I told her. "I know exactly how you feel."

"You couldn't possibly understand," she said, shaking her head.

"We're in the same boat, Maisie. We've both lost a friend, a boss, and probably a job."

She nodded, wiping her eyes with the corner of her apron. Brenda came through the door. "Mum, you're not still crying," she said. It wasn't a question.

"I can't help it," Maisie told her daughter.

"You've got a job to do," Brenda reminded her. "We haven't been sacked yet and people still need to eat. Maybe they'll keep us on if they realize they still need us even though Annabel is gone."

Maisie let out a choked sob, followed quickly by a hiccup. "You're right, of course. I'm just having a hard time with it, that's all." She hiccupped again. Brenda came and put her arms around her mum's shoulders.

"I'm not always flighty, see?" she said with a smile. Maisie reached up and squeezed Brenda's hand. "Now that you're feeling a bit better, I've got work to do upstairs," Brenda said. She leaned down and kissed her mum's cheek. Maisie smiled wistfully as she watched Brenda leave the room.

"Brenda's absolutely right. I, for one, am starving," I announced. "You could start by whipping up something for me before I faint." Maisie chuckled.

"I've got just the thing," she said. She stood up and smoothed her apron, then got to work making me a delicious grilled cheese sandwich with a pickle, crisps, and a small bowl of fruit salad. I savored it in the warm, cozy kitchen while Maisie bustled around gathering the ingredients she would need to make dinner for the household.

I had just finished eating when Brenda came into the kitchen again. "Eilidh, the police are asking for you and Hugh. I think the ambulance is here for Annabel's body." A feeling of dread replaced the calm that had descended upon the kitchen earlier. I heaved a long sigh.

"I'll go up straightaway," I told Brenda. I hated to go up there to preside over the departure of Annabel's body. I knew she would want to stay here in her beloved castle, no matter how she died. But Hugh obviously felt differently. He wanted to know why his mother died. The more I thought about it, the more I felt it was wrong of me to begrudge him that knowledge.

I went up the stairs with a heaviness in my step. Hugh was at the end of the hallway, walking toward the sitting room. When I entered, he was talking in a low voice to the officers. They all looked at me. "What?" I asked. I was irritable already and their stares unnerved me.

"Eilidh, maybe it's best if you're not here for this," Hugh suggested. "I know you're against Annabel's body leaving the castle for the purpose of an autopsy, but I'm afraid you have no choice in the matter."

I had to force myself to remember that this man was in mourning for his mother and that he probably didn't mean to sound as pompous and rigid as he did. I counted to ten and took a breath before responding. "Hugh, I completely understand that you need to know why Annabel died. I'm perfectly capable of being here to help the officers if you have no objection." Somehow I just knew that as long as the autopsy was going to go forward without regard for my feelings, Annabel would want me here when her body left the castle. In all the time I had known her, Annabel hadn't had much to say about Hugh, and I knew their relationship had been distant and cool. I had loved and respected her, and it was fitting that I be there to say goodbye if Andreas, her favorite son, couldn't be there.

One of the officers went to the front door to admit the ambulance driver and his assistant, who were wheeling a gurney. When they all came into the sitting room, the driver wasted no time in explaining what was going to happen. Hugh had no questions, but I had plenty.

"How long will it be before we hear something from the doctor?"

"That depends on the complexity of the autopsy," the driver answered.

"Will you need anyone from the family or the household to be there to answer questions?"

"No."

"Will the doctor be contacting us with the results, or will it be someone else from the medical examiner's office?"

"That's a question for the doctor, ma'am."

I was frustrated by the driver's inability to provide any answers to my questions. Rhisiart came in while I was talking to the driver. "Are they here to take Mum's body?" he asked Hugh. His brother nodded.

I walked past them and beckoned for the driver and his assistant to follow me up to Annabel's room. The police officers accompanied us. At Annabel's doorway, I stood aside to let the authorities enter and I waited for them to do their work and bring her body out. I didn't want to see what they were doing. Somehow it seemed an invasion of Annabel's privacy.

In time they wheeled the gurney out into the hallway. I looked away, then changed my mind and looked directly at Annabel's body. It was covered with a sheet. Even her face. I guess I should have expected that, but I felt a sudden need to see her just one more time.

"Excuse me," I said, feeling tentative and timid, "do you mind if I just look at her for a second?"

The ambulance driver exchanged glances with one of the police officers, who nodded at me. I pulled back the sheet and gazed into Annabel's face. And that's when the tears started to flow. I was embarrassed to cry in front of the four men standing before me, but I couldn't help it. I replaced the sheet and turned away while they all maneuvered the gurney down the grand stone staircase.

I didn't have long to compose myself before the authorities would be ready to take Annabel's body away, and I wanted to be there when that happened. I dried my tears and joined everyone in the great hall, where the ambulance driver was signing something for the police officers. Hugh and Rhisiart stood nearby, watching the proceedings in silence. I stood by the front door waiting to open it. When the police had the required signature, they nodded briskly to the driver and I opened the door to allow them to pass through with the gurney.

I stepped outside and over to the waiting ambulance to watch while they loaded Annabel's body through the rear doors. The heaviness in my chest was almost too much to bear. I noticed Hugh and Rhisiart out of the corner of my eye, standing behind me. I was glad they couldn't see my face—I wanted to see Annabel off without them watching. The driver climbed into the front seat while his assistant hopped up into the back of the ambulance and turned around. Looking up and nodding at me, a somber look on his face, he reached out and pulled both doors closed with a soft thud.

The ambulance slowly made its way down the long drive in front of Thistlecross Castle. I watched until it was out of sight, ignoring the tiny snowflakes that were spinning in the air around me. I swallowed hard. Annabel had loved the snow.

Chapter 10

When I turned around, Hugh and Rhisiart had both gone back indoors. I was glad. Even though it was their mother who had passed away, the emotion I was feeling seemed somehow deeper than what they had expressed. *Maybe it's just different with men,* I told myself. When I went back into the castle, I went straight to my room. I needed a little more time away from people. A couple hours passed before there was a knock at my door.

Sylvie stood there, a soft smile on her face. "How are you doing?" she asked with concern. She drew me into a hug and smoothed the back of my hair while I let the tears fall again.

I stepped away from her. "Come on in," I offered, holding the door open wider. "What have you been doing today? I'm sorry I haven't been around, but I'm afraid I wouldn't have been very good company."

"That's perfectly fine. I went into the village for some of that wonderful cheese they sell in the dairy shop. We can go over to the coach house if you'd like and we'll set up a cheese tray and have some wine. It'll be like a holiday you see in a magazine." She grinned.

I smiled for the first time in hours. "I'd like that."

"Then it's settled." She opened her mouth to say something else, but then closed it again.

"What?" I asked.

"You don't have to talk about it if you don't want to, but I was just wondering what the police said about Annabel's death."

I let out a long breath. "Not much," I said. "Hugh, and possibly Rhisiart, agreed to have an autopsy performed on Annabel's body, so the police called an ambulance and they left here a while ago."

"I'm sure that was hard, but it's probably the right thing to do. It's important for her kids to know if she had a disease that was undiagnosed. If she did, it's possible they might have it, too. Plus, it's strange when someone dies for no apparent reason. I mean, she seemed fine just yesterday."

"You're right, and I know all that. It was just hard to watch her be taken away, that's all. I don't think it's what she would have wanted."

"So is Hugh in charge now?"

"He seems to be. The police are going to ring up Annabel's barrister in Cardiff to see what the will says. That might confirm that Hugh is in charge now, or it might change things. Maybe she left Rhisiart in charge. I wonder what will happen if the will says Andreas is in charge. I wouldn't be surprised if it said that."

"Would Sian be in charge then?"

"I don't know. It's not an ideal situation, because the baby is due very soon and Sian has other things on her mind. Like her husband's death and raising a baby on her own."

"Come on, let's go try that cheese." She was making a valiant effort to cheer me up, and it was the least I could do to accept her invitation. Her holiday had been a disaster so far—two deaths. What more could possibly go wrong?

I pulled on a jacket and followed her through the halls of the castle, halls that now seemed much emptier with Annabel gone. We hurried to the coach house in the blustery wind. A few snowflakes continued dancing around on the air currents, but nothing was sticking to the ground. We never got much snow at the castle, but everything looked enchanting when we did.

After we had prepared a cheese tray and poured two large glasses of wine, we sat in front of the fire, watching the snowflakes dance through the tall windows that overlooked the fields. I could see the stable from where I sat, and I thought how lovely and warm it would be in there with the horses and the sweet-smelling hay.

Sylvie had chosen not one, but four kinds of cheese from the cheese monger in the village. She had arranged them on a rustic wooden board she had found in the coach house kitchen and paired them with biscuits, French bread, and pots of fig jam, honey, and Major Grey's chutney. It was exactly what I needed. I didn't feel like being in that huge castle with only Hugh, Cadi, Rhisiart, and Sian for company. Maisie and Brenda would be there, of course, but they were busy and I didn't want to make a nuisance of myself.

I settled back into the sofa and smiled at my cousin. "I can't believe what a horrible holiday you've had," I said. "It's wonderful of you to stay when there's been nothing but tragedy since you got here."

Sylvie raised her glass in a silent cheer. "How could I go home? You need someone most right now. Have you told Mum about Annabel?"

"I hadn't even thought of that," I admitted. "I can ring her up. She's the one who got me the job with Annabel, so I should probably be the one to break the news to her."

Sylvie agreed. "She'll be so sad," she said. "They've been friends since I was little."

When we had enjoyed our fill of cheese and accompaniments and wine, I returned to the castle by myself, feeling a little cheered. As much as I had wanted to be alone earlier, it was good to have spent some time with Sylvie. I went straight to my room and rang up Aunt Margot.

As I expected, she was shocked and saddened by the news of Annabel's passing. She was silent for a moment as she composed herself.

"This follows so closely on the heels of Andreas's death. The family must be devastated."

"I suppose they are. I confess, I haven't wanted to spend time with any of them today. I've been with Sylvie. She's been trying to cheer me up."

"I know how much you loved working for Annabel. I'm so sorry."

"And I'm sorry for you and all her other friends, people who will miss her so much."

"I wish her sons and their wives had never accepted her invitation to visit the castle."

"Why not?"

"I probably shouldn't even have mentioned it. Never mind."

"Wait, what do you mean?"

"I mean, she was so worried about their visit. She wanted it to be perfect because she wanted to apologize for the things that happened in their home so many years ago. But nothing can be perfect, and I'm afraid that kind of stress wasn't very good for her health, and when I spoke to her on the phone recently she mentioned that her doctor had warned her about taking on additional stress."

"Maybe her heart wasn't strong enough for all that's happened," I mused.

"What did they say was the cause of death?" Aunt Margot asked.

"No one knows yet. They've taken her body away for an autopsy."

"She wouldn't have wanted that," Aunt Margot said softly.

"I agree, but Hugh made the decision. Or maybe it was Hugh and Rhisiart."

"Of course they'll want to know how their mother died. That's understandable."

"I hated to see them take her away."

"I'm sure that was very hard. She loved her castle."

I promised that either I or Sylvie would keep Aunt Margot apprised of the funeral arrangements, then rang off. I was restless, but felt I had nothing to do. I didn't know where things stood with Annabel's personal effects—I supposed we would have to wait for the barrister to resolve the issue of the will before I would be allowed to go through any of her files. I didn't relish the thought of asking Hugh or Rhisiart for permission to do such a thing, so I decided to wait for the barrister.

I didn't have to wait long. One of the police officers came back to the house the next morning. He had spoken to Mr. Hadley and there was indeed a copy of the will in his office. Mr. Hadley would come to the castle the following day to read the will in the presence of the family members.

Tensions in the castle were running high. Hugh was especially belligerent and he and Cadi got into another heated argument over when they would be returning to London. Hugh insisted that Cadi wait until after the funeral to go anywhere. Cadi wanted to go back to London at once, then return to Wales for the funeral. I don't know how the argument ended because they went into their room and lowered their voices, but I assumed we would all know the outcome soon enough, based on whether Cadi stayed or left.

Rhisiart was especially ungentlemanly, too. He slammed his bedroom door, spoke rudely to Brenda, and demanded that Maisie bring him a pipe in the drawing room after dinner. I opened my mouth to tell him that Maisie was not his personal servant, but Maisie shot me a look that asked me to keep my mouth shut. It pained me to do so, but I respected her obvious wishes. She did deliver his pipe to him, but took her time doing so. I was pleased to see that she was responding to Rhisiart's demands with spunk.

When Mr. Hadley arrived the next morning, he was accompanied by the police officer. The officer stood outside the drawing room door while the family gathered in the room to await Mr. Hadley's reading.

Maisie and Brenda and I were anxious to hear the outcome of the will reading because we wanted to know how our jobs were going to be affected. Would we be looking for employment right away? Would we be asked to stay on? We sat downstairs in the silent kitchen, waiting. Griff came in after a short time wondering why everyone was so quiet.

"The family is in the drawing room for the will reading," I explained.

"What brings you here?" I asked him.

He jerked his chin and motioned for me to come into the hallway with him. I joined him there. "Why the secrecy?" I whispered.

"Oh, there's no secrecy. I just wondered if you'd be interested in going for another ride later today," he said. "I just didn't want to ask in front of Maisie and Brenda, that's all."

I smiled at him. "A ride would be nice, but I have to see what Sylvie is doing. I feel like I've been ignoring her lately, what with all that's been going on. Let me see if she has any plans and I'll let you know."

He grinned and headed up the stairs to the main hallway, calling "goodbye" to Maisie and Brenda. When I went back into the kitchen, the women looked at me with quizzical expressions. But my mischievous streak reared its head and I didn't say a word about Griff's visit. I just smiled and let them wonder.

Maisie opened a cupboard and brought out tea things. "We might as well have something warm to drink while we're waiting to hear what's happening upstairs." She put a kettle on the stove and came back to the table. "Eilidh, do you have any job prospects in case we get kicked out of the castle?"

"I'm afraid not," I said, shaking my head.

"Do you think you'll go back to Scotland?"

"I don't know about that," I said. "I don't know where I'd go in Scotland. I suppose I could go to Edinburgh and live near Greer, but when I moved to the Highlands, I loved it so much up there I never wanted to live in a city again. I suppose I could go live with my mum, but she's been talking about moving to a warmer climate. Then there's Sylvie, but she lives in Cauld Loch and I'm not ready to move back there. Not yet. Maybe never. I guess I'll have to find a new job and see where it takes me. What about you two?" I asked, indicating mother and daughter with a sweep of my hand.

They exchanged glances. "It's a touchy subject," Maisie said. "I think it would be wise for us to work together. Or if not, Brenda should at least stay near the village. That way she could still live at home and wouldn't have to let a place. She could save some money that way. Maybe go back to school or save enough for a down payment on a house of her own."

Brenda rolled her eyes. "Mum, I told you a hundred times I'm ready to be out on my own." She scowled, which made her lean face look pinched and mean.

"I didn't say you weren't ready, Brenda. I said you could save some money if you lived at home. Kids do it all the time now."

"Well, I'm not a kid."

"You act like one," her mother snapped. Thankfully, the water began to boil and Maisie stood up and poured three cups. She brought them back to the table on a tray while Brenda retrieved the sugar, cream, and lemon slices. They were an efficient team, those two. If only they could stop sniping at each other long enough to realize it.

"*Lechyd da*," I said, raising my cup to toast my companions.

"Lechyd da," they repeated, then we all sipped the hot tea in silence, each one of us probably thinking about what the future held.

It wasn't long before we heard shuffling and other noises in the hallway upstairs. I looked at Maisie, who looked at Brenda. "What should we do?" Maisie asked. "Should one of us go up there and find out what happened?"

"Let's wait," I suggested. "I have a feeling we'll know soon enough."

Indeed, we didn't have to wait long before we heard a door slam somewhere on an upper floor. We all exchanged glances, then I pushed away from the table. "You two stay down here, out of the line of fire. I'll see what I can find out." They nodded and Maisie crossed her fingers.

By the time I reached the drawing room, only the police and Mr. Hadley were left. The family members had already scattered.

"Good afternoon, Eilidh," Mr. Hadley said, reaching out to shake my hand. He shook his head. "That's a volatile group you have here."

I smiled knowingly. "I agree. Is there anything you can tell me about the will?"

"It's public knowledge now, so I suppose I can tell you that Hugh and Rhisiart are to split the value of the estate with Sian's unborn baby, one-third each. Andreas would have received a third upon Annabel's passing, but since he predeceased her Annabel's wish was that his share of the estate will pass to his child. I believe Sian is to make decisions on behalf of the child until he or she reaches the age of majority."

"What does that mean for everyone here?"

"It means, of course, that Annabel's two sons are, shall we say, displeased that they have to share the estate with Sian's baby. And until the two sons, and Sian on the child's behalf, decide what they want to do in the future, I don't know that it means anything for anyone who worked here in the castle for Annabel."

"So should we just keep doing what we've been doing?"

"Annabel's cook and housekeeper can continue with their duties as long as Hugh and Rhisiart and Sian agree, because people need to eat and live in a clean home. But I don't know about you. You were the one who handled the accounts for the castle, and whether you continue in that capacity is going to depend on the direction those three decide to take with the castle."

"But there are still going to be bills that have to be paid," I said, "including paychecks for Maisie, Brenda, Griff, and the other men who work in the stables part-time."

"I will approach Annabel's heirs about the issue," Mr. Hadley said. "They've agreed to retain my services for the duration of the estate proceedings. After that I may be looking for a new client."

I hadn't thought about that. Between her financial investments and her substantial land holdings in the county and in Cardiff, Annabel had been one of Mr. Hadley's best clients. There was always legal work for him to do. Now he might have to find another client as loyal as Annabel, or perhaps a number of clients whose combined work would equal that of Annabel's. A daunting prospect, I was sure.

The police officer had been silent during our brief conversation, but I was quite sure he had missed nothing. I wondered if he had heard anything about Annabel's autopsy.

We all turned toward the main hall when we heard shouting. It sounded like a man and a woman. We all walked to the doorway and peered down the dim corridor.

Indeed, it was Hugh and Cadi, yelling at each other while Cadi pulled on a long overcoat.

"That's ridiculous!" Cadi shouted.

"How could I have known?" Hugh asked. "I didn't make out the bloody will!"

"She gave her money to a *baby*? That's insane!"

"How many times do I have to tell you?" Hugh yelled. Then his voice quieted a bit. We could still hear him, though. "Andreas was supposed to get a third, but the will provided for his children, including unborn children, to inherit in the event he died before Mum."

"How much is there?" Cadi asked angrily.

"We have no idea."

"Well, find out. I'm going back to London whether you like it or not. I'll be back for the funeral." She picked up a large satchel that sat on the floor by her feet and swept out the front door before slamming it behind her. Hugh clenched his fists and let out an expletive. Then he looked in our direction, noticing for the first time that he and Cadi had had an audience.

"What are you looking at?" he snarled.

"Nothing," the officer replied calmly. "Nothing at all." We drew back into the room and looked at each other for a moment. Life in the castle was about to change drastically. Somehow Hugh and Rhisiart and Sian were going to have to cooperate in order to move the castle into the future.

I wondered what that meant for Griff, too, if Rhisiart got his way and expanded the stables for racing horses.

It was then I remembered Griff's invitation to go riding. I excused myself from the drawing room and put on a coat, then walked over to the coach house to see what Sylvie was up to. She was reading in front of the fireplace.

"What's going on?" I asked.

"Not much," she said with a sweep of her hand. "Just some holiday down time. Have a seat."

"Do you have plans for this afternoon?" I asked.

"Not really. I thought I'd take my camera and get some shots in the village and around the castle. Want to go with me?" she asked. "Or do you have something else you need to do?"

"I might go," I answered. "I was wondering because a friend asked me to go riding for a little while this afternoon."

"You can go with me anytime to take pictures. Go with your friend and have fun. You don't have to entertain me." Her eyes twinkled. "Who is this friend?" she asked with a grin.

I smiled self-consciously. "Griff, the groom, asked me this morning."

"He's cute!" Sylvie squealed. "He's so rugged!"

"Calm down. You're married, remember?" I said.

"Yeah, but you're not," she pointed out. "And Griff seems nice. And he's a *groom*, get it?" She giggled. I ignored her reference to marriage.

"I thought the last man I dated was nice, too, remember? And now we're divorced."

"That was just bad luck," Sylvie answered.

"Bad luck? I would say it was more than that," I replied. "Bad luck is having a flat tire when you're in a hurry to get somewhere. Bad luck is *not* marrying someone you had no idea was a criminal."

I went back to the castle and texted Griff on my way. He told me he'd have Penelope ready for me after lunch.

Maisie had made a delicious meal of thick chicken soup for those of us who remained in the castle, and we gathered in the dining room for lunch with somber faces. I realized that I was lunching with the three new owners of the castle and I was suddenly uncomfortable.

Maisie came into the dining room bearing a tray of fruit. Facing away from the others, she winked at me and rolled her eyes. I had to bite my lip to keep from giggling. She liked Annabel's family about as much as I did.

I ate quickly so I could get out of the dining room and away from the sour faces around the table. A tiny trill of excitement had found its way into my mood and I was happy to get outdoors and talk to Griff.

Dressed warmly, I walked briskly to the stables and found Penelope ready to go. Griff had also saddled Caesar and walked out of the stable office with a handful of carrots. "We'll take these with us," he said. "We'll stop halfway and give them a snack."

He gave me a boost onto Penelope's back and swung up onto Caesar, then we set off in the opposite direction from where we had gone on our first ride. We went round to the front of the castle and continued across the land between the castle and the main road leading to the village.

"Where are we going?" I called out to Griff. Caesar was leading the way and Penelope was taking her time following.

"A place I think you probably haven't seen," he called back. He reined in Caesar to wait for me, and after that our horses ambled side-by-side across the uneven ground.

When we came to the road leading into the village we turned to the left and began moving along the low stone wall that marked the edge of the land belonging to the castle. Eventually we reached a break in the wall; we passed through it and I found myself in a verdant glen populated with thousands of evergreen trees. The gray from the sky dappled the graceful branches and pine needles underfoot softened the sounds of the horses' hooves. Fronds from the crispy-looking ferns, quite brown by this time in the season, swayed in the gentle breeze. The earthy scent of the pine needles almost immediately transported me back to Christmas as a child in Scotland. I breathed deeply and exhaled. Griff turned to look at me. "Smells wonderful, doesn't it?"

"I love it," I said softly, almost afraid that talking in a normal tone would break the spell of the place.

"Have you ever been over here?" he asked.

"No, I've seen the woods from the house, obviously, but I've never ventured over here."

"Then I'm glad I brought you. I thought you'd enjoy it. It's peaceful, don't you think?"

"Heavenly," I replied. The horses kept walking, as if they knew the way. A narrow path had been worn across the ground and their steps took us farther into the woods. "Who owns this property?" I asked.

"It's village land. Occasionally I see other people while I'm riding through the glen, but mostly no one comes here."

"If I had known about it, I would have been out here all the time," I said. "Thanks for bringing me."

"It's my pleasure," he said, turning and smiling at me. "Just wait—it gets even better."

Penelope followed Caesar along the uphill path while I tried to take in every detail around me. It was nice to leave the walking to the horse so I could focus on my breathtaking surroundings. It wasn't long before I heard the sound of rushing water. It reminded me of the last time Griff and I had gone riding, when he showed me the stream in the woods. I experienced a moment of hesitation, recalling that Rhisiart had met us on our ride and interrupted a pleasant afternoon.

"What's up ahead?" I asked, noting the sound of the water getting louder.

"You'll see," Griff replied.

We rounded a bend in the path and the horses stopped suddenly. In front of us was a huge waterfall. Bright, clear water tumbled from a perch high above us, spilling over rocks and pooling into swirling eddies at the base of the fall.

Chapter 11

I swung off Penelope's back and tied her to a tree without waiting to see if Griff was getting off Caesar. I laughed as I dipped my hands into the pool again and again, feeling the cold water tingle my skin. Griff walked up behind me, a wide smile on his face. "You like it, eh?" he asked.

"It's amazing! I had no idea this was here!"

"For the few people who come into these woods, even fewer of them know about the falls. It's pretty far back along the trail."

"Thank you for bringing me here," I said again. "How could I live so close and not realize this is here?"

"You need time if you're going to explore, and I don't think you've had lots of time to do that," he said.

"And now with Annabel gone..." My voice trailed off.

"Any word on what's happening with the castle? And the employees?" he asked.

"Only that Hugh, Rhisiart, and Andreas's baby are going to own the castle together. And Sian is making decisions on the baby's behalf."

Griff whistled. "That promises to be ugly," he said, shaking his head. "They don't get along on a good day."

"I know. I ate lunch with all three of them earlier and there wasn't much conversation. And Cadi is furious. She's gone back to London until the funeral."

"Why is she mad?"

"She's always mad about something. But this time it's because she can't believe a third of the property was left to an unborn baby and that Sian will be making decisions on the baby's behalf. I suspect she's mad because she and Sian are both Annabel's daughters-in-law, but only Sian will be able to participate in making decisions about the castle."

"But Sian wouldn't be making any decisions if Andreas hadn't died."

"I know that, and you know that, but Cadi doesn't often listen to reason."

"What does Hugh have to say about it?"

"Not much, at least so far. He was just listening to Cadi's harangue right before she left for London, and I haven't heard him say anything about it since then."

"So any word about your job? And everyone else's?"

"Not yet. I imagine we'll hear something soon. They can't keep us in the dark forever. Mr. Hadley, the barrister, thinks Maisie and Brenda should just go on as they've been doing because the family will want the castle to be clean and they need to eat. But as for me, he said I'll have to wait to see what the family decides about the castle's future, since I'm the one who pays the bills, answers letters, that sort of thing. And I don't know about you and the stable hands—I would think you're rather like Maisie and Brenda. If they want to have horses, they need grooms."

"But Rhisiart wants racehorses, and I want nothing to do with them," he answered, an edge of anger creeping into his voice.

"I guess we'll have to wait and see what happens. But in the meantime, even if they want to sell the horses, they still need someone to feed them and care for them until that time comes."

"I guess you're right. Sounds like I don't need to pack my bags tonight, but I won't be surprised if it happens in the near future." He stroked Caesar's muzzle. "I'd buy Caesar, no doubt, if Rhisiart wanted to get rid of him. Heck, I'd try to buy all the horses. But I certainly don't have that kind of money and I don't have a place to keep them. I'd hate to see these horses get sold off."

"Me, too. If I could scrape enough money together I'd buy Penelope. But maybe Rhisiart will want to keep the horses that are in the stables now, even if he does want to expand to include race horses."

Griff cocked an eyebrow at me. "Maybe, but I doubt it."

Griff had brought a snack in a saddle bag and we ate sitting on a big boulder by the side of the pool, watching the water cascade into it. The rushing sound it made was simultaneously soothing and enervating. Griff had sliced vegetables and brought a jar of homemade hummus, and it was just what I needed after the ride. We fed the remaining vegetables, as well as the carrots Griff had brought with him, to the horses after we finished eating and the horses seemed to enjoy their snack as much as I did.

"Do you live in the village?" I asked, suddenly realizing I didn't know much about Griff personally.

He nodded. "I have a small cottage on the road leading out of the village. You'll have to come by sometime."

"I have a lot more time to do things like that now that Annabel's gone," I said ruefully.

"Any word on when her funeral is going to be?"

"No. I suppose that'll depend on how long the autopsy takes."

"Do I need to ask..." he began.

"No. The ambulance driver who took her to the medical examiner's office told me it depends on the complexity of the autopsy."

"So we're in a holding pattern right now," he stated.

"Yes."

"Come on over here. I want to show you something," he said, beckoning me near him. I walked over to where he stood and looked where he was pointing. There was a mossy log lying on the ground, and nestled inside a knot in the log was a tiny gold star. It was made of metal; the elements—the wind, the rain, and spray from the waterfall—had deadened its gleam, but it was enchanting.

"Oh!" I exclaimed. "It's beautiful! Someone must have left it here," I said, stating the obvious.

"There's a belief among the villagers that if visitors to the falls leave something shiny for the fairies, the fairies will keep the water in the forest clean and in good supply."

"What a lovely story," I said. Then, looking around, I began to notice more gold baubles I hadn't seen before. There was a string of gold beads looped around the branches of a tree overhanging the falls, a group of gold trinkets scattered about the ground, and a once-sparkly Christmas ornament hanging from another tree nearby. I patted my pockets. "I wonder if I brought anything sparkly with me."

"Here, I've got something," he said, fishing in his coat pocket. He held up a one-pound piece. "Leave this for the fairies," he said, handing it to me.

"Thank you! I don't have anything shiny on me," I said, taking the coin from him. "Where should we leave it?" I looked around, hunting for a good spot.

"Over here," he said. There was another log lying on the ground near his foot. He took a sharp stick and carved a tiny slice in the soft log. "Put the coin right in that slice," he suggested. "It should be secure in there."

I placed the coin in the log and stood back to admire our handiwork. "We'll have to come back here again sometime to make sure the coin is still there," I said.

"I've never known anything to be stolen from this place," he replied.

"Do you bring all the girls here?" I teased.

"No, just you," he said, smiling. I felt a funny tingle and I could feel my face flushing.

He had been standing near me when I bent down to put the coin in the log. When I straightened up he reached for my hand to help me, though I didn't need the help. His hand was warm. He pulled me close to him and kissed my lips, then held me away from him and looked at me intently. "I've wanted to do that for a long time, Eilidh. Do you mind?"

I knew I was blushing. More than anything I wanted him to do it again. "I don't mind at all," I said with a smile. "You can do that anytime you want!"

He obliged, kissing me again, then we walked over to where the horses were tethered. "I suppose we should be getting back, though I wish we could spend hours here."

"We can sometime," Griff answered. "But you're right. We should get back and see what's going on at the castle. I get the feeling we're in for a roller coaster of a ride with those three in charge."

When we were both on our horses and ready to leave, I took one long backward look at the waterfall and the fairy glen. I could hardly wait to visit again.

The horses walked a bit faster on the return trip to the stables as if they, too, sensed the need to get back and learn what may have transpired in our absence.

And there was plenty, as it turned out. I left Penelope in Griff's care and hurried back to the castle to get an update from Maisie and Brenda. When I opened the huge front door and stood in the front hall listening for any sounds, I heard nothing. Silence prevailed, as it had done earlier.

I went in search of Maisie and Brenda and didn't have to look far. They were in the kitchen, talking in strained voices.

"What's up?" I asked, walking into the warm, cozy room.

"You'll never guess, Eilidh," Brenda said breathlessly.

"What?" I asked.

"Brenda was upstairs dusting the sitting room when the call came in about the autopsy results," Maisie said.

"I can tell her. I was the one who heard," Brenda said, shooting her mum a frustrated look.

"Okay, you tell her," Maisie said.

"Tell me what?" I asked, exasperated.

"Annabel was poisoned." Brenda's words fell like a rock. I sat down in the nearest chair and stared at her.

"That can't be right."

"It's true," she insisted. "Hugh came into the room while I was dusting and he asked me to come back later to finish. I was telling him I was just finishing up when the phone rang. He shooed me out of the room, but I stood in the hallway to listen. He talked to the person on the phone and I heard him say, 'Yes, I'm Annabel's son.' Then he listened for a minute, then he said, 'You're kidding. She was poisoned? By what? Who did it?'"

"Did you get the answers?" I asked.

She shook her head. "No. I left and came down here to tell Mum right after I heard that. I didn't want him to know I was listening. He'd sack me for sure if he knew that."

"I can't believe this," I breathed. "How could she have been poisoned? Who would have done such a thing?" I looked at Maisie. "Do you suppose someone in the castle did this to her?" *Which one of her sons, or her daughters-in-law, could have done this?*

"This is all going to come back to me," Maisie said, her voice rising with anxiety. "People are going to think I put something in the food." She was breathing heavily and I was afraid she was going to faint. I stood up quickly, took her arm, and led her to the chair I had vacated.

"Brenda, will you please get her a glass of ice water?" I took the dish towel Maisie was clutching and tossed it over to the counter. "Maisie, look at me," I directed in a stern voice. "You have to pull yourself together. There's no reason for anyone to think you poisoned Annabel. The police are going to be looking at every possibility, and there are lots of ways Annabel could have been poisoned."

"Name one," she said.

I thought for a moment. The truth was, if Annabel had really been poisoned, it certainly seemed plausible that the poison was administered in her food. That would put Maisie in the crosshairs of the police investigation even if we all knew neither Maisie nor Brenda would ever have done such a thing. If the poison had been administered in Annabel's food, then either Hugh, Cadi, Sian, or Rhisiart could have done it. Even *I* would have had an opportunity to do it.

"Well, even if she ingested the poison, it could have come from any of the ingredients you used."

"But other people would be sick, too," she said.

"Okay, then maybe Annabel got something in her system when she ate a meal at a restaurant with one of her friends."

"Don't you think we would have heard if there were an outbreak of poisoning deaths? Wouldn't we know if one of her friends was poisoned, too? No, Eilidh, I appreciate what you're trying to do, but there's no getting away from it—this looks really bad for me."

There was nothing else I could say. I couldn't think of any words to placate her troubled mind and soul, so it was best for me to stop talking. I put my hand over hers and we sat at the table like that for several minutes. Brenda sat down with us and stared into her lap. I wondered what she was thinking. She hadn't been sniffling as much since Andreas's death, but I found myself thinking that could be for two reasons: she was getting used to Andreas being gone or she wasn't using cocaine because Andreas wasn't there to sell it to her.

I immediately felt ashamed for believing the worst could be true of Brenda. More than anything I wanted to think she was moving past the grief she felt when Andreas died and wasn't crying as much.

I vowed to keep a closer eye on Brenda, for her own sake. I was sure Maisie was doing the same thing, but it couldn't hurt to have two sets of eyes looking out for her.

Rhisiart came down to the kitchen just a few minutes later. "Eilidh, can you come upstairs, please? We'd like to talk to you about something."

I could feel Maisie and Brenda watching me as I left, but I didn't look at them. They knew I would share with them whatever I learned. Or whatever was asked of me.

Rhisiart led the way into the drawing room and closed the door behind us. Hugh and Sian were already in there. Hugh greeted me and motioned for me to have a seat.

"We've heard from the police about the results of Annabel's autopsy," Rhisiart began. I raised my eyebrows, hoping he wouldn't realize I already knew that.

"The medical examiner has concluded she was poisoned."

"That's terrible," I murmured. "With what? How?"

"They haven't given me that information yet," he replied. "But I expect we'll learn before very long. If they know she was poisoned, they must know what poison was used. But that's not why we asked you to come in here."

I glanced around the warm, dark space. Anyone locking in would have wondered why such a somber group had gathered. There was a dichotomy in the room I didn't care for: Hugh and Sian sat together on a divan and Rhisiart stood behind them. I, the interrogee, sat across from them in an armchair. I wasn't sure where this discussion was leading, but I didn't like it. I waited for someone to speak.

Finally Rhisiart cleared his throat, then addressed me. "Have you had any discussions with Maisie or Brenda, but Maisie in particular, regarding her relationship with Annabel?"

So that's what this was all about. They were already trying to blame Annabel's death on Maisie and Brenda.

"No," I answered. "I haven't spoken to either of them about it."

"We still have to speak to the police about the situation, but it seems likely that poisoning would have come from something Annabel ate," Rhisiart said.

I nodded, unwilling to divulge the conversation I had shared with Maisie and Brenda. I hadn't lied to Hugh or Sian or Rhisiart—Maisie and Brenda and I had not discussed Maisie's relationship with Annabel. I was simply answering questions truthfully. If my interrogators didn't ask the proper questions they wouldn't get the answers they sought.

"The police will likely be here soon," Hugh said, and at that moment the door gong reverberated through the front of the castle. We all looked at each other, no one saying a word. Brenda would answer the door and announce the visitor. Or visitors.

Indeed, Brenda came into the drawing room just moments later, escorting two police officers. She left, closing the door behind her, after taking tea orders from Hugh and Sian. She would probably not be eavesdropping on this conversation. I wasn't sure I should even be there.

One of the officers mentioned that immediately. "We will need to have a word with each of the household staff, but perhaps we should just speak with the family for now," he said, giving me a pointed look.

I took the hint. "I'll be in my room if anyone needs me," I announced. I was glad to leave the room, though I wondered what the others would say once I left. It occurred to me for the first time that I might be questioned as a suspect simply because I had enjoyed such a close relationship with Annabel.

But they certainly wouldn't view me as a suspect, would they? The thought would be laughable if it weren't so horrifying.

I wanted to go straight down to the kitchen to warn Maisie and Brenda that Annabel's sons and Sian were looking in Maisie's direction as having poisoned Annabel, but I didn't dare leave my room after telling the police that was where they could find me. I would have to be more careful about the family seeing me speaking to Maisie or Brenda. If I wanted to help the two women, I would have to downplay our friendly relationship.

The first thing I did once my bedroom door was shut and I had pulled out my mobile phone was text Sylvie.

Bad news.

What?

Annabel poisoned. Family asking questions.

Who poisoned her?

Don't know.

With what?

Don't know. Can you come over?

Be right there.

When she got there we sat on the floor in my room in front of the fire, talking over the shocking news.

"Who could have done such a thing?" she asked.

"I don't have any idea. Everyone liked Annabel. She didn't have any enemies that I knew of, and I knew just about everything there was to know."

"You mentioned there had been abuse in the house growing up. Do you suppose Hugh or Rhisiart finally snapped and killed her because of what happened when they were little?" Sylvie suggested.

I spread my hands wide. "I have no idea. It scares me to think there could be someone in this castle who hated Annabel enough to kill her. And how does that person feel about me? I was closer to Annabel than anyone."

"Don't say that," Sylvie said with a shiver. "The person who did this to Annabel obviously had a problem with Annabel, not you."

"I hope you're right." I paused for a moment.

"Could one of her boys, or Cadi or Sian, really hate her enough to kill her?" Sylvie had no answer.

Chapter 12

The doorbell sounded again, reverberating through the halls. I went to see if someone was answering it and I saw Brenda pass the end of the hallway on her way to the door. She led a police officer and an older woman toward the drawing room. I pulled my door shut and spoke to my cousin.

"It's another police officer and some woman I've never seen. I wonder what's going on now."

"No doubt the police officer is here to help ask questions," Sylvie said. "I shouldn't be surprised if the castle is crawling with them before evening."

And as if the police force of the village heard her, the doorbell sounded again. I repeated my actions from a few moments ago—I looked to see if Brenda was going to answer the door, then watched as she led a phalanx of officers toward the drawing room.

"It won't be long before I'm summoned to answer questions," I said miserably. "It's hard enough around here with Annabel gone, but now with everyone suspecting everyone else, it's going to be positively ghastly."

"Should I stay? I'm sure the police are going to want to talk to me, too," Sylvie said.

"I'm not sure," I answered. "I don't want them to find you in here and think that we're colluding and comparing our stories."

"You're beginning to sound paranoid. I'll go back to the coach house and wait for them to either come over there or call me over here."

"Maybe you should leave through the kitchen door downstairs," I fretted.

"I have nothing to hide, and neither do you. How is it going to look if someone sees me trying to sneak back over to the coach house? They'll think I'm guilty of something, that's for sure. No, I'm going out the front door. If anyone asks, I came to see you because you got some bad news, and that's the truth whether they like it or not."

My phone buzzed. I looked at the screen—it was a text from Griff.

What's going on?

I didn't answer right away. I wanted to make sure Sylvie was out of the castle and back in the coach house without facing a gauntlet of questions from the police.

She left without incident and I resisted the temptation to listen at the drawing room door to try to learn what the police were telling the family.

Instead I returned to my room to wait. My stomach churned and rumbled, my hands were sweaty. Brenda knocked softly on the door at one point and raised her eyebrows when I answered, a silent request for information, but I merely shook my head slightly and whispered "later." I knew she and Maisie, especially Maisie, were desperate for information, but I didn't want to get them in trouble and I didn't want to get myself into trouble if the police or any member of the family were to see us having a whispered conversation.

For that same reason I didn't respond to Griff's earlier text. I longed to tell him what was going on in the castle, but I didn't want to cause any trouble for him. If the police were going to question him, it would be better for him and for me if he heard the news of the poisoning from the authorities.

I didn't have long to wait before a police officer knocked at my door and requested that I accompany her to the drawing room. As we got there Hugh, Rhisiart, and Sian were leaving, also accompanied by an officer. I didn't know where they were going.

The officer motioned for me to sit down. The older woman who had come into the castle earlier with one of the police officers was also in the room, seated at a desk, pen and pad in hand.

"I am Officer Beckton and this is Dr. Thomas, the medical examiner," the police officer began. "The doctor and I have some questions for you. It's highly irregular for the medical examiner to accompany the authorities to question people regarding a person's death, but in this case we thought we should have Dr. Thomas with us because of the community standing of the deceased and the fact that her death so closely follows the death of a close family member."

The officer asked her questions first, taking me through the events of the past several days, and in particular the thirty-six hours leading up to Annabel's death. I repeated all the information I had previously given the other officers who questioned me. The officer seemed satisfied with my answers, but how was I to know what she was really thinking? For all I knew I was a suspect in Annabel's death.

Then it was Dr. Thomas's turn to ask questions.

"Eilidh, I'm sure you've been told that Annabel's cause of death was poisoning."

"Yes. The family told me."

"Are you aware of the poison that caused her death?"

"No."

"It's called 'monkshood.'"

"I've never heard of it."

"Sometimes it's called 'devil's helmet.'"

I shook my head.

"How about 'wolfsbane?'"

I started. "Wolfsbane? That grows in the English cottage garden right outside the castle."

The doctor wrote something on her pad. "Are you sure?"

"I'm positive. Annabel had mentioned before that it's poisonous, but still very popular in cottage gardens. It's a beautiful plant."

"How long has Annabel been growing the wolfsbane?"

"I don't know. It's been there since I started working here."

Dr. Thomas made another note on her pad and nodded at the police officer, who spoke to me. "I'm sure we and Dr. Thomas will have more questions for you, so please stay nearby."

I nodded and left the room. I had to resist the urge to break into a run going down the hallway, and I longed to tell Maisie and Brenda what I had learned from the doctor. But it wouldn't be wise to talk to them before the police did. I thought again about texting Griff to tell him of the developments in the castle, but I refrained. Same with Sylvie. If the police were going to talk to Annabel's other employees and my guest I didn't want anyone, including me, to get in trouble for talking about the investigation prematurely.

Instead I went online to research wolfsbane. It seemed incredible that such a pretty plant could cause such harm and suffering. The plant in Annabel's garden was more purple than blue, though the plant had bluer varieties, as well as yellow-ivory varieties. It was highly toxic when ingested and there were even stories of its use in ancient times as an aid in euthanasia.

What interested me the most was the evidence that the taste of wolfsbane was so bitter that accidental poisoning was rare. In other words, if someone had slipped the plant into Annabel's food, she would have been able to taste it and she wouldn't have eaten the food. Maisie would be very happy to learn that.

There were also instances of people becoming ill and dying after merely touching the plant. Annabel had told me once that she avoided pruning the wolfsbane because of its toxicity. Since she was so careful around wolfsbane, it seemed unlikely that she would have gotten sick by coming into physical contact with the plant out in the cottage garden.

Another interesting fact I learned about wolfsbane from my wee bit of research was that it often causes severe stomach pain and upset, followed by a slowing of the heart rate and heart failure. I didn't know for sure whether Annabel died from heart failure, but it made sense. After complaining of a sour stomach in the morning, Annabel had experienced worsening gastrointestinal pain throughout the day. Then something had caused her to collapse on the floor of her bedroom and death had apparently come quickly. It had happened in the time it took me to go down to the kitchen for tea. I shuddered at the thought of Annabel suffering from the effects of the poison. From what I was reading, it sounded like an agonizing death.

How could someone have done that to her?

There was a knock at my bedroom door. When I answered it there were two police officers standing in the hallway with Dr. Thomas.

"We'd like permission to search your room, miss," said one of the officers.

"Certainly," I said, stepping aside. One officer and Dr. Thomas came into the room while the other officer remained in the hallway.

"Miss, I'd like you to step out here with me," he said. "We'll have you remain in the hallway while your room is being searched."

I grimaced. "Fine." He stood next to me, not saying a word, while his partner and Dr. Thomas could be heard rummaging through everything in my room. I heard the armoire doors opening and closing, bureau drawers opening and closing, and furniture being moved around. I was impatient to get back into my room to reorganize everything after the officer and the doctor were done making a mess.

When they emerged from my room they were carrying a large paper bag that obviously had something in it. "What is that?" I asked, pointing to the bag.

"We have taken some items that may be necessary as evidence," the officer said. My blood ran cold.

"What items? What evidence?" I demanded, my voice rising. I could feel my heart beating faster and my hands were clammy.

No answer. The two officers and the doctor walked away without a backward glance. I was frantic wondering what they had taken. I threw my door open and went first to the nightstand. As I suspected, nothing seemed to be missing. I went through my desk next, noting immediately that my laptop was missing from its drawer. I rifled through mail that had been on the desk and couldn't recall everything that had been there, so I didn't know if anything was missing or not.

When I went to my vanity I found there were several items missing. Moisturizer, foundation, eye makeup, lip balm, perfume, and lotion. In the bathroom, I found the police had taken other items, too: creams, medicines, and dental floss. I wondered what about my possessions had so interested the police and Dr. Thomas that they felt the need to confiscate them.

I could feel the heat rising in the back of my neck. Why was I being treated like I had done something wrong? And worse, what if the police actually believed I had done something wrong? I knew I shouldn't be contacting anyone else who might be in the police's sights at the moment, but I couldn't bear to be by myself. I rang up Sylvie. She didn't answer. I tried Griff and he picked up the phone.

"This is unexpected," he said when he answered the phone.

"Are you busy?"

"No. Why? What's wrong?" The stress in my voice must have been more obvious than I thought.

"I've just had my room searched by the police and the doctor they've brought in, and they took stuff from my vanity and my desk and my bathroom." My words were terse.

"What types of things did they take?"

"Lotions, perfumes, things like that. And my laptop. Do you suppose I'm a suspect?"

"I doubt it. What reason would they have to think you killed Annabel?"

"There's no reason. That's what I can't figure out."

"Have they taken stuff from other people's rooms? Or the kitchen?"

"I don't know. I haven't left my room yet."

"Well, let's figure that out before you panic. Maybe they're taking those items from every room." I felt a tiny surge of hope. Of course they would take items from everyone's room. At this point, all of us were probably suspects.

"Do you want me to come up to the castle?"

I wanted him to, but it was not a good idea. "You probably shouldn't," I answered. "I'm sure the police will want to talk to you, too, and I don't want them to accuse either of us of obstructing or colluding or whatever it is they might think."

"You're right. Do you know yet how Annabel died? I assume you have at least an idea because of what the police took."

"I do know how she died, but maybe I should keep the information to myself until the police tell you. That way when the police talk to you there won't be any question that I shared information without their permission."

"All right. I guess I'll just wait in the stables for the police to come find me. They won't be long, I shouldn't think. I'll call you the minute they leave."

I tried Sylvie again, but she didn't answer the phone.

I had nothing to do and I didn't want to be alone in my room. Several police officers still scurried through the halls of the castle, visiting various rooms and carting items away in large bags identical to the one they took from my room. I breathed a sigh of relief when I saw that my room wasn't the only one with suspicious contents. I wanted to visit the sitting room first to find a book I might take to my room in case I could settle down enough to read. There was an officer right outside the sitting room.

"Can I go in there?" I asked.

"Yes, ma'am. We have cleared this room of evidence."

I brushed past him and went to one of the floor-to-ceiling bookshelves that lined the sitting room walls. I stared at the book spines for a long time before finally picking out a biography of Welshman George Everest, of Mount Everest fame. Normally I loved mysteries, but I just couldn't summon the enthusiasm for a mystery, since I was living in one.

Tucking the book under my arm, I left the sitting room. But I wasn't ready to go back to my room yet. I wanted to see what the police were doing, where they were looking for evidence in Annabel's death. I walked upstairs. There was a police officer standing outside Annabel's bedroom door.

"Can I help you?" he asked as I drew nearer.

"I'm just taking a walk," I replied. "Can I go upstairs?" He nodded. There was a room above Annabel's that was fully and beautifully furnished. It had been meant as a private sitting room for the family of Annabel's second husband, but when her second husband died the family no longer came for extended visits. They would stop in to see Annabel occasionally, but there was not much need for a sitting room furnished especially for them. Annabel had loved the way the room was decorated, though, and she had sometimes gone up there to curl up with a good book or a cup of tea.

I pushed the door open and peered into the room. The curtains had been drawn to protect the carpet and the furniture from fading, so the first thing I did was to slide all the drapes open and let the sunshine stream in. The room was chilly, so I chose a blanket from a large chest against one wall and lay down on the cushy sofa in front of the fireplace. The sofa had a tall back and sides, so I felt protected and cozy, like I was in a cocoon. There was no fire in the grate, but I knew the blanket would warm me in no time.

I opened the book and began to read, but I found my mind wandering. As much as I wanted to learn more about George Everest, I couldn't stop the questions swirling around in my head—what had the police found in other rooms? Did they think the person who poisoned Annabel was in the castle? Were any of the family members under suspicion? Did they think her death had anything to do with the death of Andreas?

I had no answers. I tried reminding myself over and over again that there was nothing I could do at the moment to glean more information or to convince the police I had nothing to do with Annabel's death, and eventually I was able to read the first chapter of my book. But I was exhausted from the stress of the day, and I was asleep before I began chapter two.

I don't know how long I had been sleeping when I was awakened by a soft sound. Groggy and confused, I sat up and peered around the side of the sofa to see what had made the noise.

Brenda was in the room. I don't know how she had come in without me hearing her. Her back was to me and she obviously didn't know she wasn't alone. Something about her stance warned me not to reveal my presence just yet. She was hunched over a table on the other side of the large room. I heard again the sound that had awakened me.

She was sniffing. One long sniff, followed by another. I realized with horror that she was doing lines of cocaine. I was shocked.

I didn't know what to do. *Should I let her know I'm here? Should I shrink back down and hide on the sofa? What if she finds me here? How will she react?*

Finally my desire to stop her from destroying herself propelled me off the sofa. "Brenda, what are you doing?" I asked softly.

She spun around, her red eyes wide with surprise, and started coughing. When she was able to catch her breath she straightened up and stared at me, clearly unsure of what to do. I solved the dilemma for her.

"Brenda, don't do it. You're hurting yourself."

She recovered her voice and sneered at me. "What do you know?"

"I know what you're doing, and I know the damage you're causing to yourself. What I don't know is why."

"It doesn't matter why."

"How are you getting the cocaine?"

"None of your business."

"It is my business, though, because I care about what's happening to you. You're destroying your future."

"What future?"

"You're young, Brenda. It may seem right now like things are hopeless, but they're not. You'll find another job."

"It's not just my job. It's everything."

"Like what?"

"Like Andreas being dead. Like my mum not understanding anything."

"Your mother loves you. She wants the very best for you."

Her eyes widened, as if she had just come to some realization. "You're not going to tell Mum about this, are you?"

"I should."

"Don't."

"She probably already knows, Brenda."

"How could she know?"

"The sniffling, the red eyes. She knows, believe me."

"Just don't tell her that you saw me. Please."

"Tell you what. I won't tell her for now, but you have to kick this habit. It's obvious to everyone, not just me. Everyone sees your eyes, your nose. They know what you're doing. In fact, *they* told *me*. I wanted to believe you were just distraught over Andreas's death."

"I am."

"I know that, but it's not just Andreas's death that's causing those things. Was he the one selling to you?"

She looked at me sullenly, not answering.

"Brenda? Was he? Did you buy cocaine from him his first night here, the night he left and slammed the door behind him? It doesn't matter now, since he's dead." No response.

"I'm going to take that as a 'yes.' So where are you getting the cocaine now?" I knew better than to expect a response from her.

"Just don't tell Mum, okay? I'm going to try to get off it. I promise."

I gave her a skeptical look. "I'm not promising that I won't tell your mum," I said. "But I'm going to be keeping an eye on you. I can't stand the thought of you ruining everything because of some white powder."

She looked at her feet, then up at me again. "I didn't ask for this."

"I know that. But now that you're using, you're the only one who can make the decision to stop." She nodded. "You should probably get back to work," I said.

"Okay." She turned around and was leaving when I had a thought.

"Brenda, were you looking for cocaine in Andreas's bureau when Sian caught you in there?"

She gazed at me for a moment, her eyes and nose red and raw-looking, and gave me a short nod. I could only shake my head and she left without another word. I returned to the sofa and lay down, hoping to be able to rest again, but I knew it wouldn't happen. My mind was wide awake again, reeling with thoughts of Brenda, cocaine, and the horrors I knew could accompany addiction. I didn't know if Brenda was addicted, but it could happen easily. I tried reading again, too, but I couldn't focus on the words. Eventually I closed the book, folded the blanket and put it away, and closed the drapes again before returning to the main floor of the castle. The room that had held so much warmth and comfort for Annabel and for me was tainted now with the sight of Brenda sniffing lines of cocaine from an antique table inlaid with mother-of-pearl.

When I went back to my room Griff was leaving me a note. "I couldn't find you," he said with a smile. "How are you doing?"

I mustered a smile in return. "I've been better," I said. I knew he would think I was talking about Annabel's death and its aftermath, and I let him think it. I didn't want to betray Brenda's trust by revealing her secret to Griff, even though I knew he could be trusted.

"Did the police come out to the stables to talk to you?"

"They did, and they searched the office out there, too. They took my laptop, which I keep on the desk."

"Why do you think they took that?"

He shrugged. "Same reason they took yours, I suppose. They told me Annabel had been poisoned with something that grows right here on the property, so they probably wanted to know if anyone has done any online research about how to poison someone using wolfsbane."

"I did research on it after they told me she had been poisoned," I said with a gasp. My body broke out in a cold sweat.

"I wouldn't worry about it," he said in a soothing voice. "They'll be able to see the date and time you looked it up and that it was after Annabel had already died."

Thank goodness he was keeping a cooler head than me. All I could think was that I would somehow be targeted by the police as the main suspect in Annabel's murder.

"You're right," I said. "I'm just nervous, that's all. I think I'm still a bit shocked about everything that's happened."

"So how does one kill someone with wolfsbane, exactly?" Griff asked.

"I don't know. That's why I looked it up online, but I didn't get very far. I read mostly about its history. I assume you grind up the flowers or the leaves or something."

"It's a terrible thought, isn't it, that someone in the castle might have been grinding up roots or leaves or something in the night like a mad scientist," Griff said. I shuddered.

"I don't even want to think about it."

"Then let's not. Let's think of something else for a while. What are you doing tonight?" Griff asked. "Care to go into the village for a dinner at the pub?"

I grinned. "I would like that, but I should see what Sylvie is doing."

"Why don't you invite her to come along? That way she's not left out and I still get to have dinner with you." He smiled at me.

"All right. I'll text her and let you know."

I felt guilty for being happy in the face of the circumstances in the castle, but some tiny nugget of warmth and happiness was beginning to stir in me. I hoped Sylvie didn't have plans, because I wanted to spend time with her and at the same time I wanted to go to dinner with Griff. Inviting her along would be a lovely solution.

When I rang up Sylvie she told me she had, in fact, hoped to go to dinner with me at the pub. I'm sure she could hear the smile in my voice when I suggested we go to dinner with Griff.

"That sounds wonderful," she said. "Let me know when I have to be ready and I'll meet you in the front hall of the castle."

Chapter 13

Talking to Griff and Sylvie and having dinner plans gave me a welcome boost of energy. I didn't want to be alone in my room so I grabbed a heavy coat and went for a walk around the grounds just outside the castle. The English cottage garden was roped off by the police and there were still two officers there, pointing to different plants and holding up mobile phone photos next to the plants, presumably comparing the ones in the garden to photos online. They glanced up as I walked past, but didn't seem to care that I was outside.

I walked around the back of the castle and was startled to see Maisie outside the kitchen door. She sat on an upturned barrel on the ground and looked up as I approached.

"Aren't you cold out here?" I asked.

"Nay, it feels good to me," she replied.

"I guess you've talked to the police?" I asked. I was in the mood to talk, though I couldn't tell if she shared the feeling.

She sniffled, sounding for a moment like her daughter. "Aye."

"Did they take anything from the kitchen?"

"Aye. You should have seen the bags they took away. You could feed a hundred people with all that stuff."

I nodded in sympathy. "You're not alone," I told her. "They took quite a few things from my room and from all the others' rooms, too."

"They did?" She looked at me in surprise, her expression brightening a bit. "You mean I'm not the only one under suspicion?"

I shook my head. "No, it seems we're all under suspicion, at least until they go through the evidence and start narrowing down the possibilities."

"Have you talked to anyone else?"

"No one in the family, though I did talk to Griff. They didn't take anything from the stables but his personal laptop. They took mine, too."

"Why do you suppose they did that?"

"Probably to see if anyone did research on poisoning with wolfsbane."

"I told Annabel long ago that she shouldn't plant that nasty stuff in her garden. Now look where it's gotten all of us."

"It's really a pretty plant. I can see why it's so popular in English gardens. But you sure have to be careful around it."

She nodded, seemingly lost in thought. "Have you seen Brenda?" she asked suddenly.

I froze for just a moment, wondering if Maisie knew I had seen Brenda upstairs in the castle. Then I realized she probably wasn't referring to that incident at all and I recovered myself. But should I lie and tell her I hadn't seen Brenda? Or tell the truth and not elaborate?

I decided to lie. "I haven't seen her."

"I've been looking for her. She's supposed to help me clean the cupboards now that they're almost totally bare." The tone of her voice held an edge of anger. I didn't know if the anger was because she couldn't find Brenda or because the cupboards, normally bulging with good things to eat, were empty.

"If I see her I'll tell her you're looking for her," I said a little too brightly.

"Thank you." Maisie looked into the distance, away across the fields behind the castle. Our conversation was apparently over. I felt a pang of sympathy for her. I knew she was worried about being a suspect in Annabel's death because of her position as the person who fed everyone in the castle, but she was probably concerned about her daughter, too. If she knew of Brenda's drug habit, and I assumed she did, she was no doubt worried sick about it.

I didn't see anyone else as I continued my walk around the outside of the castle. When I went back inside I felt better, more refreshed. I went to my room and was able to read the Everest biography for a long time before putting it aside to get ready to go to dinner in the village.

I didn't mean to, but I spent a long time getting ready for dinner. Part of the problem was that many of my usual beauty products were missing, having been confiscated by the police. The other part of the problem was that I was finding myself taking extra care with my hair and the little bit of makeup I still had. I was certainly old enough to realize that I didn't want to be in a relationship with Griff if he only liked what he saw on the outside, but I couldn't help myself. I wanted to look nice.

And Sylvie confirmed it for me when I greeted her in the great hall just a little while later. She let out a long whistle. "Look at you!" she exclaimed. "Maybe we should let you and Griff eat dinner alone!"

I could feel myself blushing, and I smiled broadly. "Do I look okay?" I asked, turning in a circle.

"You are beautiful inside and out. And Griff sees it, too. I know he does." How did she always seem to know just what I was thinking?

"I'm starving," she said. "I can stand here all night telling you how lovely you are or we can go meet Griff at the pub. I hope they have fish and chips on the menu tonight."

I led the way out to the parking enclosure and drove us over to the pub, where Griff was already waiting at a booth. I hesitated for just a moment, then slid in next to him while Sylvie sat across from us. Votive candles flickered on the tabletop and a fire crackled in the huge fireplace that took up the far wall of the pub. The place was crowded because the food was so good.

The three of us enjoyed a hearty meal. Sylvie pronounced her fish and chips the best she'd tasted since leaving Scotland. I had a juicy cheeseburger with fried onions and Griff had a large bowl of mutton stew. Everyone agreed we should meet there more often for dinner.

Talk, of course, centered on the actions of the police and the medical examiner. We speculated as to how Annabel could have been poisoned and who might have done such a thing. Sylvie wondered whether she would be allowed to return to Scotland at the end of her holiday if the police didn't have a suspect in custody.

"I would think so," Griff said in answer to Sylvie's concern. "Even if the police don't have a suspect in custody, at least they can rule out certain people." Again, I appreciated Griff's level-headedness. He could cut through the emotion of a situation and see it more rationally than I could.

"I don't even want to think about you leaving," I told Sylvie. "How is Seamus doing without you, anyway?" I asked. I turned to Griff. "You should meet her husband. He's wonderful." Griff smiled and looked at Sylvie expectantly as he slipped his arm around my shoulders across the back of the booth. I felt a tiny flutter of butterflies in my stomach and I noticed Sylvie grin ever so slightly.

Our talk turned to Seamus. We spent a long time entertaining Griff with tales about Seamus and his work.

As the hours stretched into the late evening, I noticed several patrons had left the pub, leaving the cozy space less crowded. I noticed for the first time that someone was listening to our conversations from a nearby table. Rhisiart.

He was alone, nursing a pint of Guinness and keeping an ear cocked toward our table. I wondered if he had been there all evening, just listening. I couldn't believe I hadn't noticed him before, but I had been enjoying myself with my two companions, not paying attention to anyone else in the pub.

He saw me looking at him and he raised his glass slightly toward me in a silent toast. I realized I had missed whatever Sylvie was saying.

"Eilidh?" she asked. "Do you remember that?"

"Hmm?" I asked, turning back to the others. "I'm sorry. What did you say?"

Sylvie had followed my eyes and saw Rhisiart. She lowered her voice. "How long has he been here? He gives me the creeps."

"Why do you suppose he's sitting there all alone?" Griff asked. "Do you think he's been listening to us?"

"I don't know," I replied, "but suddenly I'm ready to go back to the castle. It's a good thing I didn't spot him until now, or he would have ruined my appetite." The vehemence of my feelings toward Rhisiart's appearance surprised even me.

We called for the check and it took us a few minutes to figure out the bill. We all chipped in and left the server a hefty tip, considering we had commandeered the table all evening. When we stood up to leave, Griff helped me with my coat. I glanced over at Rhisiart, who gave me a sardonic grin.

I wondered about Rhisiart all the way back to the castle, where Cadi was just arriving from London as we drove up to the front. She was standing near the door and waiting for the taxi driver to unload her bags from the boot. I let Sylvie out of my car and she walked away to the coach house in the darkness. I pulled the car around to the parking enclosure and stepped into the cold night air. Normally I would have gone inside using the door that led to the enclosure, but for some reason that door was locked. It was a rule below stairs in the castle that if anyone was out using one of the cars, that door would be left unlocked so the person could get back inside without having to walk all the way around to the front, particularly in the darkness and the cold. But this night it was locked, so I had no choice but to trudge across the enclosure and out along the wide stone path that led to the front.

I hadn't gone far when I heard a noise in front of me. I stopped for a moment to listen, but the noise stopped. It was a soft rustle, like a sound the wind would make blowing through tall, dead grass.

I took a tentative step forward, then heard a different sort of a noise. This was a whisper. And it was whispering my name.

"Eilidh. Eilidh."

I stopped again and looked around, squinting to see anything in the darkness and wondering for the first time why all the lights were out on this side of the castle.

"Who's there?" I called in a loud whisper. I didn't know why we were whispering.

"It's me. Cadi." She stepped out of the shadow of the castle and stood on the path in front of me. I started, giving a little gasp.

"Cadi, you scared me. What are you doing?"

"Hugh doesn't know I'm back yet. I didn't tell him when I would be arriving from London. What's been going on?"

"Nothing. It's just the same as when you left. You weren't gone very long."

"I know. I got to feeling bad about leaving so I turned around and came back almost as soon as I got to London."

"Annabel's service is the day after tomorrow. You were going to come back in time for that anyway, weren't you?"

"Yes." I could see her a bit better now that she wasn't hidden in shadow.

"So why are you out here? Why didn't you just go inside and unpack?"

"I wanted to talk to you. Have they found out how Annabel died?"

"Yes. She was poisoned."

She gripped my arm. "Poisoned? With what? Who did it?"

I gently released my arm from her grasp and began walking toward the front of the castle, hoping she would follow. I was cold and I was a little uncomfortable whispering with her in the dark.

"She was poisoned by a plant called wolfsbane, which has grown for years in the English cottage garden along the western side of the castle. The police and the medical examiner are trying to figure out who did it and how."

"They've talked to everyone? Even Sian?"

I noticed the changed tone of her voice right away. It was lower, more conspiratorial. "Yes, they've talked to all of us, including Sian. They haven't announced their suspicions, though I hardly expect them to do that. I'm sure they'll want to talk to you now that you're back."

"I'll have no choice but to tell them what I know," she said. I knew she was dying for me to ask her what she knew, but I found suddenly that I didn't want to be involved in whatever Cadi was planning. I didn't want to know what she knew or what she was going to tell the police.

"I suppose you need to tell them the truth," I said noncommittally, quickening my steps. She took my arm again and held me back, and I knew before she said anything that she was going to tell me her secret about Sian.

"You know Sian is an avid gardener, right? We visited her and Andreas once and their house has plants all over the place. Lush, thriving plants. She knows her way around a garden, believe me. Of course, I would never imply that Sian was responsible for Annabel's death, but I do think it bears investigation by the authorities, don't you?"

I didn't say anything and she kept talking. "I know you probably don't want to know all of this, given how close you were to Annabel, but we all deserve the truth." *And if the truth happens to involve implicating someone Cadi doesn't like, then so much the better for her,* I though with a grimace.

"Cadi, I'm freezing. Could we talk later, maybe? I'd really like to go inside," I said.

"Oh, yes. Forgive me. I wasn't thinking. This whole thing has me tied in knots," she said. "Let's get inside where it's warm. We can talk later."

I nodded and walked briskly in front of her until we reached the front door of the castle. I opened the door and stepped back to wait for her to cross the threshold, then I followed her inside. The warmth felt delicious after the frigid air outside. When she bent down to rifle through one of her bags I saw my chance to make my escape. "Brrr. I'm going to go build a fire first thing and crawl into bed. Goodnight, Cadi." She grunted in return, still looking in her bag. I made a beeline for my room and closed the door firmly behind me, double-checking to make sure it was locked.

Once I was alone I got ready for bed while I mulled over Cadi's words. I didn't know very much about Sian; Annabel hadn't known her well, either. Was it possible she knew a lot about plants? Was it even possible she was familiar with the toxicity of wolfsbane? I wondered if she had told the police everything she knew about gardening. I remembered with an uncomfortable jolt that I had seen Annabel and Sian leaving the cottage garden the day Andreas went missing. No doubt Annabel told Sian about the wolfsbane plant, knowing it could hurt the baby if Sian touched it.

Had Sian killed Annabel? And if so, why? Of course, it was possible that Cadi was not telling the truth, or at least not telling all of it.

I didn't sleep well that night. My dreams were filled with visions of Andreas's body, of Annabel's last moments, and of Brenda's surprise at finding me in the room where she was doing lines of coke, where she thought she was alone. Maisie cried throughout my dream, lending a melancholy note to all the mixed messages my brain was trying to process. I woke up several times throughout the night, each time sadder than the last.

When I finally dragged myself out of bed before dawn, I went downstairs for a cup of tea. Maisie was already working, having arrived at the castle an hour previously. She invited me to sit down with her at the kitchen table while we waited for the rest of the household to awaken.

"This is my favorite time of day," she confided when we were both seated with steaming cups of tea before us. "It has been for years. It's the only time of day when I feel everything is at peace. When Brenda was a baby I used to treasure the few minutes I had to myself in the morning. Not much has changed, really, even though Brenda has grown. I still love the minutes I spend alone each morning."

"And I went and spoiled it by coming downstairs," I said.

"No, no," she hastened to assure me. "I'm glad you came down. I wanted to ask your opinion about something. Someone, actually."

I gave her a wary glance. Memories, still fresh, of last night's whispered conversation with Cadi sprang up unbidden. "What do you want my opinion for?" I asked.

"There's a reason Annabel liked having you as her assistant so much. You're trustworthy. And you have good instincts. I just want to plumb those instincts for a minute or two."

"All right," I said, wondering where this was leading.

"I want to know what Brenda has been up to. She likes you and she knows Annabel loved you. She trusts you because you're closer in age to her than the rest of us. You remember most clearly what it was like to be a teenager," she said with a rueful chuckle.

"I do remember," I said. "It's hard to be a teenager. So many temptations, so many things to remember, so many people telling you to do the right thing."

"That's exactly what I'm concerned about. I'm her mother. She doesn't tell me anything. Of course I know she's been doing drugs and I know she used to get them from Andreas, but I don't know much other than that. I thought Andreas's death might shock her into kicking her habit. But I don't think that's happened. I'd like your take on it."

"How did you know she was using drugs?"

She gave me a sidelong look. "A mother knows those things."

"How do you know she bought the drugs from Andreas?"

"I stumbled upon them one day on his last visit. They were in the middle of a 'transaction' and I read her the riot act afterwards. But I don't think it helped. I've left pamphlets for her to find about the dangers of drug abuse, but I find them in the rubbish bin. I've tried talking to her calmly, but she's not listening."

"Maisie, I'm not sure I can help you. I only found out very recently that Brenda was using drugs, and I don't think I'm the one to ask about whether she's continued to use."

"But surely you've noticed the red, rheumy eyes, the sniffling, the mood changes."

"I have," I said with a nod, "but honestly I thought the occasional red eyes and mood changes were from crying jags that are normal among girls her age. You know, unrequited love. I had no idea drugs played a part in her behavior at all." I hoped my answer was ambiguous enough to stop Maisie from probing any further. I had promised Brenda I wouldn't reveal her secret. Yet. I wondered now how I would handle the stickiness if Brenda didn't stop using and I had to go to Maisie to tell her what I knew about Brenda's cocaine habit. Maisie would accuse me of deceiving her, of knowing full well about Brenda's drug use and not being forthcoming with the information. And could I blame her for feeling that way?

Everything was becoming more complicated by the day.

"Maisie, can you try talking to Brenda again?" I asked gently. "She's the only one who can do anything about the drugs."

"I know," her mother said, her eyes glistening with tears. "But I'm the last person she wants to talk to and I can help her. If she would only ask for help. Or even realize she needs it. She's ruining her life, but she won't listen when I try to tell her that. But here's what I want to know—have you noticed anything about her behavior that would lead you to believe she's still taking drugs?"

"I haven't noticed a change in Brenda's behavior, if that's what you're asking," I said. It was true. I knew she was still using cocaine and in my opinion her behavior didn't suggest anything different.

"Would you tell me if you see anything?" Maisie asked. I gave a slight nod. She was getting dangerously close to asking me flat-out if I'd seen Brenda using drugs. I didn't want to lie to my friend, especially when all she wanted was to help her daughter, but I had made a deal with my young friend, too. She would try to kick her habit and I wouldn't tell her mother what I knew. But going forward, I wouldn't be able to lie to Maisie. I would tell her the truth if I saw evidence of Brenda using any illegal drugs, since that was part of my deal with Brenda.

We sat in silence for several long minutes after that, each lost in our own thoughts in the quiet and warmth of the kitchen. But reality intruded before long and there was a ringing, the signal that someone upstairs wanted something from Maisie. The bell system was a relic from old days in the castle, much like the foot button upstairs that Annabel had used occasionally, and Annabel had insisted that it remain in place because it was one of the quainter relics of the castle's history. She found other ways, more courteous ways, of summoning Maisie when she needed her, including mobile phone calls and texts. Annabel's heirs, however, didn't feel the same way. Maybe it was the novelty of the bell system, but it smacked of an upstairs-downstairs caste system to me. Maisie rolled her eyes at its jingle. "I do wish they'd find a nicer way to let me know they need tea. I also wish they would take their tea in the dining room like it's been done for years around here. But with Annabel gone, I suppose lots of things are going to change," she said with a sigh.

"I'm sorry, Maisie. Do you want me to say something? Who's calling you, anyway?"

"All of them. Andreas never did that. Sian has only started since Annabel died. But please don't say anything. I don't want you to get in trouble for stirring up the help," she said with a grimace.

"All right. I'm here for moral support, though," I told her. When I went upstairs the first person I saw was Cadi. She was down the hall and didn't see me. I ducked into my room quickly to avoid another awkward conversation with her. My mobile phone was ringing. I grabbed it from the nightstand.

"It's Sylvie," my cousin greeted me. "What are your plans today?"

"I don't have any, I guess. Hugh and Rhisiart are taking care of the funeral arrangements and they haven't asked me to help or to leave, so I have nothing to do. Why?"

"I thought I'd take a ride into Cardiff and look around for a few hours. Want to go with me?"

"Sure! I'll be ready in a little while. I know Maisie's making breakfast, so why don't you come over and eat before we go?"

She hesitated, then said, "All right. I'll come as long as someone knows I'm invited."

"What do you mean? Why would anyone care whether you were invited?"

"Rhisiart came over to the coach house last night to tell me that he's not sure how long I'm going to be able to stay."

"What? What did he say that for?"

"I don't know. I told him I can leave anytime. Then he became nice suddenly and made it seem like he was doing me a favor by letting me stay. 'I'll see what I can do,' he said."

"That's unbelievable. You're here as Annabel's guest, not just mine. She invited you here. He can't make you leave. You're welcome to come over to the castle anytime you want."

"Don't say anything to him. I don't want you to get in trouble. I'd just be more comfortable if we eat out, okay? I'll meet you by the car in a half hour. Is that enough time?"

"Yes," I said absently. I was fuming over Rhisiart's treatment of my cousin.

"Don't be mad, Eilidh. Don't let him ruin your day. I can't stay forever anyway. Once Annabel passed away, I decided I should probably head home soon after the funeral. That way I won't be underfoot and no one will have to worry about me overstaying my welcome."

"You could never overstay your welcome. That's how I feel and I know that's how Annabel felt. I'll be down in a bit and we'll grab breakfast together on the way to Cardiff."

After I rang off I took a quick shower and put on warm clothes. The day promised to be cold and raw. Still angry, I stalked to the front door hoping I wouldn't meet anyone.

Chapter 14

But Rhisiart was standing in the massive front hall, scanning the newspaper. I stopped short when I saw him. My sudden movement announced my presence and Rhisiart turned. "Good morning, Eilidh. I trust you enjoyed yourself at the pub last night."

"I did."

"Maybe you'd like to go with me some evening."

"I don't think so, Rhisiart. I'm not sure you and I are well-suited."

"You don't really believe that, do you?"

"Yes, I do."

"Well, maybe you'll come around in time. Where are you headed right now?"

"Out. I'll be eating breakfast with my cousin because apparently someone has told her she's not welcome in the castle." I hadn't intended to say anything, but his high-handedness was getting out of control.

He winced dramatically. "I believe I'm the guilty party. My brother and sister-in-law and I have discussed the matter and it has nothing to do with your cousin, trust me. It's just that we may be repurposing the coach house soon and we need to have an architect come to look at it. And, of course, there can't be any guests in the coach house when the work starts. It may move very quickly once the architect has seen the property."

I gave him a skeptical look and hoisted my bag over my shoulder, not wishing to continue the conversation. He put his paper down and opened the door for me with a flourish. I stepped outside without another glance at him and walked down the broad front steps. Sylvie was just coming around the western turret of the castle.

"Are you ready?" she asked, a forced cheery note in her voice. She was taking her own advice and clearly had no intention of letting Rhisiart ruin her day. We walked in silence back to the parking enclosure.

"I think he likes you," Sylvie said.

"You might be right. The one time I went to the pub with him it wasn't terrible, but that was before Annabel died and he's been different since then. I don't like the way he treats people."

"I don't either," Sylvie agreed. "But we're not going to talk about him, remember?"

"You're right. Let's talk about something much more pleasant," I said.

"Like Griff," Sylvie said with a wicked smile.

"He is more pleasant, that's for sure, but let's stay away from the topic of men for a wee bit. Pick something else." So Sylvie told me about some of the photographs she had been taking.

After breakfast talk turned to the things we were going to do in Cardiff. Sylvie had made a list of the places she thought we'd enjoy. And she was right. We visited the National Museum Cardiff and St. Fagan's Walk, and the Cardiff Indoor Market. Rhisiart's name didn't come up once, nor did the name of anyone in Annabel's family. We steered away from any topic involving Maisie and Brenda, too.

But Griff was another matter. Sylvie seemed keen to know more about him, to analyze everything he said to me, to speculate about the future. A future that included him.

"Sylvie," I said, laughing, "I don't really know him very well. I know he has a cottage in the village, but that's really about it."

"You don't have to know much about him to know he's a great guy. But you know more than you realize. You know he loves animals, or at least horses. You know he cared about Annabel. You know he cares about what's done with the stables. He wants them to remain low-key and doesn't want them converted to housing for race horses. You know he doesn't like Rhisiart because of the way Rhisiart treats everyone. So see? There's a lot you know about Griff. Plus we both know he's cute," she added with a grin.

She was right. I knew I liked Griff, but I hadn't given much thought to *why* I liked him. And Sylvie had put it all out there for me to see clearly. Suddenly I was anxious to get back to the castle to see him.

It was dark when we left Cardiff and headed back to the village. We stopped at a chippy for supper on the way back so I wouldn't have to eat in the dining room under the scrutinizing eyes of Annabel's family. I hated to think of Maisie and Brenda stuck back in the castle without the freedom to come and go that I enjoyed, but the time would come when

I would probably be looking for another job and I wanted to spend time with Sylvie while she was nearby. I could commiserate with Maisie and Brenda after Sylvie left.

When I got back I found the household in a flurry of preparations for Annabel's service the next day. Or rather, Maisie and Brenda were in a flurry of activity while the three new owners of Thistlecross Castle made lists and barked orders to the two harried women. I jumped in to help them as soon as I walked in the door and realized what was happening.

Hugh and Sian had decided that a home cooked meal would be more "comforting," as they put it, for the guests who would be arriving to pay their respects after the service. This included Annabel's matronly—and quite wealthy—friends from the village as well as people from her church, people involved with the charities Annabel had supported and sponsored, and friends with whom her sons had grown up.

I went downstairs to help Maisie in the kitchen first. "Wouldn't it be smarter and easier to use a caterer for this?" I asked.

"It certainly would," Maisie grumbled. "Annabel used her caterer friend for the meal after Andreas's service and things went very smoothly. Brenda and I worked hard, but we weren't treated like mules. And we were able to pay our respects to Andreas, too, even though I didn't know him well and what I knew of him I didn't like. But it was important to show our support for the family because of the way we felt about Annabel. And now this—Brenda and I aren't going to have one minute to formally grieve for Annabel. We won't even be able to go to the service because we've got so much work to do here to prepare for all those people."

"Do you want me to talk to them?" I asked. I didn't relish the thought of approaching Hugh and Sian and Rhisiart about this, but someone had to stand up for Maisie and Brenda.

"What good would it do?" she asked grumpily. "The service is tomorrow morning and it's too late to hire anyone else to do the cooking or to help with the cleaning. No, we're stuck. We'll just get through the day and maybe we can do something to remember Annabel in private."

I felt sick at the prospect of Maisie and Brenda missing Annabel's funeral service. After several minutes of helping her in the kitchen, I concocted a story about something else I had remembered and I went in search of Rhisiart.

In hindsight, it probably would have been smarter to look for Sian or Hugh, but I was worried one of them might give me the brush-off. I knew Rhisiart would at least listen to my request.

I found him in the drawing room, working in a notebook. I knocked on the door even though it was ajar and he grunted, "Who is it?" without looking up from his work. *Perhaps I should have waited,* I thought, *but I'm already here and I've already disturbed him. Might as well go through with it.*

"It's Eilidh."

He pushed his notebook away and leaned back in the chair. "To what do I owe this pleasure?"

"I've come to ask a favor of you." He raised his eyebrows and cocked his head toward the sofa. I sat down on the edge of it, leaning forward stiffly. He just looked at me. I plunged into my request.

"It's just that Maisie and Brenda are working so hard to get the house and the food ready for tomorrow that they're not even going to be able to attend the funeral. They both loved Annabel and it seems a shame they're not able to say goodbye to her properly."

"Hmm," he said, nodding his head slightly.

"Do you think you could let them take just a short break to go to the funeral? All they want to do is pay their final respects."

"But they're needed here," he said finally.

"I know, but maybe they could just take an hour or so to go into the village. They do such a wonderful job in the castle and they have for years. They deserve this."

He leaned his head back and closed his eyes, and I got the uneasy feeling he was going to say something I didn't like.

And I was right, but what he said still came as a shock

"I'll tell you what. I'll agree to let Maisie and Brenda come to the funeral tomorrow. For an hour," he added, pointing in my direction, "if you go to the pub with me for a drink this evening."

Was he suggesting I go on a date with him in exchange for a favor? The very idea was revolting. I didn't say anything. There were plenty of things I would do for Maisie and Brenda, but I had to draw the line somewhere and Rhisiart's request was cheeky to an unbelievable degree.

He was waiting for an answer. I sat and stared at him and he met my gaze steadily. Neither of us said anything while my mind raced, trying to decide if I should make a counter-offer or say yes or say no.

I was distracted for a moment by a soft sound. I glanced toward the door and saw Brenda peek into the room, her haggard face revealing how tired she was. "I'm sorry to disturb you," she said in a quiet voice. "I was just wondering when I might be able to dust in there."

"Just give us another minute, Brenda," came Rhisiart's reply. She turned away, her shoulders stooped. I thought for a moment of her mother, working herself to exhaustion down in the kitchen, making everything perfect for the guests who would be in the castle tomorrow. All those people would be talking in low voices about Annabel and her good works, not giving much thought to the people who worked so hard to feed them so sumptuously.

"All right, I'll go for a drink with you," I said. "When shall we go?"

"How about thirty minutes?" he asked.

"That's fine." My voice sounded flat in my own ears. I hoped Brenda wasn't listening because I didn't want her to report to her mother that I was going on a date with Rhisiart just so the two of them could have an hour off to attend the funeral the following day. Maisie wouldn't forgive herself if she knew what I was doing.

He gathered his notebook and pencils, then excused himself and walked out of the room, glancing back and winking at me. I winced inwardly. It was going to be a long evening.

Brenda came into the drawing room, her dust cloths bunched up in her hand. "Can I dust now, Eilidh?" she asked, her voice a little louder than when she had spoken to Rhisiart.

"Sure, Brenda, come on in. I was just leaving," I said. Something in my voice must have warned her that all was not right. She tilted her head and gave me a hard look. "Is something wrong, Eilidh? You don't look like yourself."

"No, nothing's wrong," I hastened to assure her. "I guess I'm just wishing I didn't have to say goodbye to Annabel tomorrow, that's all."

"I know how you feel. She was just the nicest lady. I wish me and Mum could go to the funeral, but I think we'll be too busy here."

I didn't say anything. I figured Rhisiart would tell them they could have the time off to go to the funeral, so I didn't want to give any hint that I knew his plans.

"Take a break now and then, Brenda," I advised her. "You'll be more productive if you're not so tired."

"I will," she said, reaching up to dust a sconce on the wall. "See you later."

I turned and left her to her work. I went to my room to brood for twenty minutes, then grabbed a coat and went to the front hall to wait for Rhisiart.

He was already there, waiting for me. He looked dapper in his khaki trousers, white Oxford shirt, and navy toggle coat, but I knew his looks were deceiving. "Ready?" he asked. He held out his arm for me to take and I pretended not to notice. He opened the door for me and we went out to his car, which was already parked in the circle out front. He hurried around to the passenger side of the car and again opened the door for me, this time with a comical flourish. He seemed a different man, softer and more playful.

But I still didn't trust him. I sat in the front seat of the car, pressing my body as much as I could to the left so I wouldn't touch his arm accidentally. He didn't seem to notice, though I got the feeling that not much escaped his keen writer's eyes. He didn't say much except to comment on the chilly weather as we drove into the village and parked at the pub, apparently having decided to respect my wishes not to talk just yet.

When he had parked the car he ran around the front and opened my door, again offering me his arm to help me out. It was indeed a very low-sitting car, so I took his arm. He gave me a sideways smile as I released his arm.

Once in the pub, he pulled out my chair for me and helped me off with my coat. We sat down and a server brought us menus. Rhisiart offered to look at the wine list, but I didn't feel like drinking wine. I wanted something hearty to drink, and that called for a pint.

We both ordered pints and then Rhisiart sat forward and I sat back in my chair while we waited for our drinks.

"So what do you think of all that's going on in the castle?" he asked.

"What do you mean?"

"I mean the change in ownership, the possible changes in staffing. Everything."

I hadn't noticed any changes yet except that Hugh and Sian and Rhisiart seemed to be relishing their new positions as lords and lady of the manor. I chose my words carefully when I answered him several moments later.

"Change is hard, especially when it comes as a result of the death of someone so beloved, as Annabel was. It's also hard when people aren't kept apprised of what's going on." I gave him a pointed look.

"Are you saying you and the other staff don't realize what's happening?"

"Is there anything to realize?" I shot back. "Annabel died. Someone has to own the castle, so it's you and your brother and your sister-in-law. There really haven't been any changes other than that, have there?"

He sat back and regarded me with barely-concealed amusement. I fumed under his gaze. Whereas his behavior before we drove away from the castle and since coming into the village had suggested he might try to be a gentleman tonight, this was quickly turning into a tête-à-tête for which I had no stomach.

"I suppose you're right about that," he acknowledged, toying with his fork. "But mark my words, things are going to change soon."

"Things like what?"

He leaned forward and lowered his voice conspiratorially. "Once the funeral is over and the barrister has completed the necessary paperwork to transfer ownership of the castle to me and Hugh and Sian's baby, and to set up the baby's trust so Sian can make the necessary decisions, we're going to turn the old place into a brand-new venue for breeding race horses. And not only that, but we're going to open it up to the public."

I stared at him in horror. "You're kidding."

He smiled, self-satisfied and smug. "You see, Annabel never made full use of the property after her second husband died. We've been trying to get her to make some changes for years. The old castle could become a world-class destination for horse breeders, horse aficionados, and people who are interested in learning more about the breeding process and horse racing in general."

I couldn't hold my tongue any longer. "I think that's horrible," I said flatly. "Annabel would hate it—you know that."

"Annabel isn't here any longer," he said flatly.

"But how could you dishonor her memory like this?" I asked.

"You're forgetting, I think, that when Brian was alive the castle grounds were used for polo games. Brian kept his polo ponies in the stables."

"But that was because Brian had a passion for polo," I said, making a pleading gesture with my hands. "He used part of the estate for a polo ground because that's what he loved to do. He and his friends spent their free time playing polo."

"And I have a passion for breeding and racing horses. How is that any different from what Brian did?"

"It just is," I insisted. "Brian didn't convert part of the estate to a polo ground to make money. In fact, he lost money. He did it for fun and the love of the sport."

"Who said we're doing this for money?"

"Ha!" I scoffed. "Of course this is all about money. I'm not stupid. You're not a horse breeder or a horse racer—you're a writer. And you're good at what you do. Why would you put your energies into something that is so disrespectful of your mother?"

"And what did she ever do that was respectful of me?" he hissed, leaning close to me so that other people in the pub wouldn't hear him. "Why does she deserve so much honor from me or Hugh or Andreas's wife or child?"

I was taken aback. "Because she loved you," I said quietly.

"She had a funny way of showing it," he said, his nostrils flaring and the vein in his neck bulging. "She let our father beat us senseless and never did a thing about it. We got where we are today not because of her, but in spite of her. And if we want to change the course of the castle's future and make it into something we want, that's our prerogative and we don't have to worry about your so-called 'honor' getting in the way." He heaved a long breath, as if he had been waiting to say those words for a long time.

I didn't know what to say. There was an anger in this man I hadn't known existed. And the more I thought about it, the more I realized it was unfair to argue with him, to try to convince him of his mistaken thoughts.

"I know what you're thinking," he said. "You're trying to reconcile the Annabel you knew with the Annabel I knew, the Annabel my brothers knew."

He was right. I nodded slowly.

"You have no idea what it was like growing up in our family. Our father was a monster. We were kids. There was nothing we could do to stop it short of running away, and where were we going to go that our father wouldn't find us?

"Don't you see? We were dependent on Annabel to protect us from him. But she didn't. She was a miserable failure. And now you expect us to hold her in some great regard for the wonderful, charitable, community-minded woman she turned into in her later years. But we don't know that woman. We knew the woman she was when we were kids, the weak, insipid woman who couldn't save us from our own father."

"I'm sorry. I never thought about it that way."

"I wouldn't expect you to. No one but me and Hugh and Andreas can know what it was really like. All we ask is that you and everyone else who wants to voice their opinions remember that Annabel wasn't always the beloved saint she was when she died."

"I knew about the abuse, of course, but maybe you need to give it some thought, too. Your mother was scared. She didn't know how best to protect you and your brothers and she was afraid that if she did anything against your father's wishes she and your brothers and you might have ended up in much more dire circumstances, ostracized by the community and having nowhere to go."

He shook his head vigorously, as if to rid himself of such thoughts. "No. You don't get it. She had a choice—she always had a choice. We wouldn't have cared if we were poor, if we had to depend on the kindness of strangers when we were small. She would have gotten back on her feet, though it may have taken her a little while."

"You can see that now, through the lens of adulthood and a lifetime of experience, but when you were small you wouldn't have understood. You would have resented her for taking you away from your comfortable home and putting you in uncertain circumstances."

"All she would have had to tell us is that we were safe, we wouldn't have to worry about our father hitting us anymore, and we would have understood. A very young child can understand things like that."

"I don't know what to say," I told him. "I'm sorry for everything you and your brothers had to go through as children. But do you realize how much her heart ached for the three of you? Do you realize that your visit to the castle this time was supposed to be an apology for her failures during your childhood?"

He nodded, his face somber. "I do realize that. But there are some things that a mere apology can't solve. This goes too deep and it goes back too far for it to end so simply and comfortably. Even though she said she was sorry before she died, there was still too much left unsaid, too many hurt feelings not addressed, for any of us to feel the urge or the need to forgive her."

"You told her you had forgiven her," I pointed out. "And I wish that had been the truth. Forgiving her would make you feel better. It wouldn't be for her, don't you see? It would be for you. So you might not feel so much anger anymore."

"I'll think about it. But don't hold your breath."

The pints had come and we drank slowly, each of us mulling over the things the other had said. I hated to admit that he had a point. Had my respect and admiration for Annabel clouded my beliefs about her? I hadn't given much thought to the way her children must have felt growing up, in a household where they had no protector, no one to soothe their fears about their father. I suddenly felt an overwhelming sadness for both Annabel and her three children.

"I don't know what to say about any of this," I told Rhisiart.

"You don't have to say anything. It's not your fault. All I ask, all any of us ask, is that you keep an open mind where Annabel is concerned. Everyone has things about them they aren't proud of, even her."

When I agreed to go to the pub with Rhisiart, I had envisioned the evening unfolding in a very different way. I thought I would spend the entire time listening to Rhisiart's bombastic, self-absorbed rhetoric. I didn't expect to have my feelings about Annabel challenged in such a thoughtful, and thought-provoking, manner.

We both ordered another pint and talked about the childhood memories he cherished—visiting his mother's friend Margot, Sylvie and Greer's mum. He always enjoyed visiting their house, he said, because his father never accompanied them and because the atmosphere in their home was happy and relaxed. I knew Sylvie would be happy to know her childhood home held such happy memories for Rhisiart, regardless of her feelings for him as an adult.

He was in the middle of telling me about one of his visits to Margot's house when something made me look up and glance toward the door of the pub.

Griff stood in the doorway, holding the door for one of his friends. They walked toward the bar and stood at the burnished oak rail and Griff held up two fingers when the bartender looked at him. Both men shouldered their coats off and Griff took them to the coat rack in the corner near the fireplace. He turned around to go back to the bar and that's when he spotted me. And Rhisiart. Together.

I smiled at him, an embarrassed I'll-tell-you-about-it-later smile, but he gave no indication that he had seen me except for the briefest look of confusion and disappointment that crossed his face. He didn't look at me again.

Chapter 15

I had stopped listening to Rhisiart. The background noise of the pub faded into a murmur of hushed sound as I focused on the blood rushing in my ears. I knew I cared for Griff, but the extent of my feelings for him suddenly hit me when he looked away, pointedly ignoring my presence in the pub with Rhisiart. I hated to think I had upset Griff, and I was sick to think I might have ruined the very young, still-fragile relationship I was building with him.

"Are you even listening?" Rhisiart cut into my thoughts with a frustrated question.

"What?"

"Did you even hear what I was saying?"

"No. I'm sorry, something caught my eye and I got distracted."

"Yeah. I saw him, too. I don't know what you see in him, Eilidh."

I couldn't explain my feelings to Rhisiart, nor did I care to. My relationship with Griff was none of his business, and I cursed myself thinking that my "date" with Rhisiart, agreed to solely so Maisie and Brenda could attend Annabel's funeral service, could spell heartache and disappointment for me. And for Griff, too.

"This would be good material for a book," Rhisiart was saying, "if only I wrote sappy romances."

I gave him an angry look. "Rhisiart, please don't be so callous."

"He's nothing but a stable boy, Eilidh. You can do better than that."

"Rhisiart, I've had enough. I'm going back to the castle. You can't make statements like that about other people, and especially about other people I care for. Are you taking me back, or am I going to find someone else to give me a ride?"

"Find someone else," he said, examining his fingernails. "Maybe your boyfriend would like to take you back." I was so angry I couldn't even answer him without sputtering and embarrassing myself, so I stalked away from the table and headed straight for the front door of the pub. I didn't look at him again, nor did I look in Griff's direction to see if he had noticed me leaving. I didn't care—I just had to get out of there, away from my mistakes.

Once outside I whipped out my mobile phone and rang up Sylvie. She was shocked to hear I needed a ride home from the pub.

"What are you doing there? How did you get there? Are you drunk?"

"For God's sake, Sylvie, I'm not drunk. I'll explain everything when you get here. Can you just come and pick me up, please?"

"I'll be there in just a couple minutes." She rang off.

"What on earth is going on?" Sylvie asked when she pulled up less than ten minutes later.

I took a deep breath to think, to steady my voice, to calm down. "I came here tonight with Rhisiart." She gasped.

"I can't believe you would actually go out with him," she said in a bewildered voice.

I explained the agreement I had made with Rhisiart in order to let Maisie and Brenda go to Annabel's funeral service while she listened in silence. I couldn't tell if her silence was disapproving or sympathetic or both. Then I went on to explain that Griff had seen me there with Rhisiart and had ignored me after that.

"Does Maisie know this?" Sylvie asked.

"No! And don't tell her. She would be mortified to think I did such a thing so she could go to the funeral."

"Couldn't you have suggested some other arrangement?"

"Does it matter?" I shot back, then was immediately sorry for my tone of voice. I spoke more calmly after that. "The fact is that I made the agreement with Rhisiart, so it doesn't really matter what I *should* have done. Now I have to live with the fallout, whatever that may be."

"I'm sorry. You're right," Sylvie said, a note of contrition in her voice. "What can I do to help?"

"There's nothing anyone can do. Hopefully Griff will listen to me when I try to explain why I was out at the pub with someone he hates."

"He'll understand, I'm sure." I hoped with all my heart that she was right.

When we pulled up to the castle, with its forbidding façade and its missing matriarch, I felt a sadness that I couldn't explain or shake off. I missed Annabel, I missed the happiness that used to reign in the castle, and I missed the cozy, contented feeling I used to experience every time I walked into the massive front hall.

I thanked Sylvie for coming to pick me up. I hugged her before going into the castle, feeling again an overwhelming gratefulness for her presence and friendship.

I stopped in the kitchen to see if Maisie needed help before going to my room for the night. She and Brenda were in a frenzy of activity, trying to get everything done before morning. I pitched in to help for a little while, putting canapes on trays and mixing ingredients for finger sandwich fillings, but it soon became clear that I was much better at moral support than at kitchen duties. Maisie thanked me for helping, but tactfully suggested that I get a good night's sleep before the grueling activities of the following day.

Giving her an apologetic smile, I bid them goodnight and went to my room. I sat in front of the fire, trying to warm myself from the outside in, but found that there was still a cold nugget of worry in the pit of my stomach—worry that Griff might not understand why I was at the pub with Rhisiart earlier, if he even gave me a chance to explain.

Staring into the fireplace made me sleepy, and I finally went to bed and fell asleep without much trouble. The last thought that I had before drifting off was a happy one—Maisie and Brenda were going to get to say their goodbyes to Annabel in the morning.

But when I went into the dining room in the morning, Rhisiart was there. He fixed me with a cold stare. "I see you made it home last night. The stable boy stayed at the pub, so he obviously wasn't the one who brought you back to the castle. Did you find some other willing man to help you?"

"That's none of your business," I told him. "Have you told Maisie and Brenda that they have time off to attend the funeral?"

"Ah, but they don't."

I wheeled around to glare at him, my mouth agape. "You told me you would let them have time off to attend Annabel's funeral if I went to the pub with you last night. You broke your end of the deal!" I said hotly.

"And you broke your end of the deal when you left in a huff," he shot back.

"Our deal was that I would go to the pub with you for a drink. I went to the pub with you and we had a drink. Sounds like I upheld my part of the bargain just fine," I replied.

"You were supposed to come home with me, too, not leave me there looking like an arse while you found another ride back to the castle," he seethed.

"That wasn't part of the deal."

"It was an implied part of the deal."

"That's ridiculous. You can't do that to Maisie and Brenda. They've worked here for years, especially Maisie. She was Annabel's friend."

"Watch me." He picked up the newspaper he had been reading and blocked out any view of me with it. I should have known he would pull such a stunt. I stalked out of the room without having anything to eat or drink.

I went downstairs to the kitchen in search of food that I could eat without having to look at Rhisiart. Maisie and Brenda were hard at work again. Though they shared a cottage in the village, they also had rooms in the castle, where they stayed overnight if the weather was especially bad or if there was a special event and they had extra responsibilities that kept them working late.

"Did you two sleep at all last night?" I asked.

"We each took a catnap," Maisie replied, hurrying from the refrigerator to the counter with a jug of cream. "Brenda," she ordered, "take this up to the second floor to Miss Sian's room."

"Why can't she come down for breakfast?" I asked.

"She called for tea this morning. It's no different from any other day."

Brenda hurried out the kitchen door with the cream and I rummaged through the fridge looking for yoghurt, trying to stay out of Maisie's way. I sat down to eat the yoghurt and a piece of fruit at the kitchen table, where I watched Maisie, admiring her efficiency and deft skills in the kitchen. I was just finishing the fruit when Brenda came back downstairs, breathless. Her face looked flushed.

"What's the matter?" her mother asked.

"Miss Sian doesn't feel well," Brenda answered. "She wants a different kind of tea. Peppermint this time."

Maisie rolled her eyes and rifled through the cupboard that was filled with different varieties of tea. She pulled out a tin of peppermint tea leaves. "Got nothin' better to do today than wait on these ingrates," she muttered. Then she gave me a sheepish look, saying, "I'm sorry. I shouldn't talk like that."

"Don't apologize on my account," I said. "I agree with you completely."

Maisie handed the tin to Brenda. "Give this to her and see if that satisfies her." Brenda took the tea and scurried back upstairs. It made me angry to think that as hard as these two women were working, the family members in the castle were still making unreasonable demands on a day such as this.

But when Brenda came back to the kitchen, her hands shaking as she set her tray of unused tea things on the counter, her words tumbled out in a rush. "I think the baby's coming early!" she exclaimed.

"Not today, of all days!" Maisie wailed. "How are we going to manage this?" She turned to me, her eyes pleading. "What should we do? You're the manager."

All thoughts of anger toward Sian and even toward Rhisiart dissipated in the face of the impending birth of Sian and Andreas's baby. "Maisie, you go upstairs to Sian and call a doctor if that hasn't already been done." I looked toward Brenda, who shook her head. Maisie threw down the towel she had been holding and raced out of the room. "Brenda, you go upstairs to the dining room and tell Rhisiart what's happening. Then find Hugh and Cadi and tell them. They're going to have to decide who goes to the hospital with Sian and who represents the family at the funeral."

Hugh and Rhisiart decided Maisie should accompany Sian to the hospital. Maisie wasn't happy about the arrangement, since she felt someone with at least some small bit of fondness for Sian should go to the hospital, but Hugh and Rhisiart, in their typical thoughtless fashion, felt the most senior woman in the castle would be the greatest comfort to Sian in the hours before her baby's birth. I had made such a mess of trying to get Maisie time off to go to Annabel's funeral that I thought it best not to interfere with the brothers' decision this time. And without her mother around to direct arrangements, Brenda was left to her own devices in the castle trying to ready the rooms and the food for the luncheon following the funeral. I was tempted to spend some time feeling sorry for myself, fuming that I had gone out with Rhisiart for nothing, but I decided to stay busy and help Brenda while the family attended the funeral. I knew Annabel would understand why I stayed behind rather than say a final public goodbye to her.

Brenda and I worked well together. I asked her to make a list of everything that had to be done before the guests began to arrive, then we divided the tasks and conquered them one-by-one. Maisie was in frequent contact from the hospital, letting us know that Sian was still hours away from giving birth. As this was her first child, it would likely be a long labor.

The morning sped along in a rush of activity and as Brenda put the finishing touches on the buffet in the dining room, Hugh, Cadi, and Rhisiart returned from the funeral. Brenda and I hurried to change into clothes more appropriate for the luncheon and we returned to the dining room to survey our work just as the doorbell rang, signaling the arrival of the first guest.

After that, mourners arrived in droves to pay their respects to the family Annabel had left behind. Ladies from Annabel's social clubs came with husbands in tow, long-time friends of Annabel's sons came to offer their condolences, and people from Annabel's church and from the village stopped by. Sylvie was there, too. My Aunt Margot had been unable to attend the funeral because she was battling bronchitis.

Griff was there, too, looking uncomfortable in a suit and tie. He stayed in a corner of the dining room, talking to one of the stable hands. I caught his eye once, but he quickly looked away, a frown turning down the corners of his mouth. I longed to go talk to him, to explain why I had been out with Rhisiart the previous evening, but I was so busy helping Brenda and talking to people who had come to express their sorrow at Annabel's passing that I didn't have time to talk to Griff in private.

During the luncheon Maisie phoned several times to let us know of Sian's progress. The doctor thought the baby might come a bit earlier than expected and Maisie wanted to know who else might be coming to spell her and to offer support to Sian. Apparently Sian was weepy and upset that Andreas couldn't be there with her, and as sorry as Maisie was that Sian was bringing a baby without a father into the world, she didn't feel she was the right person to offer the comfort and support that Sian needed at such a critical time.

But who was the right person? The natural answer was Annabel, of course, but she wasn't there to offer support, either. It would fall to another member of the family to be at the birth of Andreas's baby.

In the end Hugh and Cadi were in the room with Sian when the baby arrived in the middle of the night, long after the guests had left the castle.

Sian had a baby boy, whom she named André. Through her exhausted tears the next morning, when the rest of the household went to visit her and the baby, she explained that it was too painful to name the baby Andreas, which was the name she and Andreas had decided on if the baby was a boy, so she chose a similar name—one that would suggest Andreas, but might not bring up such painful thoughts every time Sian spoke it aloud. She was sure her late husband would approve.

She let all of us hold the baby. When it was my turn I gazed at his tiny eyes and his wispy dark hair and thought of how Annabel had longed for a grandchild. My eyes filled with tears that spilled slowly down my cheeks when I thought of how Annabel would never get to hold her grandson, how she would never have a chance to redeem herself in the eyes of her sons as a caring, attentive grandmother who would do anything to protect her grandchild. If only she had lived a few more days.

I was the last one to hold André. After I handed him back to Sian it was time for her to rest. Hugh, Cadi, Rhisiart, Maisie, Brenda, and I all left the room quietly and went our separate ways. Hugh, Cadi, and Rhisiart said they were going into the village for breakfast. Maisie and Brenda were going to their home outside the village, and I headed back to the empty castle by myself.

As soon as I got back I rang up Sylvie. "Want to come over for breakfast? We'll be the only ones here," I added, knowing she wouldn't want to come over if Rhisiart were around. She came over just a few moments later and we rummaged for leftovers from the funeral luncheon and ate around the cozy table in the kitchen.

"What happens now?" Sylvie asked.

I sat back in my chair. "I don't know. No one has said anything. I don't know if Sian will stay here with the baby or if she'll go back to London. I wouldn't be surprised by either. If Annabel were still alive, I think she would stay here because of the connection to Andreas. But with Annabel gone..."

"Do you think you'll stay here?"

"I doubt it, but I don't know where I'll go. I really haven't given it much thought. I suppose I should have been planning since Annabel died, but I just haven't been able to."

"Planning for what?"

"For the future. For whatever comes next," I answered. "I'll have to find a new job."

"They haven't asked you to stay on here?"

"No. And even if they do ask, I don't think I want to," I said. "They want to make lots of changes to the property and I frankly don't know that I can work with any of them."

"I think you're right to want to get out of here," Sylvie remarked. "That Rhisiart is no picnic to be around." I nodded, absently popping a strawberry into my mouth and wondering what the castle would look like in a year's time with the changes the family were talking about implementing.

"Heard from Griff?" she asked.

I emerged from my own thoughts and answered. "No. I saw him at the luncheon yesterday and he looked away like I was a sea hag."

"I think he'll come around. If he knows you at all he'll figure out there had to be some good reason you were at the pub with Rhisiart."

"He doesn't know me very well—that's the problem," I said.

"I think you're giving him too little credit," Sylvie said. "Remember we talked about all the things you know about him without even realizing it? Well, all he has to do is give it a wee think and he'll realize he knows more about you than he thought he did. And it's all good stuff."

I smiled at Sylvie, marveling at her ability to turn a dim outlook into a rosy one. "What do you want to do today?" I asked.

"Let's go for a hike," she suggested. "We could both use one, I think."

I agreed quickly because I wanted to show her the place Griff had shown me—the fairy glen with its sparkly things and the clean, clear rushing water. "I know just the place," I said. "We'll have to leave now, because the last time I went I was on horseback and this time we'll be walking, so it's going to take longer to get there."

Sylvie was eager to see the place I told her about. We packed lunches from the bounty in Maisie's kitchen, then she went back to the coach house to grab her rucksack and I got mine from my bedroom. Just a few minutes later we were walking across the huge field in front of the castle, heading for the woods.

We talked the whole way. I shared Rhisiart's tales of his visits to her house as a child and told her how much he enjoyed spending time with her family. She was happy to hear it. She could remember times when Annabel brought her sons to visit her family in Dumfries, Scotland, and she was pleased to learn that, as much as she didn't care for Rhisiart, he had enjoyed his time with her family.

Then Sylvie said she had a surprise for me.

"What is it?"

"Seamus wants to come down to visit for a few days. I'll go back to Cauld Loch when he goes."

"I don't believe it! When's he coming?" I cried, already excited for his arrival.

"Well, since you're obviously so anxious to see him, how about tonight?" she asked, a mischievous gleam in her eyes.

"You're kidding!" I shrieked, breaking the silence in the air as we entered the woods.

Sylvie laughed, clearly pleased with herself for keeping the secret. "You've been so down and Seamus has been looking for an excuse to join our girls-only holiday, so I invited him and he's on his way now. Do you suppose it's okay with Rhisiart and the rest of them?"

"Who cares what Rhisiart and the rest of them say? I'll talk to them if they dare to say anything."

Her face turned somber. "Unfortunately, he can only stay for a day or two, then he has to return to Cauld Loch, and I have to go with him. Our shop assistant, the one who took your place, is sick and I need to get back to help out."

"I'm sorry you'll be leaving, but it'll be wonderful to see Seamus." I put on a bright smile so Sylvie wouldn't know how disappointed I was that she was going home.

Seamus, big and burly Seamus, was beloved by everyone who knew him. Well, almost everyone—he had gone to prison once for hurting someone badly in a bar fight, even though he was defending himself, so I suppose there were people in his past who weren't fond of him. With his wicked sense of humor and his artistic talent and his teddy-bear ways, though, one would never guess he had been in prison. And it was easy to forget his past when confronted with the man in the present.

Already looking forward to the end of the hike when I would be closer to seeing one of my favorite people, I led the way through the woods and pointed out some of the interesting things Griff had shown me on my first trip. When we reached the fairy glen, I found it every bit as enchanting as I remembered. The water tumbled over rocks and whooshed around eddies, cold and refreshing. I showed Sylvie all the shiny objects people had left behind, including the coin Griff and I had placed in the log. She was fascinated. She must have taken a hundred photos. With her talent and penchant for getting the perfect shot, I couldn't wait to see her prints from the glen.

"Shall we go back to the castle?" I asked after we had enjoyed a leisurely lunch.

We returned through the woods the way we had come. The rays of sunlight that penetrated the trees slanted lower to the ground on our way back, and we hadn't gone far when we heard a whinnying from up ahead. There was a bend in the path so we couldn't see what—or who—was up ahead, so we slowed our pace just a bit.

I was startled to see Griff come around the curve in the path, riding Caesar. He pulled up short when he saw us.

"Hi, Griff!" Sylvie called cheerfully. I was relieved she had recovered herself quickly enough to say something. My embarrassment was already beginning to burn my face. I felt like a bird caught in a cage—I wanted to get away as quickly as I could, but Griff and Caesar were blocking the way forward and Sylvie was standing behind me and would surely prevent me from running back to the wood if I suddenly made a run for it. I had no choice but to stand still and bear the shame of being out in the woods where Griff had taken me so recently.

"How's everyone?" he asked, no trace of warmth in his voice. It had always held a rich timbre for me, but now it sounded cold and distant.

"We're just fine. Eilidh wanted to show me the place you took her—the fairy glen, is it called?—and I thought it was just beautiful. Thanks for showing it to Eilidh."

He nodded. "You're welcome." He guided Caesar into the brush along the trail. "I'll get out of the way so you can get back," he said. He clearly didn't want to stand around chatting. I knew I had ruined his afternoon, just as Rhisiart had ruined ours when Griff and I had visited the fairy glen.

We skirted Griff and Caesar and continued walking, this time in silence. Sylvie knew better than to talk to me just then. I longed to turn around to see if Griff was watching us leave, but I was in front of Sylvie and I didn't want her to see my disappointment if he wasn't looking. I was quiet for the rest of the way back to the castle, the excitement at Seamus's impending arrival fading in the raw hurt of Griff's brush-off.

But as we neared the castle, I could feel the excitement building again. Seamus was a good friend of Callum, and he would be able to tell me how Callum was doing in prison and what life was like for him now. I had a soft spot for my ex-husband, even though I wasn't in love with him anymore, and I was eager for news of his well-being.

But Seamus texted Sylvie that he had been delayed, so we would have to wait a bit longer for him to arrive at the castle. He would stay in the coach house with Sylvie, obviously, but I knew he would love to take a look around Annabel's home, too. I even looked forward to introducing him to Rhisiart and Hugh, just to see what he thought of them.

It was snowing by the time we arrived at the castle. Snowy days were my favorite days in Wales, and particularly at the castle, because the snow softened the military-style effect of the home's architecture. Sylvie took out her camera and snapped a few photos as the snow began to fall more thickly, then asked if we could visit the gardens, where the fallen snow on the flowers and garden sculptures might provide interesting photo opportunities. Sylvie preferred sweeping landscape photography, but her interests were branching a bit as she was learning more about photographing small, close subjects.

We took our time walking through the gardens. Like me, Sylvie loved the snow. We wandered through the gardens, laughing as the snow fell and trying to catch the flakes. When she ventured near the wolfsbane I asked her not to take a photo of the plant that had become so hateful to me, and she readily consented.

She even climbed onto a wrought iron table to reach up and place her camera on top of a high stone fence that surrounded one of the gardens. She positioned the camera and used a remote control to shoot pictures from there. When she retrieved the camera and scrolled through the pictures, she gasped.

Chapter 16

"What is it?" I asked.

"Look at this," Sylvie instructed in a whisper, holding the screen of her camera in front of her. My mouth fell open. Sylvie had shot a photo of Rhisiart. He was standing directly outside the garden where we were. He must not have realized Sylvie had placed her camera up high to take pictures from a different angle, so he probably didn't know we were aware of his presence.

I motioned for her to lean in closer. "He wants to hear something good? Let's give him something," I whispered.

In a louder voice I said, "Sylvie, did I tell you what Annabel told me before she died?"

"No," she answered, moving away so it didn't sound like she was standing right next to me. "What did she say?"

"She said there's another will hidden somewhere."

Sylvie gasped loudly. "Did she say where it was?"

"No, only that it's in the castle somewhere," I answered.

"Why didn't you tell the barrister?"

"Annabel didn't want the boys to know about it," I said, trying to keep from giggling.

"It must be different from the will everyone knows about," Sylvie suggested, playing along.

"I'm sure it is. Otherwise she wouldn't have told me about it."

"Maybe she leaves her money to you!" she exclaimed. She was enjoying this.

"I seriously doubt it," I replied.

"Have you looked for it?"

"No."

"Why on earth not?"

"Because it doesn't matter to me. What would I do with all Annabel's money?" I asked with a grin. This was going better than I could have imagined.

"You could give it to me," Sylvie suggested, laughing.

We started walking toward the garden entrance and kept up the pretext of Annabel's mysterious missing will. By the time we reached the garden gate I peered around the corner and saw just the tails of Rhisiart's overcoat flying as they disappeared around the front of the castle.

Sylvie laughed. "That'll teach him to follow us and eavesdrop."

I grinned, happy because we had put one over on Rhisiart, whose superior smugness infuriated me. Let him wonder whether another will existed, one that left me as the sole heiress of Annabel's estate.

Sylvie bid me goodbye where the path to the coach house parted from the walkway to the front of the castle, but promised to let me know the minute Seamus arrived. I went inside the castle, still chuckling to myself over our practical joke.

The sight that greeted my eyes upon entering the main hall of the castle was enough to make me laugh out loud. Hugh ran past me to where Rhisiart stood waiting by the sitting room door, his phone to his ear. I had a feeling he was talking to Sian, who was still in hospital. He had apparently wasted no time in warning his co-heirs about the possibility of another will being hidden somewhere in the castle.

I pretended to take no notice of them and went straight to my room, where I showered and changed out of my wet, snowy clothes and into jeans and a warm, dry sweater. I was still in a good mood and I sat in front of the fireplace, my feet toasty, reading a book and finally being able to concentrate on the words. I only stopped reading when I got hungry and went downstairs for something light to eat. Maisie was taking stock of the cupboard contents, something Hugh had asked her to do. I didn't know where Brenda was.

I ate a sandwich and returned to my room. I saw that I had gotten a text in my absence. Seamus had arrived! I threw on a coat and dashed over to the coach house, and when he opened the door I flung myself into his arms, giving him a great bear hug. He laughed with his deep booming voice, and Sylvie came to watch the happy reunion, her face alit with a wide smile. She knew how much I had missed my old friend.

"So tell me about Callum," I said as we all sat in the great room. I got all the news about my ex-husband; Seamus went to visit him regularly, at least once a week. He told me Callum was studying art history while he was incarcerated and wanted to get a job in Edinburgh when he got out, possibly in a museum or art gallery. I was happy to hear that he had plans to change careers and move to the city. He would miss the Highlands, but his opportunities would be better in Edinburgh, and maybe Seamus could even introduce him to people who might give him a job. I asked Seamus to pass on my wishes for his success. I hadn't had much contact with Callum since our divorce, and it seemed better that we not communicate directly. Seamus had told me it hurt Callum the few times we had talked, so I tried to avoid anything that would cause him more heartache.

"Seamus, you have to see the castle. You'll love it. Annabel bought some fabulous pieces of art during her lifetime and they're displayed throughout the castle. Some of her things are still in storage rooms. I'll take you through the castle tomorrow and you can spend all the time you like looking around."

"Sounds *cracking,*" he said, rubbing his hands together. "Now, how about a snack?"

Since I had already eaten, I left the couple to their meal and I returned to the castle, where I was not surprised to find Rhisiart leafing rapidly through a book in the sitting room when I poked my head in there.

"Anything I can help you find, Rhisiart?" I asked, knowing perfectly well he was looking for Annabel's alleged hidden will. He hadn't realized I was standing in the doorway. He whirled around, a startled look on his face, like a child caught with his hand in the cookie jar.

"No, no. I'm just trying to decide what to read," he explained hastily, his eyes darting to and fro along the bookshelves. He was probably contemplating how long it would take him to leaf through every book on the shelf for something I knew didn't exist. The idea of it was delightfully sneaky.

"Well, good luck. If you need any recommendations, let me know. I've read a lot of them," I said. I gave him a little wave and left the room, laughing to myself.

I returned to my room and slept well that night for the first time in a long while. It wasn't just the good feeling I had from having hoodwinked Rhisiart and the others; it was a combination of the long walk through the woods, the fun I had with Sylvie in the snow, and the excitement over seeing Seamus again after two years away from Cauld Loch. Griff didn't even cross my mind that night.

He was front and center the next morning when I awoke, though, along with a nervous feeling in the pit of my stomach. I missed seeing him and talking with him and I worried what would happen when we crossed paths again, as we inevitably would. After I obtained permission from Hugh, I spent some time in the sitting room going through bills and making arrangements to pay them. I was using the estate's money to pay bills now, so all the checks had to be approved and signed by Hugh, Rhisiart, and Sian.

I took a break from paying and filing bills to visit Maisie in the kitchen. She was still taking inventory of everything and she was glad for an excuse to take a break, too. She made tea for us while I found some biscuits in a cupboard and arranged them on a plate. "Where's Brenda?" I asked. "We should ask her to join us."

Maisie flashed me a look that was a combination of pain and anger. "I don't know where the lass is," she said in a flat voice. "She didn't come home last night and she didn't come in to work this morning."

"Have you tried phoning her?"

"Aye. Her phone goes right to voicemail."

"You don't seem too worried. Do you have an idea of where she is?"

"I suspect she's stayed overnight with one of her 'friends,'" Maisie said, using air quotes.

"Do you think she's all right?"

"I hope so," Maisie said with a sigh into her teacup. "I don't know what to do about her. I hoped she would stop taking the drugs when Andreas died, but I don't think she has. I have tried everything I can think of to get her clean, but she ignores me." Maisie's voice broke. "She's destroying herself and she can't see beyond the end of her nose. It's so hard to watch your kids make mistakes like that. Big mistakes."

I laid my hand on Maisie's shoulder. "Maybe Brenda is trying in her own way," I said. "Maybe she just has to figure it out for herself, without anyone's help. That might explain why she's not here yet."

Maisie sniffled and wiped her eyes. "I hope you're right. Could you let me know if you see her come in?"

I nodded and gave Maisie a hug. "Hang in there," I told her. "I think everything's going to be all right for Brenda. She probably just needs some time."

And as if to prove my words, Brenda appeared in the kitchen doorway. "Are you cryin', Mum?" she asked, her eyes wide. Maisie turned away and busied herself at the sink, rinsing our tea things.

"I'm all right," she said. "Where have you been all morning? And where were you last night?"

Brenda glanced at me, her eyes silently pleading with me to remain silent. "I stayed at a friend's house last night. We had a nip of the hard stuff, you know?" she said with a nervous laugh. "You always said I shouldn't drive home if I've been drinking."

Maisie turned around. "I'm glad about that. But why didn't you answer your phone?"

Brenda fished around in her handbag and looked at her phone. "Dead battery. I'm sorry if I worried you, Mum. I didn't even check the phone last night." She looked over her shoulder toward the stairs. "I'd better get to work before I get in trouble." She walked lightly over to Maisie and gave her a peck on the cheek. "Don't worry, Mum. I'll make sure I don't let the battery run down again."

Maisie watched Brenda turn and go. She turned to me. "What do you think?"

I was happy to be able to answer her honestly. "I think she proved that she *does* listen to you. You told her not to drive home if she's been drinking, and she didn't. She doesn't look glassy-eyed or confused, so I'd say she's telling you the truth. And if she'll listen to you about drinking and driving, maybe she's listening to the things you tell her about drugs, too. Maybe she's trying."

Maisie gave me a grateful look and I returned to the sitting room. I wasn't ready to start filing again, so I glanced at my mobile phone. No missed calls. I swallowed hard and dialed Griff's number.

As I had feared, he didn't pick up. He would have seen that I was calling and he didn't want to answer the phone. I sighed and resolved not to call him again.

Next I called Sylvie. "Is Seamus ready to see the castle?" I asked.

"He's been pacing around here this morning like a caged bull," she said with a laugh. "He couldn't wait for you to call." She said she wanted to pick up a few last souvenirs in the village. "Take Seamus and entertain him for as long as you want," she said. "He won't be able to get enough of the castle and all its artwork."

Just a few minutes later the doorbell echoed through the hallways. I ran to let Seamus in. He stood in the main hall, looking up and around and taking it all in.

"I've not been in a private house like this before," he said. "I've visited the castles in Scotland and England, of course, but those are for tourists. This is the real deal!" I was delighted that he was so excited to see Annabel's home.

I took him through the main floor and he lingered over every artifact, every statuette, every painting. He knew some of them and was intrigued by everything he didn't recognize. He took photos with his mobile phone to peruse later. We were finishing our tour of the dining room when Rhisiart came in. I introduced the two men quickly, explaining to Rhisiart that Seamus was an artist and interested in the artwork in the castle. Rhisiart eyed Seamus with an air of suspicion. "Do I know your work?" he asked.

"I don't know," Seamus answered, a gleam in his eye. "Do I know yours?"

"I write thrillers. You've probably seen my stuff in bookstores."

Seamus made a show of thinking about Rhisiart's words. "Sorry, doesn't ring a bell," he said cheerfully. "I'll be on the lookout next time I'm in a bookstore, though."

Rhisiart could barely conceal the disdain in his voice. "Eilidh, Hugh and Sian and I need to speak to you sometime. Sian will be coming back tomorrow. Tomorrow evening I'd like you to join her and Hugh and me in the dining room about fifteen minutes before dinner." I had a strong feeling this would have something to do with the "missing will" Rhisiart had overheard me discussing with Sylvie and I smiled inwardly, wondering how they would broach the subject without revealing that Rhisiart had been listening in on a private conversation.

I nodded and put my hand on Seamus's arm to steer him out of the room. I covered my mouth to suppress a giggle when we were in the hallway. Seamus rolled his eyes and mimed holding a teacup with his pinky finger pointed up. "Quite a fancy gent," he whispered. "Do you think he'll follow us around to make sure I won't steal anything?"

"Probably," I replied.

"I've heard of him, of course," Seamus said. "But I didn't want to give him the satisfaction." He gave me a devilish grin. "How did I do?"

I laughed. "Perfect. Now let's go upstairs and I'll show you around up there."

We spent hours going through the rooms upstairs. We didn't go into any occupied rooms, but I was able to show him much of the artwork Annabel had kept in storage. He enjoyed the tour and thanked me profusely for showing me around.

He and Sylvie and I had dinner together that evening, a cozy meal in the coach house. We kept the conversation light so we wouldn't dwell on their departure, which they had told me would be in two days. I got up early the next morning, thankful that it was going to be a busy day so I couldn't feel sorry for myself until Sylvie and Seamus left. There was work to do before Sian was discharged from hospital with André and I was helping Brenda prepare the nursery before Sian's arrival at the castle. Brenda and Annabel had begun decorating the nursery, but progress had come to a halt upon Annabel's death. It didn't matter very much because the baby would spend his first few months in the same room with Sian. She had decided to remain at the castle for the foreseeable future, so the nursery would be put to use eventually. We put the finishing touches in the baby's room just as Sian and André arrived. Everyone in the castle went to greet them, then Sian went straight to her room, taking André with her. She looked exhausted and André was crying. They both needed some time to rest.

But later on that afternoon, I was upstairs getting something out of a storage room for Brenda when I passed one of the big sitting rooms. Sian was in there with André, who was crying as though the world might end. Sian was crying, too.

I poked my head in the room. "Sian, can I spell you for a while? It looks like you could use a little break. Want me to watch André while you take a walk or a nap?"

She wiped her eyes and heaved a heavy sigh as she stood up from where she had been rocking the baby in a cradle. "Thank you, Eilidh. I'm exhausted. What I really need is a long nap, but I could do with a walk outside to clear my head." She left, her steps slow and heavy. I felt sorry for her—no husband, no mother-in-law, and a fussy newborn.

I discovered that what André wanted was to move about. I picked him up and walked up and down the length of the sitting room, then out into the hallway. I remembered Greer saying that sometimes movement could calm a baby. Rocking him in the cradle clearly hadn't worked, so I tried something else. He seemed fascinated every time we passed a window or a wall sconce. The changing shades of light must have given him something interesting to look at.

When Sian returned, her color was better and she seemed in a happier frame of mind. I was rocking André in my arms when she came back into the room.

"You got him to stop crying," she said in relief.

"He likes to walk, to look at the light coming in the windows and from the wall sconces in the hallway," I said.

"I know he does, but I'm just so tired," she said in a weary voice. "I don't have the energy to walk around with him just now."

"Tomorrow I'll watch him for you while you get a nap," I offered.

"Would you do that for me?" she asked. "I'd appreciate it very much."

I spent the afternoon running errands. I had received a call from the police station informing me that I could pick up my laptop, so I stopped to get it. I was thrilled to have it back not only because I liked to use it, but because it meant the police hadn't found any incriminating evidence on it. They hadn't discovered how Annabel was administered the poison, but they were continuing their investigation, they said.

After I left the police station I remembered that I had an appointment with the family before dinner. When I entered the dining room, the three of them were standing around the table, each holding a beverage. Rhisiart offered me a glass of wine, but I declined. He motioned for me to sit down at the long table, and I also declined that. I knew what they were trying to do—they were exhibiting a show of force, much like animals in the wild would do, to intimidate me. If I were the only one sitting down, I would feel like I was at a distinct disadvantage. So the four of us stood around the table looking, I felt, rather like idiots.

"We have been talking, the three of us," Rhisiart began, "and we want to assure ourselves that Annabel's true wishes are being followed. Hugh brought it to my attention that we never really searched the house for any other will Annabel may have written, so we wanted to do that. Just to make sure, you understand, that the property is being taken care of in a way that Annabel would have found acceptable."

I had to resist the urge to roll my eyes at his ridiculous speech. All of us knew Annabel would turn over in her freshly dug grave if she knew the castle and its surrounding property were turned into a venue for breeding race horses, but we all continued with the pretense.

Rhisiart continued. "What we want from you is to know whether Annabel ever mentioned the existence of another will, one that would supersede her wishes in the will that was at Mr. Hadley's office in Cardiff."

I took my time answering. I put on a serious face, my lips screwed in one direction and my eyes with a faraway look, to prove how hard I was thinking about Rhisiart's statement. Finally I spoke, surprising myself with the ease of my lie.

"This is something that has concerned me, too, since it's entirely possible there was a will that Annabel made after the one in Mr. Hadley's office. But I don't know where it might be. She had a few hiding places in the castle, so it could be in one of those, I suppose. Will you need help looking for it?"

Rhisiart exchanged a glance with Sian. "Don't worry yourself about it. We'll take care of that. What with all your duties around here just running the place, I'm sure you don't have time to go looking for a will that probably doesn't even exist." He laughed.

"So I assume you want me to keep running things until the will is settled?" I asked.

"Of course, of course," Hugh answered. "I don't know how the place would run without you. You know, for the time being, at least."

They were going to look for the will and they didn't want me to participate. That much was clear. I suppose I should have felt a twinge of guilt for sending them on a wild goose chase, but maybe it would teach Rhisiart a lesson about eavesdropping and give me and Maisie and Brenda a brief reprieve from our job hunting.

We ate dinner in relative silence, though Cadi joined us and regaled us with her typical snide comments about the food not being up to London standards and André, in a pram next to Sian, made occasional soft noises in his sleep. I longed to hear what they all had to say to each other once dinner was over, but I knew they wouldn't say a word with me around so I spared them the discomfort of waiting in silence and went to my room as soon as I finished eating.

I curled up in my armchair with the book I had begun reading, but soon unsettling thoughts began to worm their way into my mind and I couldn't concentrate on the words in front of me any longer.

What if Hugh and Sian and Rhisiart realized I was lying to them? What if they realized my ideas about another will were nothing more than a practical joke? They could make finding another job very difficult for me.

It turned out to be far worse than that, though.

I reached for my mobile phone and, without even thinking about what I was doing, dialed Griff's number. I realized with horror what I had done when the phone began to ring, and while my mind frantically tried to decide whether I should hang up or let it keep ringing, Griff answered the phone.

"Hello."

"Hi, um, sorry to bother you. I called you by mistake."

"I see. Well, if it was a mistake, then I'll talk to you later."

"Wait. I mean, I just wanted to see if everything is okay with you."

"Everything's fine."

"Look, I feel like I should tell you what happened that night I saw you in the pub and..."

"You don't need to tell me anything," he interrupted. "It's really none of my business."

"No, you don't understand," I said miserably. This was not going well.

"What's there to understand? You were there having a drink with Rhisiart, someone you previously loathed. There's no law against that. He's rich, he's good-looking. I can't blame you for that."

"But I wasn't there because I wanted to be," I tried explaining.

"Oh, I get it. He forced you to the pub at knife-point. Now it all makes sense."

"Griff, would you stop it? I'm trying to explain something to you!"

"I don't really want to hear it, Eilidh. I thought you were someone different, and I was wrong. I hate it when I misjudge people."

"You didn't misjudge me, Griff."

"It seems I did. Are we done? I have things I have to do."

"I guess we're done. Bye."

He rang off. I pushed the "end" button on my phone a wee bit too hard. Tears stung the backs of my eyes. I slammed my book closed and tossed it on the floor. I had no interest in reading any longer. I had only myself to blame for the mess with Griff, and he was clearly not interested in listening to my excuses and pleas for understanding. I couldn't really blame him—I'd probably react the same way if our situations were reversed.

If Annabel were still alive, I would go straight to the sitting room to find something to do. There had always been work to do, whether it was arranging a luncheon with her friends or making calls to set up a charity fête or making lists of vendors for fundraisers she was spearheading. But when she passed away all the work went away, too. She wasn't there to direct the events so I had nothing to do. And even if there were work I could be doing in the sitting room, I dreaded the prospect of seeing the family again tonight. I had no choice but to try to go to sleep.

But sleep did not come easily. It was over an hour before I fell into a fitful sleep; I couldn't find a comfortable position and my thoughts refused to quiet themselves. It must have been in the wee hours of the morning when I thought I heard a soft sound coming from the direction of the hallway. I turned over to face the wall, unsure of whether I had actually heard anything or whether I had dreamed the noise.

But it happened again, this time a bit louder. I turned back toward the door and squinted through the darkness. A sliver of dim light under my door was growing into a wedge. I sat up quickly and scrambled to the floor on the side of my bed farther from the door.

The wedge of light continued to grow. I couldn't tell who was behind the door, but I wasn't going to wait to find out.

"Who's there?" I called in a hoarse whisper.

Chapter 17

The door stopped moving immediately and I heard footsteps retreating rapidly down the hall. I rushed over to the door, which was still slightly ajar. I looked up and down the corridor, but the person had disappeared. I gave chase, running in the direction of the great hall, where the only light burning was the small lamp on a side table. I stood still, listening for any sound, but I heard nothing. Maybe it was the semi-darkness, maybe it was being alone in the great hall, but I had a creeping sensation that someone was watching me. I couldn't see who it was or where he or she was hiding, but I knew someone was there. I was afraid, but the longer I stood there listening, the angrier I became.

"Listen, you. I don't know who you are or what you want in my room, but you'd better think twice before doing it again," I spoke stridently into the dim. "I don't have anything you want, so leave me alone." I surprised myself by the strength of my voice—that would never have been possible back in Cauld Loch.

I stalked back down the hallway, yearning to check behind me to see if anyone was there, but refusing to give in to the temptation and signal to the person that I was afraid. I wished I had the moxie to go along with my strong words, but the truth was that I was terrified.

When I returned to my room I barricaded the door with the armchair and I moved my desk in front of it, too. No one would be able to get into my room without waking everyone in the castle.

Even so, there was no way I was getting any more sleep that night. I sat on the edge of the bed and reached for my phone. I wanted to talk to Griff, to have him reassure me that everything was going to be okay, but I couldn't call him. Not after the conversation we'd had earlier in the evening.

I thought about texting or calling Sylvie, but I knew she and Seamus would be sleeping and it seemed selfish to wake them up, especially knowing they had a long day ahead of them driving back to Cauld Loch.

There was no one for me to talk to. I was scared, alone, and still feeling sorry for myself. I tried reading again, but couldn't concentrate. Eventually I gave up, grabbed my laptop, and began a search for estates in Wales and Scotland that were advertising for managers. Until I worked for Annabel I would never have considered myself qualified to be an estate manager, but I was confident in my abilities now and liked the idea of continuing in the same type of job.

I emailed my CV in response to several of the adverts and was just closing the laptop as the sun began to rise above the horizon, painting the sky with strokes of purple, pink, and gray. I hadn't realized how long I spent on the computer. Everything always looks better in the morning than it does in the dead of night, and I felt less afraid than I had just hours before. I took a shower and ventured down the hall to the dining room, where I found Rhisiart and Sian deep in discussion. They stopped talking immediately when I entered the room.

"Don't stop on account of me," I told them. "I'm just getting a cup of tea."

Sian was staring at me. I met her look with one of my own, challenging her to admit she was the one in the hallway the previous night.

"Are you all right, Eilidh?" she asked.

"I'm fine. Why?" I countered.

"You just seem a bit flustered this morning."

"I'm fine," I repeated. *Did I really appear flustered? That was the last thing I wanted.* "My cousin and her husband are leaving this morning. I suppose I'm a little blue about that."

"Would you still be interested in watching André for a little while this afternoon so I can take a nap?" I had forgotten volunteering for the job yesterday.

"Sure," I said, faltering over the word. I had expected something completely different from her this morning, perhaps an apology for scaring me last night if indeed she had been the one trying to get into my room.

"Will you be around after lunch?" she asked.

"Yes. Shall I come upstairs?"

"Yes. Thank you." She seemed in control of herself, not giving the slightest indication that she knew what had transpired in the night. That left me with fewer suspects.

Rhisiart was watching my exchange with Sian with interest but didn't say anything. He sipped his coffee and pretended to read his newspaper, but I could tell his eyes were on us. I glanced at him and he looked away quickly. Was he the one who had tried coming into my room in the night?

Hugh and Cadi came into the dining room while my tea was steeping and they sat down across from each other at the long table. Hugh grunted a "morning" to the rest of us, but Cadi ignored us, choosing instead to flip open a magazine she had brought with her. I often wondered why she and Hugh never spoke, at least in public. They didn't seem a terribly well-matched couple.

Rhisiart cleared his throat. "What did your friend think of the artwork in the castle, Eilidh?"

"He was impressed," I answered. I couldn't resist bragging about Seamus a wee bit. "He's had shows in some of the big London galleries and he loves looking at art of all kinds. Annabel's collection was a treat for him to see up close and in private. Thanks for letting him look around."

"Our pleasure," Rhisiart said, indicating the others in the room with a short sweep of his hand.

Sian pushed her chair back. "The baby is sleeping, finally, so I'd better get back upstairs. See you after lunch, Eilidh, and thanks again."

Cadi looked up from her magazine. "What are you and Sian doing after lunch?"

"Nothing," I replied. "She's going to take a nap and I'm going to look after André for her."

Cadi nodded and went back to her reading. Had it been her, or maybe Hugh, who had scared me last night? I didn't know Cadi very well, but she didn't seem the type. Hugh, on the other hand...

Cadi must have left the dining room in a hurry after I did because she hailed me in the hallway just a moment later. "Eilidh, come here," she said in a loud whisper. *What now?* I wondered.

"What can I do for you, Cadi?" I asked, plastering a fake smile on my face and turning to talk to her.

"Nothing. I was just wondering if you've learned any more about Sian's, shall we say, gardening propensities."

I gave a slight shake of my head. "No. No one has said anything, and I haven't asked. I'm sure the police would have asked about it if they thought Sian poisoned Annabel."

"But how would the police know to ask if they haven't seen her flat back in London?"

I grimaced. Talking to Cadi like this was making me uncomfortable. It was like she was gleeful at the prospect of her sister-in-law being accused of killing Annabel. I couldn't imagine Sian doing it—why would she do such a thing knowing she could go to jail for years, leaving a fatherless newborn baby behind? Sian was not my favorite person, but she didn't strike me as being cold-blooded or dumb enough to do something like that.

"I'm sorry, Cadi, but I really have a lot to do today. Can we talk about this some other time?"

She gave a dramatic shrug. "If the police ask you about it, send them to me. I can tell them everything they need to know."

I was glad to see her go back to the dining room. I wondered if she had always felt such antagonism toward Sian. I went back to my room, wishing I really did have something to keep me busy. I texted Sylvie and she invited me to go into the village for breakfast with her and Seamus before they got on the road back to Scotland. I agreed since I had only had a cup of tea, wanting to get out of the dining room as quickly as possible.

I met them in the parking enclosure and they followed me to the village. At breakfast I explained what had transpired overnight and told them about my conversation with Cadi back in the castle. They were astounded that someone had tried getting into my room.

"Och, Eilidh, you can't stay there," Seamus cautioned.

"Seamus is right," Sylvie declared. "You'll have to stay in the coach house after this. There's plenty of room and you're not safe in the castle by yourself. You don't have a friend over there."

"I have Maisie and Brenda," I protested.

"But they go home at night," Sylvie said. "They're not around to help you when you most need it. Promise me you'll stay in the coach house. Maybe we should stay," she said, looking at Seamus. "I hate for Eilidh to be going through this all by herself."

"I agree," Seamus said gravely.

"No. You two go home. This is something I can handle on my own."

"But why should you handle it on your own if we can stay to help you?" Seamus asked.

"Because I want to deal with this myself," I said, hoping my voice sounded convincing. "I've been researching jobs that are available near here," I added. "I love Wales, and especially Thistlecross. It's quiet and quaint, and I've gotten to know lots of the people in town. I've made quite a few friends here."

Sylvie smiled. I'm sure she was remembering the way I used to be. When I lived in Cauld Loch I was a homebody. The only people I ever went anywhere with were her and Seamus and Callum. Now I could go into the village and see friendly faces everywhere.

We said our goodbyes outside the restaurant after I assured them that I would be all right. I waved to them until they drove out of sight, then dried my tears and returned to the castle, where I packed a bag to take over to the coach house. Looking around my room to make sure I hadn't forgotten anything, I knew something wasn't right but I couldn't put my finger on it.

But when I turned around to take one last look at the room, it came to me. The drapes were open. I was sure I had left them closed when I went to the village.

Someone had been in my room in my absence.

I put my bag on the floor just inside my door and closed it again, locking it for good measure. Whoever was in my room must have been looking for something. What could it have been? I strode over to the bureau and yanked open the top drawer. The contents of the drawer were *almost* the way I had left them. I liked my things in neat piles and rows, and these were the slightest bit jumbled, as if someone had rifled through them and attempted to put everything back the way it had been. I went through the bureau drawers one by one, and each one was just like the top drawer.

The person or persons who had been in my room had gone through my desk and my nightstand, too. The contents of those, like the bureau, were just a wee bit misplaced. I went into my adjoining bathroom and saw that the medicine chest hadn't been ignored, either. Nothing seemed to be missing from any of the places the intruder had looked, but it unnerved me nonetheless to know my room, my personal and only sanctuary in the castle, had been violated. I couldn't wait to get over to the coach house.

I couldn't imagine what anyone wanted in my room, then I realized with a start that someone had probably been looking for the alleged missing will.

I went downstairs to the kitchen to tell Maisie where I was going. She gave me a look of understanding. "I know how you must feel, living here with all of Annabel's family," she said. "At least Brenda and I can go home at night. You're stuck here."

"It's not just that, Maisie. Someone went into my room while I was in the village this morning." She gasped, her eyes wide with surprise.

"I can't believe someone would stoop so low," she said, shaking her head. "No one will have any privacy around here."

"Just watch your back," I warned her. "Don't leave your personal things lying around."

"I never do," she said. "I've been locking up my handbag every day since the family arrived. I don't even know what prompted me to do it that first day they visited—just suspicious, I guess."

"Well, I wish my bedroom door locked from the outside, then I could lock it anytime I'm not here," I said ruefully. "I don't think there's anything missing, but just having someone burrowing through my things is enough to give me second thoughts about staying in my job for even one more minute."

"Oh, don't say you're leaving yet!" Maisie cried.

"I'll stay for a bit longer, but I've sent out my CV to places in the area looking for an estate manager. I hope I can get another job soon. Have you and Brenda been looking?"

Maisie looked around, as if she thought someone might hear us. "We think we've found a place that will take both of us. I wasn't sure we should do that, but it so happens there's a house that needs a maid and a cook. That would be perfect for us—it's not far from the village."

"That's wonderful! Have you visited yet or spoken to the owners of the home?"

"Yes. I've spoken to them on the phone and Brenda and I are both going over there tomorrow to talk to the lady of the house."

"I'm so happy for you, Maisie. I hope you get the job and you and Brenda can get out of here as quickly as possible." I smiled at my friend.

"Should I ask if they need a house manager?" Maisie asked.

"No, don't do anything that might hamper your own chances of getting the job. Don't worry about me. I'll find something." And I truly believed I would.

I went over to the coach house. Sylvie had made sure that the other guest room had clean sheets and plenty of fresh towels. I deposited my bag on the bed and slumped on the sofa, where I leafed through magazines until I was hungry again. Seamus had thoughtfully left me a delicious sandwich in the fridge, so after lunch I returned to the castle to look after André while Sian rested. I found mother and son in the upstairs sitting room. André, as I expected, was wide awake and making soft noises in the cradle. Sian looked exhausted, sitting next to him and rocking the cradle with one limp arm. The skin around her eyes was dark from lack of sleep and she blinked slowly when I entered the room and she looked up at me.

"Sian, I hope you're planning to take a nice, long nap this afternoon. You look worn out."

"I'm going to sleep as soon as I get back to my room." She nodded toward her baby. "He's been awake practically all night, every night. I haven't been getting any sleep."

"I'll take care of him now, so you go and lie down. Don't worry about a thing." I already knew where she kept his pram, so I intended to take him outside for some fresh air while she slept.

She didn't need to be asked twice. She left just a moment later and I heaved a sigh of relief that André was still too young to experience separation anxiety. Otherwise I might have a screaming baby on my hands. But he was a delightful infant, quiet and happy, with dark, expressive eyes just like his father. I bundled him up and carried him downstairs to the main hall, where I knew the pram waited, mostly unused, in an alcove generally reserved for coats and hats. He was interested in everything that went on around him. He watched me closely and I smiled at him, tickled his chubby chin, and sang to him. He was still too little to appreciate my singing, and I was glad there was no one else around to hear me.

I pushed the pram out the huge front doors and onto the stone steps in front of the castle. Very carefully I lifted it down the steps and placed it on the ground. I made sure the visor was up so the bright sky wouldn't bother André's eyes, then I pushed him first around to the gardens.

We had a lovely walk through some of the gardens. The starkness of the boughs against the sky probably made them easier for him to see, and he seemed fascinated. He looked around everywhere we went. I took him round to the rear of the castle where the undulating fields stretched out to the woods beyond.

I shifted my eyes toward the direction of the stables and noticed a person walking toward us. I recognized that familiar gait—Griff. I was torn between staying where I was to wait for him, since he had surely spotted me, too, or keep walking. I chose to keep walking. Surely he wasn't coming up to the castle in search of me, so there was no reason to stay to talk to him. I pushed the pram the long distance around the front of the castle and noticed that Griff had come around the other side and with his long strides, we had reached the front of the castle at the same time. Suddenly and unexpectedly, I felt shy when I saw him. Thankfully I had André to focus on or I don't know what I would have done with myself while Griff stood holding the front door open for me.

"Thank you," I said primly. The words sounded stuffy. I gently laid André against my shoulder and walked past Griff and into the main hall. The pram was still outside on the landing and Griff grabbed the handle and pulled it inside behind him.

"I can hold the baby while you put this away," he offered, indicating the pram with a nod of his head.

I handed André to him, warning him to be careful to support the baby's head and keep him wrapped warmly. I hurriedly put the pram back in the alcove where Sian kept it and turned around to take André back.

Griff was staring at the baby, grinning as if he didn't have another care. The sight of the two of them stopped me where I was. I was struck with the memory of the conversation I had with Sylvie about Griff—that I knew more about him than I realized. The way he gazed at André told the story of a man who cherished other people and who would go great lengths to protect those needing protection. Then Griff looked up at me and his expression changed to one of ambivalence. I felt a pained hopelessness—I had made a huge blunder in spending one miserable evening in the pub with Rhisiart. But I had to try explaining myself one more time.

"Griff, do you have a minute? I'd like to talk to you."

"I'm pretty busy," he answered. "Rhisiart wanted to meet with me. I don't know what it's all about."

"After you're done talking to Rhisiart then?" I asked, sounding more hopeful than I wanted to.

"I don't know about that. It depends on what he wants." He handed André back to me carefully and I got a whiff of his cologne—masculine and light—mixed with the comforting scent of horses.

Griff went down the hallway in search of Rhisiart and I took André upstairs. I found two thick, soft blankets in a chest and spread them out on the floor in the sitting room where Sian liked to stay with André. I placed him on the blankets on his back and sat next to him. He watched my movements as I reached for a squishy block that was on the floor nearby, then I moved it in the air above his head where he could see it. He was still too tiny to grasp things on his own, but he waved his arms upward and touched the block. His bright eyes didn't miss anything.

Before long there was a soft sound in the doorway. I turned my head toward the noise and saw Brenda standing just inside the room.

"Hi, Brenda. Is everything all right?"

She stood still, her eyes darting from one side of the room to another. Something was wrong.

"Brenda? What's going on?" I raised my voice to get her attention. I glanced at the baby, who was happily gurgling to himself.

I stood up slowly and walked toward Brenda with uncertain steps. I kept my eyes focused on her to make sure she didn't move without warning.

When I reached her I waved my hand in front of her eyes, which appeared unfocused and bleary.

"Brenda, what's going on? Come sit down." I led her to the settee in front of the fireplace, trying to keep one eye on André, who was moving his little body on the blankets but certainly wasn't going anywhere. He was too small to turn over by himself.

Brenda let me pull her gently to a seated position, then gave a slight shake of her head. "Eilidh. What are you doing here?" she asked, her voice sounding far away.

"I was in here playing with the baby. What are you doing here?" I had a feeling I knew where this conversation was headed and I didn't like it at all.

"I don't know. How did I get in here?" she asked, looking around as if realizing for the first time where she was.

"Brenda, what have you been doing?" I asked, a warning tone in my voice.

She looked down at her hands in her lap. "Nothing."

"It doesn't look like nothing to me," I said. "Is there something we should talk about?"

She slouched forward, her head resting in her hands. "Don't tell my mum, please, Eilidh. I need help."

"What are you on?" I asked. "Cocaine?"

She groaned, and I took that as a "yes."

"You know what has to happen, Brenda. You know we have to talk to your mum about this. You can't go on letting this drug destroy everything. I thought you were getting better."

She was getting weepy. "But with all the stress of having to look for a new job, and Mum's always talking about how I need to get out of the village and go to university, and…" She left off, shaking her head in despair.

"There are other ways of dealing with stress, ways that are much healthier." I dreaded what was coming next. "Brenda, tell me where you got the coke."

"I can't," she said with a whisper. "Something awful will happen if I say anything."

"What could happen? We get that person to stop giving you cocaine, or selling it to you, and it's done. If necessary, we call the police and they'll arrest whoever it is."

"I can't." The words came out in a barely perceptible squeak.

"You have to, I'm afraid. We can't have you going around like this, especially with a tiny child in the castle. You're going to have to tell me where you got the cocaine and I'll take care of it myself."

"But you don't understand," she said, louder now, pleading with me.

"I understand perfectly. You're the one who doesn't understand," I told her. I was getting angry now. I had believed that she was getting clean, and I was mad at myself. Mad for believing her.

But as I looked at her pathetic form, slumped down on the settee, I wondered if I had really understood the extent of her need for cocaine. Was she more dependent on it than I realized? Than anyone realized? And was it leading her down a path of other drug use? And where was she getting the cocaine? My first concern had to be for her safety and health, and then my second concern, almost as important as the first, was the safety of everyone else in the castle, especially little André. I didn't know what someone under the influence of a drug-addled brain was capable of doing, but I didn't want to wait to find out.

I stood up. "Brenda, I want you to go downstairs to my room. Stay in there until you've had a chance to sober up, compose yourself, whatever you need to do. I'll keep this between us for the moment because I'm watching André until Sian has had time to rest."

Brenda turned around to look at the door and then blinked once, turning back to me. "I'm tired."

"You look tired. Now go do what I told you to do."

She pushed herself up from the settee and made her way to the doorway, staring at André on the floor as she walked. "He's so lucky," she said with a sigh. "Not a care in the world."

I wasn't sure how lucky André was, having no father and no grandmother, but I didn't argue. I wanted Brenda out of the room, away from the baby, and downstairs where no one would see her.

Chapter 18

After Brenda left André began to fuss, so I scooped him up and walked around the room with him, bouncing him gently on my shoulder and cooing to him, but the fussing soon turned into wailing. I didn't know if Sian used a *dummy* to quiet her baby, but I didn't have one. I remembered Greer saying that Ellie used to be soothed by the tip of Greer's pinky finger, so I put my finger in André's mouth. He began sucking on it and stopped crying almost immediately. The room grew quiet again and I continued to walk with him. We walked around the perimeter of the room for many minutes. Several times I thought he would go to sleep, but he opened his eyes each time I tried to put him down. I had taken him over to the window to gaze outside when there was a scream from downstairs. I didn't want to startle André, so I walked swiftly to the staircase and looked over the railing. He began to squirm in my arms as people began to gather in the front hall, which I could glimpse from my perch.

The first one to arrive in the main hall was Cadi. "Who screamed?" she called out, looking in every direction. She didn't look up, though, and I didn't answer her.

"I don't know. Where did it come from?" The voice belonged to Rhisiart, who came running from the direction of the sitting room, with Griff close on his heels.

"I don't know," Cadi said. "You two go see if you can find out who it was." She made no move to help them, but watched as they ran down the hallway leading to my room and to the staircase going below-stairs.

A moment later there was a shout. I stayed where I was, holding the baby tighter and jiggling him gently in my arms. I wanted to know what was happening, but I couldn't leave André alone and I didn't want to take him into the confusion downstairs. As I watched Rhisiart appeared, flailing his arms. "Call for an ambulance!" he yelled to Cadi.

"Why?" she asked. He turned on her, his eyes flashing.

"Just do it and I'll tell you in a minute!" Cadi slipped her hand into the back pocket of her trousers and pulled out her phone. In just a moment she had dialed the number and had a dispatcher on the line. She handed the phone to Rhisiart.

"There's a woman here who's been cut very badly," he told the dispatcher, his breath coming quickly. "You have to hurry. She's bleeding everywhere!" He listened for a moment and then handed the phone back to Cadi. "I have to try to stop the bleeding. Where can I find a rag?"

"Run and ask Maisie for one!" I cried from my perch above them. Rhisiart looked up, then did a double-take. Cadi looked on in surprise.

"What are you doing up there?" Rhisiart asked.

"Minding the baby," I answered. "Never mind that. Hurry and get the rags you need from Maisie. Who's hurt?"

"I don't know. I thought it was you," Rhisiart answered, then took off in a sprint toward the stairs leading to the kitchen. My arms started trembling. Me? Why would he think it was me? Holding André close against my chest, I walked as quickly as I dared toward Sian's room. As much as I wanted her to rest so she could care for her baby properly, it was time for her to take André back so I could assist with whatever was going on downstairs.

I rapped my knuckles loudly on her bedroom door. I could hear a shuffling noise inside the room. After a moment Sian opened the door, her hair rumpled but her eyes bright. "Oh, Eilidh. I hope I didn't take too long." She reached for André. "Thank you so much for taking care of him. How long was I asleep?"

"About two hours," I answered. "I'd be happy to watch André longer, but something is going on downstairs and I think I should get down there to help." I was turning away from the door as I spoke.

"What's going on?" she asked, alarm in her voice.

"I don't know. Cadi just rang for an ambulance. I need to get down there." Sian gasped at my words, then held her baby closer to her as I sped down the hallway toward the stairs. I heard the *click* of her bedroom door lock as I descended into the chaos on the main floor of the castle.

Griff was running from the direction of my bedroom and he stopped short when he saw me at the bottom of the stairs.

"What... I mean, how did you... I thought that was you back there!" he said, his features morphing into a look of confusion.

"What on earth is going on?" I demanded. "Why does everyone think I'm somewhere else?"

He nodded down the hall toward my bedroom. "That scream came from your room," he said. "It's pitch dark in there and there's blood..." He trailed off. "Then who's in there?"

Brenda. Something had happened to Brenda. Only a few short minutes had passed since I first heard the scream coming from the main floor, so there were no answers yet.

"It's Brenda—I sent her to my room to, um, rest. Something awful must have happened." I couldn't stand here any longer chatting about it. I had to find out what had gone on in my room.

I yanked the door open to find utter darkness in the room. The drapes had been drawn and no one had thought to open them. From the dim light of the hallway I could see Brenda's body sprawled on the bedroom floor. Blood lay spattered around her. I ran to the windows and thrust the drapes open to let some light into the room, then turned on the light next to the bed. She lay face-down on the floor, her eyes closed, her lips white. A pool of blood was seeping around her head. I forced my eyes to focus on her head and neck to determine where the blood was coming from. I didn't want to turn her over for fear of hurting her more. I knelt next to her and finally saw the blood moving, glistening in the light from the windows. It was pulsing slowly from her neck. I yelled her name, then breathed a huge sigh of relief when she moaned.

"She's alive," I said, half to reassure myself. I took her hand in mine.

Rhisiart appeared in the doorway. "I have the rags. Do you want to do it?"

"No, you can do it." I pointed to Brenda's neck and said to Rhisiart, "Hold this rag in place. Press hard." He held the rag against the girl's neck and pressed. Brenda moaned again.

"It's all right, Brenda. You're going to be all right." I looked at Rhisiart and said in a low voice, "Where's Maisie?"

"She's on her way up. She wanted to get some hot water to bring upstairs and I asked her for more rags." Maisie probably didn't realize it was her daughter who had been hurt—I wanted to be there when she found out, so she would have a friend close by.

At that moment Maisie appeared in the doorway. She took one look at me and her gaze shifted to the body on the floor. She let out an anguished cry and flung herself beside Brenda, letting the basin of water fall to the floor. She kept her focus on her daughter as she spoke to me. "What happened?"

"We don't know. I was upstairs with the baby and I heard someone scream. Rhisiart and Griff found her in here but the drapes were drawn and they couldn't see who it was. They assumed it was me."

"What was Brenda doing in here?" Maisie asked.

"I sent her here to lie down. She wasn't feeling well," I answered. Now wasn't the time to discuss Brenda's continuing coke habit.

Brenda moaned again, this time trying to twist her body. I tried to hold her shoulders in place and Maisie held her hand. "Don't try to move, Brenda. The ambulance is on its way and you'll be at hospital before you know it. They'll get you all fixed up there," I told her.

I looked to Maisie, hoping she would say something to calm Brenda, but it was clear that Maisie was having a hard time controlling her own emotions. She blinked rapidly, obviously not wanting to cry in front of her daughter. She opened and closed her mouth several times, then looked at me and shook her head. I knew she didn't trust herself to say anything without falling apart. Griff came into the room to announce that the ambulance had just pulled up, as well as two police cars. He knelt on the floor next to me and peered closely at Brenda. "How are you doing, lass? We'll have you out of here in no time. You'll be as good as new before you know it."

Rhisiart hadn't said a word, but continued to apply pressure to the wound on Brenda's neck. It was only a moment before the paramedics came rushing into the room, wheeling a stretcher between them. They were quickly followed by three police officers. We all backed away to let the professionals do their work. In just a few minutes they had the young girl strapped to the stretcher and they were wheeling her down the corridor toward the main hall. Maisie and I followed them while the rest of the household stood silently.

"Maisie, don't worry about a thing here. Go in the ambulance with Brenda and I'll take care of everything at the castle." Ordinarily Maisie was one to worry about details, but this time she just nodded and swept into the back of the ambulance after Brenda. She had forgotten all about the castle and its inhabitants and was focused solely on her daughter by the time the paramedic slammed the back door of the ambulance.

I walked slowly back into the castle, where the police had already started to separate everyone in the main hall to talk to them in different rooms. Hugh and Cadi were each with a different officer, and the third kept watch over Griff and Rhisiart, who were both standing in the front hall, glowering at each other. Sian was nowhere to be seen.

"Miss, can you wait right here, please, until you're called for questioning?" the officer asked, gesturing toward a chair that had been placed against the wall. I sat down obediently, wondering how long I was going to have to wait. Someone had apparently told the police that Sian was in the castle, too, because she came downstairs a few minutes later holding André, who was setting up quite a wail. She handed the baby to me while she retrieved the pram from its home in the alcove, then she took him back and strapped him into the carriage. She pushed the handle of the pram back and forth while André continued to cry, but as the minutes stretched by the baby eventually calmed down. If it hadn't been such a grim situation, it might have been comical to watch Rhisiart try to control his anger at having to listen to the baby cry. He clenched and unclenched his fists, muttered to himself, and sighed loudly every time André let out an especially loud howl. Griff, as I had expected, seemed not to be bothered by the baby's noise. Sian herself was doing her utmost to keep her son quiet, but she was finding it difficult, as I could see by her increased agitation and the tears that slid down her cheeks. At one point I offered to take him and walk with him, but she declined. I think she felt more secure having him with her.

We had been sitting there about thirty minutes when one of the officers came out of the sitting room and beckoned me into the sitting room.

When we were seated across the coffee table from each other he began to ask me questions.

"Why was the housekeeper in your room? It's my understanding she wasn't required to clean your room."

"That's true," I said with a nod. "I sent her there to lie down."

"Why?"

"She wasn't acting like herself and I knew her mother would worry if she saw Brenda like that."

"Like what?"

"She was... under the weather," I answered, struggling to find words that would describe Brenda without revealing that she was high.

The officer eyed me suspiciously. "Under the weather how?"

It was obvious that he wasn't going to let this go until he had a straight answer, so I just blurted it out. "Brenda was high. I didn't want her mum to see her like that so I sent her to my room to sleep it off."

"High on what?"

"Cocaine, I think."

"Where'd she get it?"

"I don't know. I tried to get her to tell me, but she wouldn't."

"Where do you think she got it?"

"If I knew, I'd be the first one to tell you. But I have no idea."

"All right. Tell me what you think happened in your room."

"I have no idea. I heard a scream, but I couldn't go looking for the source of it right away because I was taking care of Sian's baby. I was upstairs."

"When did you come down?"

"I finally knocked on Sian's door and gave the baby to her so I could come down and help. That's when I went into my room and saw Brenda on the floor."

"Who might have held a grudge against Brenda?"

"I can't think of anyone. She kept to herself. She's a good housekeeper, but she didn't get involved in household matters."

"So you don't know who slashed her neck?"

"No." I shook my head.

"We've been called to this house quite a few times recently. Why do you suppose that's happening?"

The obvious answer was that people kept getting hurt, or worse, but I didn't think that was the answer he was looking for. "I honestly don't know."

"Why are you still around? It's my understanding that Annabel's sons and daughter-in-law own the property now. Do you work for them?"

"In a way. They've asked me to do certain things, like pay the bills and do the filing, but I'm not employed by them in the same capacity I was for Annabel. And incidentally, it's not Sian who owns a third of the property. It's her infant, André, but since he's a newborn she will make decisions on his behalf until he gets older."

The officer seemed to think this interesting.

"You haven't answered my question, though. Why are you still around?"

"I've sent out my CV to some places looking for an estate manager, but I haven't heard anything yet. At least here I'm still earning a paycheck. I can't just stop working until the right job comes along." I was annoyed that he had asked the question, as if blaming me somehow for not finding another job yet.

"Don't go too far. We may need to talk to you again."

I left the room to find that the other officer asking questions had taken Rhisiart into the dining room. Sian was next, and the officer who had spoken to me called her.

I went straight to the coach house, where I busied myself cleaning and straightening up. Maisie called once to let me know Brenda was in surgery, but had no other information for me. She hadn't been told of Brenda's prognosis.

"Do you want me to come and wait with you?" I asked my friend.

"No, you stay there to see what you can learn," Maisie answered. "My sister is here with me." I was relieved to know that Maisie wasn't alone waiting for Brenda to come out of surgery. Maisie had probably forgotten that I was staying in the coach house because of the danger of staying in the castle, but I didn't remind her. I didn't want her to think I wasn't trying to get to the bottom of Brenda's attack.

After I'd finished talking to Maisie I was obsessively cleaning the coach house when Sylvie called. Before I could stop myself I blurted out what had happened.

"Do you want me to come back?" she asked, her voice filled with worry.

"No, you stay there. I'll be fine. I just wanted to talk."

"I never should have come back to Cauld Loch," she fretted. "Maybe Seamus should stay with you. He's more protection than I would ever be."

"No, really. It's fine. I'm staying in the coach house and I'm perfectly safe over here."

"All right, if you're sure..."

I promised to keep her updated and rang off. I had cheese and crackers for dinner that night and went to bed early. It had been an extremely long day.

I was almost asleep when a horrifying thought occurred to me. I didn't know why I hadn't realized it sooner.

The person who attacked Brenda probably expected me to be in the bedroom. That attack had been meant for me.

In an instant I felt like I couldn't breathe. I turned on the light next to the bed and despite that, the edges of my vision started to turn black. I reached for my phone and dialed Sylvie. She answered on the first ring, sounding like she was wide awake.

"That attack was meant for me. I'm sure of it."

Her voice told me she had expected this. "We didn't want to say anything. That was the first thing I thought of when I heard the news about Brenda and the first thing Seamus said when I told him. I'm sorry. Maybe we should have said something so we could talk about it rather than having you figure it out for yourself alone and in the dark."

"That's all right," I said miserably. "Poor Brenda. She was just in the wrong place at the wrong time. I'll never forgive myself."

"You couldn't have known what would happen," Sylvie pointed out. "Remember the time back in Edinburgh when I was beaten so badly? That guy thought he was attacking Greer because we look so much alike. But I never once blamed her for it. She couldn't have known what would happen." Sylvie referred to an incident back before she and Seamus were married. The two sisters shared a flat in Edinburgh and during the awful time when Greer's daughter was missing, a man had broken into the flat hoping to scare Greer and attacked Sylvie instead. And though it was a comfort to have Sylvie's side of the story, I still didn't know how I would face Brenda or Maisie after this.

Sylvie talked with me until she thought I would be able to fall asleep. Once she rang off, though, I got up and sat in front of the smoldering fire for a short while, thinking about everything that had happened. I had planned to continue working at the castle until I found another job, but was that wise? I had some money saved. Perhaps it was time to leave the castle for good, dip into that fund, and use the money to find a flat and buy necessities while I looked for another job. But that wasn't the only reason I was staying: I wanted to be there as long as Maisie and Brenda stayed, since I was the only friendly face they saw in the castle. But that would likely change, since Maisie probably wouldn't want to work in the castle after this experience and Brenda would likely never want to set foot in the castle again.

I would have to talk to Maisie about it before packing up my things and leaving the castle, but I had a feeling that she would be ready to leave. And if that attack had been directed at me, then she would want me to leave, too.

I could hear my mobile phone ringing in my room.

"Hullo?"

There was a muffled sound on the other end and I couldn't make out a voice. "Who is this?"

A snorting sound, then a deep breath. "It's Maisie. Brenda just passed," Maisie said in a choked voice.

I hung up the phone and let out a howl that echoed through the coach house. I was shaking, screaming, weeping into my hands. I heaved choking sobs as I rocked back and forth on the sofa. I couldn't open my eyes. I wanted to die. I called Sylvie again.

"She's dead!" I cried when Sylvie answered. "It should have been me," I moaned over and over. "It's all my fault she's dead!"

Sylvie said something, but I couldn't hear her. I was alone, afraid, and unspeakably grief-stricken. Then everything went black around me and the voice of my cousin faded into a soft nothingness. The last thing I heard was Sylvie saying, almost in slow motion, "Stay with me, Eilidh. Seamus and I are on our way."

I don't know how long I was unconscious, but I was still crying when I came to. I couldn't stay in the coach house. Its walls were pressing in on me. I needed to get out, to go somewhere, to do something. I didn't know what I had to do or where I had to go, but I had to get out.

Still in my pyjamas, I grabbed my coat from where it hung on a rack inside the front door and thrust my arms into it.

I wrenched the door open and stepped outside into the whipping wind and the sleet falling from the inky black sky. Slamming the door behind me, I stalked away.

My feet took me to the English garden where Annabel had so loved to go. There were stone benches scattered around, and I sat on the one farthest from the garden gate, not really feeling but somehow aware of the biting cold of the stone. I buried my head in my hands, wishing tears would flow, but they wouldn't. I had cried them all out back at the coach house.

I sat on the bench for quite a long time, then got up and wandered along the gravel paths that led from one vignette of plantings to another. I knew right where the wolfsbane was, but I didn't go near it. I had planned on having the wolfsbane cut out of the garden completely after Annabel's death, but I hadn't made the arrangements yet. I wondered if I would ever do it or if I would just pack up and leave the castle when morning came. Shivering, I finally made my way to the garden entrance. I was beyond tired and could only think of going to sleep to escape everything. I walked slowly toward the coach house feeling numb and empty. As I approached, though, I heard a noise and in an instant all my senses were on alert.

"Who's there?" I asked.

"It's Griff," came the unmistakable voice.

He's the last person I want to see right now, I thought with a groan.

"Sylvie called me," he said. "She told me about Brenda. I thought you could use some company." I walked slowly toward him, not sure whether I really wanted this, but I stood to face him. He stared at me for several moments.

"It's all my fault," I said. "She's dead because of me."

"Come on, let's go inside," Griff said. He followed me into the coach house and we sat down opposite each other by the fireplace. "Why do you think it's your fault?"

"I told her to lie down in my room because she was high and I didn't want her mother or anyone else to see her like that. So she did. And now she's dead. I'm sure that the person who killed her thought it was me in that bed."

"You don't know that."

"I'm pretty sure. What are you doing here with me, anyway? I thought you wanted nothing to do with me." In my frame of mind I didn't feel like being gentle or diplomatic.

"When Sylvie called tonight to tell me about Brenda, she also told me about Rhisiart. She said you went to the pub with him that night because you wanted Maisie and Brenda to be able to go to Annabel's funeral. Is that true?"

I nodded mutely. Leave it to Sylvie to try to patch things up between Griff and me. I couldn't decide if I was relieved or furious.

"Why didn't you just come out and tell me that?"

"I tried, but you weren't interested in hearing it."

"I'm sorry," he said softly. "I was jealous and angry."

"It doesn't matter now, anyway. I'm done at the castle. I'm leaving, so you and I won't be seeing each other anymore."

"I don't blame you for leaving. You stayed longer than I would have if I had to be stuck inside the castle with that family. Where are you going?"

"I don't know. Wherever I can find a job."

"There must be places around here that are hiring."

"I've sent out my CV to several places, but I haven't heard anything yet."

"Don't leave just yet. I mean, I think leaving the castle is a good idea and you should have done it before now, but don't leave the area. A job is bound to open up for you."

"I don't know about that, Griff. I'll have to give it some thought. I have to go where the jobs are."

"Just don't make any rash decisions."

"I won't." Suddenly I was bone-weary. It became too much work to continue talking and all I wanted was to crawl into bed, perhaps with the aid of a sedative so I could stay asleep. "I'm exhausted."

He didn't move and I went to my room. I turned around to look at him before I closed my bedroom door behind me. "I'm staying to make sure you're all right," he said. "Turn off your phone and sleep well. I'll text Maisie and tell her to get in touch with me if she needs anything."

"Thanks. See you later."

I had almost shut the door when he spoke again. "Wait. Just tell me—am I forgiven for being such a clod about you and Rhisiart?"

I smiled wearily. "Yes. You're forgiven. But next time make sure you listen if I'm trying to explain something to you."

"I will, promise." He smiled.

In addition to being so tired, I was cold and sore. I found a bottle of nighttime pain reliever and took two, hoping I would be able to have a long sleep.

Chapter 19

And it was, indeed, late in the morning when I woke up to the smell of bacon and toast. My first thought was one of despair, but I forced myself out of bed. As much as I didn't want to get up and face the day, I knew staying in bed to think would drive me mad. I wandered out of my room, rubbing my eyes. Griff was in the living room, drinking a cup of coffee in front of the fireplace.

"How are you doing?" he asked, fixing me with a look of concern.

"I feel better now that I've slept, but that doesn't change what happened last night. I don't think I'll ever get over that."

"Someday it won't be as painful as it is now," he said, standing up and following me into the kitchen. "You can't go back to the castle, Eilidh. It's dangerous for you there."

"I won't go there except to pack up all my things," I said. I helped myself to bacon and toast with jam while the water boiled for tea. There was a knock at the door as I was pouring the tea. Griff went to answer it and a moment later Sylvie and Seamus came bundling into the kitchen, each of them carrying a rucksack. I was astonished. I had completely forgotten Sylvie saying she and Seamus were coming.

"You really came?"

"We drove all night to be here with you," Sylvie said, reaching out to wrap me in a big hug. I had held everything together until she did that, but once my face was buried in her shoulder, I became unglued, crying as though my heart was broken.

Seamus and Griff stood there awkwardly until I disengaged myself from Sylvie's grasp, then I poured tea for the newcomers and we all stood in the kitchen talking.

"Have you talked to Maisie today?" Sylvie asked.

"No. Griff was going to text her last night to tell her to get in touch with him if she needed anything. And thanks for smoothing things out between us, Sylvie." I gave her an embarrassed smile, glancing at Griff.

"Yes, thanks for that," Griff added.

"I was getting right sick of waiting for you to do something about it, and he's clearly too stubborn to do anything," she said, smiling at both of us. "Now what's the plan for today?"

"I have to go see Maisie, then I think I'm going to start packing my things to move out of the castle."

Seamus offered to drive me over to Maisie's house, but I wanted to go by myself. I had only been to her house a couple times, but I knew I could remember the way. When I pulled into her drive, I was relieved to see it full of cars. I had been so afraid Maisie would be alone. Working in the castle, it was hard to remember sometimes that she had friends and a life in the village, too.

I knocked on the door and a woman let me in. "How's Maisie?" I asked. The woman wiped her nose with a handkerchief and pointed toward the back of the house.

"She's back there. She's holding up, but this has been a horrible blow to her."

I made my way through clusters of mourners to the kitchen, where Maisie was at the sink, rinsing a plate.

"Maisie?" I asked tentatively.

She turned around slowly, then her face crumpled when she saw me. She came over to where I was standing and we held each other in a long embrace. The other people in the kitchen seemed to fade away and it felt as if the only two people in the room were Maisie and me.

She sat down at the table and held my hands. I cried like a child; I told her how sorry I was, how I knew the whole thing was my fault, and how much I would miss Brenda. She assured me through her tears that Brenda's death wasn't my fault—that the blame lay solely on the person who had committed this violent and horrible act.

She introduced me to the other people in the kitchen, mostly women. They were members of her church, she said. They were all very kind, and they murmured sympathetically when Maisie told everyone that I was the one who had been with Brenda when the paramedics arrived.

Maisie squeezed my hand as other people made their way into the kitchen to pay their respects. It seemed Maisie and Brenda had a lot of friends in the village and I was thankful to count myself in that group. I felt better after talking to Maisie and when I left about an hour later, my foremost thought was thankfulness for Maisie's friends and family whose presence would be so essential to her in the coming weeks and months.

As my thoughts turned to the things I needed to do once I returned to the coach house, I couldn't escape the jittery feeling that enveloped me. I knew I needed to go over to the castle to retrieve all my belongings, but I was anxious about going into my room. Would I even be allowed to go in? Would I have to talk to any of the family members? I drove up to the castle and wasn't surprised to see police cars parked out front. I pulled my car into the parking enclosure. As long as there were police inside, there was no reason for me to be afraid to go into the castle. I could ask about getting my things and maybe one of the officers could wait while I packed everything in suitcases.

But as soon as I set foot in the front hall, I was accosted by noisy confusion. There were at least ten or twelve police officers heading in different directions. Sian was standing in the hallway holding André, who was screaming. Rhisiart and Hugh were arguing with one of the officers about access to the sitting room—Rhisiart and Hugh wanted to go in; the police wanted to keep them out.

Now that the attack on Brenda had turned into a murder investigation, the police would need to search every inch of the castle for any information that could lead them to the killer. They had apparently started in the sitting room and in my bedroom, as I discovered when I tried to go into my room and was stopped by one of the officers in charge.

"What are you doing?" he asked.

"This is my room, but I'm moving out. I need to get my things."

"I'm afraid you can't get in here right now. We're conducting a search and it's going to take a while."

I turned around, dejected, dreading the thought of having to come back to the castle again. The officer thought they might be done in my room by the next morning, so he suggested I return then.

I returned to the coach house to find Sylvie and Seamus working. Sylvie was on her laptop, working on a photo collage, and Seamus was online, doing research about a place he wanted to visit to do some painting. And though they offered to set their work aside to spend some time with me, I didn't want to disturb them. I went into my room and found a book that looked interesting. I had just settled onto the bed to read when my mobile phone rang. It was Griff, with an offer to spend the afternoon horse riding through the woods where we had seen the fairy glen.

I accepted immediately, thinking a ride would tire me out and ensure that I slept through the night, but also thinking it would be nice to spend some time with Griff. It had been a while since he and I had done anything together.

I met him in the stables several minutes later. He had saddled Penelope for me and Caesar for himself. We rode side-by-side to the woods, through the fields in front of the castle. I looked back at the castle once. It was shrouded by fog, its turrets just barely visible through the white mist that covered it. It looked almost haunted, like a place out of the past where ghosts might roam. I would miss that beautiful old place and hoped that Rhisiart and Hugh and Sian wouldn't ruin its charm and sodden its rich history.

But Griff was up ahead waiting for me, and it was time to ride with him and try to forget all that had happened to dampen my love for the old castle. I couldn't forget Annabel or Brenda, both of whom had died within its strong walls, but I could try to push the memories of the violence and the pain from my mind.

"Shall we walk for a while, give the horses a rest?" Griff called, turning in his saddle to look at me.

"Sure."

We slid down to the ground and walked a good distance into the woods, holding the reins so the horses would follow us obediently. Griff reached for my hand and I let him hold it in his, the grip sure and warm and steady.

We rode again before we came to the fairy glen, and this time the waters were rushing and swollen with recent rains. We sat down to talk when we reached the waterfall, tying up the horses near the stream so they could drink their fill.

I told him about my visit to Maisie's house and how happy I was to see that she was surrounded by people who loved her, people who would help make the future a little brighter for her. He listened as I explained that I couldn't get into my room to take away my belongings and made me promise that I would take either him or Seamus with me when I returned to the castle the next day.

Finally, as if reading my mind, he reached out and stroked my face with his finger and leaned in to kiss me. It felt right, just as it had before, and when he sat back and gazed at me, I knew with certainty that I couldn't leave the village. I had to stay.

When we returned to the coach house Griff said he couldn't come in. He needed to get back to the stables. I went inside and found Sylvie and Seamus still hard at work. Sylvie closed her laptop after a couple minutes and leaned back into the sofa with a sigh. "I saw you come up the walk with Griff. It looks like things are smoothed over," she said with a grin.

"They are. Normally I'd be furious that you butted in, but I'm grateful for it." I returned her smile and sat down next to her. "I'm not leaving. I've decided to stay."

"In the castle?" The look she turned on me was one of confusion and shock.

"No, just in the village. I can't stay at the castle any longer, but I realized when Griff and I were at the fairy glen that he means more to me than I even realized."

"And it's all because of me," she said, winking and releasing a contented sigh. I pushed her arm and she fell sideways onto the sofa, laughing. Then she sobered. "Rhisiart called while you were out. He wants to talk to you."

"Ugh. I wonder what he wants."

"He didn't say. Just asked me to tell you to come over to the castle when you got back from your walk."

"I'm not going over there. I'll call him, but I'm not going to talk to him face-to-face."

"Good for you," Sylvie said.

I dialed Rhisiart and waited for him to answer.

"Yes?"

"Rhisiart, it's Eilidh. Sylvie tells me you called looking for me."

"I did. I'd like you to come over here so we can get some things straightened out."

"What things?"

"We need to discuss your salary going forward, what your duties are going to be around here when everything calms down and the police allow us back into the office." He referred to the sitting room.

"Actually, I wanted to talk to you about that, Rhisiart. I'm afraid I won't be coming back to the castle."

There was silence on his end. Then, "Did I hear you correctly? You're not coming back?"

"That's right. I guess you can consider this my notice."

"Well. This is unexpected."

"Are you serious? How can you expect me to come back to work in the castle when someone has been murdered in my bedroom? It's time for me to find someplace else to work."

"But you weren't hurt at all."

"Maybe so, but I think we all know that attack was meant for me. And I won't stay around waiting for it to happen again." I glanced over at Sylvie, who was listening to my side of the conversation. She pumped her fist in the air and I smiled.

"You'll get a substantial raise if you come back to work here."

"Rhisiart, you don't understand. I'm not coming back."

His tone changed from mere incredulity to hard and cold. "I don't know who's going to hire you around here now that your name is mentioned in connection with Brenda's murder."

Was he threatening me? "I'm not worried about that, Rhisiart. I have to go now." I rang off and leaned back. "That call wasn't what I expected."

"What did you expect?" Sylvie asked.

"I don't know, but not that."

The phone rang. I looked at the screen—Rhisiart. "I'm not answering that."

"The nerve of him."

"Do you think Seamus will go over to the castle with me in the morning to get everything out of my bedroom?"

"Of course he will," Sylvie said.

The evening was a quiet one. We watched a movie in the living room; it was a comedy. I think Sylvie chose it because she wanted to cheer me up a bit. As the darkness approached I had become more melancholy, weepier about Brenda. I texted Maisie to see how she was holding up, and she answered that the first night without Brenda had been hard. Her sister and brother were staying with her, though, so she had company.

Seamus was coughing during the movie, so much so that Sylvie told him to go into another room if he couldn't stop bothering us with the noise. I felt bad for him. He excused himself to go into the kitchen every time he had a coughing fit, so he ended up missing parts of the movie.

So I wasn't surprised when he was so sick the next morning that he couldn't drag himself out of bed. Feverish and groggy, he staggered into the living room to ask me to wait for a few minutes. He said he would get dressed and walk me over to the castle.

"Seamus, you're going straight back to bed," I told him. Sylvie stood nodding next to me with her arms crossed over her chest. "Even if you went with me this morning, you'd probably collapse even before getting to my room."

"I'm sorry, lass," he mumbled, feeling his forehead. "Can we do it tomorrow?"

"Of course," I answered. He turned and went back into the bedroom, coughing and moaning.

"I'm sure he'll feel better tomorrow. He never gets sick," Sylvie said. She went into the kitchen to make Seamus a mug of tea. I had gotten up that morning with a feeling of determination to get over to the castle and retrieve all my belongings, and a sickly Seamus wasn't going to stop me. I pulled out my phone and called Griff.

But there was no answer, and my call went straight to his voicemail. I was in a quandary. I didn't want to wait to get over to the castle, but I was a bit worried. Perhaps the police were still over there.

The answer came in a phone call from Maisie. She was in the castle, she said, packing up the few personal things she and Brenda had left there, and she asked me to come over to say goodbye. She told me she couldn't work in the castle any longer after what had happened, and she was leaving as quickly as possible. I couldn't say no.

I slipped out the front door of the coach house unnoticed by anyone. I hurried down the path leading to the front of the castle and stood looking at its magnificent Norman façade with sorrow and apprehension.

The massive front door creaked as I pushed it open. I stood in the main hall, listening for voices, sounds, anything that would tell me where the family members were. But I heard nothing. I made a beeline for the stairs leading down to the kitchen and I found Maisie in the warm, comforting space, packing a small bag with a few kitchen utensils and jars of vegetables she had brought from home after canning them herself.

"They don't deserve all these canned goodies," she muttered to me when she saw me standing in the doorway. "I brought them to share when Annabel was still alive, but I can't abide the thought of those people eating them." She looked upward, as if she could see Rhisiart and Hugh, Cadi and Sian as she spoke.

"I'll miss you," I told her.

"I'll miss you too, my dear," she said. "But surely you're leaving too?"

"Yes. In fact, I'll probably clean out my room upstairs while I'm here this morning. Have you seen any of the family about?"

"No. It's been silent since I got here."

"Are you going to be here for a little while?"

"Probably. I have to find Brenda's personal things and pack them up."

"All right. As long as you're going to be around I'm going to head upstairs and pack up my things. It shouldn't take very long. I have suitcases up there that I can fill."

"I'll be down here. I really don't want to go back upstairs," she said.

I went upstairs into the dim hallway and walked to my room, my footsteps echoing on the stone floor. I was as quiet as I could be, since I didn't want to draw attention to myself if any members of the family happened to be nearby.

There was no police tape across my doorway, so they must have finished processing the scene. *Good*, I thought. *I should be able to get out of here in no time.*

I opened the door to my bedroom and was immediately taken aback by the visceral reaction of my mind and body to the sight of the place where Brenda had been so brutally attacked. My stomach lurched and I swayed, holding onto the door frame for support. Maybe it hadn't been such a good idea to return to my room.

But I had to get my things and go. Now that I was here, I wasn't backing down only to have to come back the following day.

Taking a deep, steadying breath, I closed the door behind me and took my suitcases from the closet, lining them up under the window. I began taking clothes and other belongings from the bureau and placing them into the suitcases, then I turned toward the nightstand to remove all my things from it.

It was then I noticed the door opening ever so slightly. I stopped and stood silently, hoping whoever was there would just go away. I chided myself for leaving it unlocked. I couldn't go anywhere and I couldn't hide—the person had probably heard me moving around in the room.

Chapter 20

The door swung open fully and Rhisiart stood in the doorway, a smirk on his face.

"What're you doing here?"

"I came to pack up my things."

"You need permission from me or Hugh or Sian to be in the castle."

"Why?"

"Because you gave notice that you're quitting your job. That makes you a trespasser."

"Rhisiart, I can assure you there's nothing I want from this building except the things I brought here with me."

"I'm busy right now," he answered. "I'm working on a new book. I think I'll ask Hugh to come keep an eye on you." He left and I could hear his footsteps quickly receding down the hallway. It wasn't long before Hugh arrived, looking smug and angry.

"Rhisiart tells me you're leaving our employ. How are we supposed to get the bills paid and the filing done and find anything if you're gone?" he asked.

"I have no idea. You'll find someone to take my place, I'm sure. In the meantime you may just have to do some of that work yourselves."

He closed the door behind him. My eyes darted to the lock, which he deftly clicked with a slight movement of his wrist. I was stuck in here with him. My phone lay on the bed and by then I was working on getting my things out of the big desk; it would have been too obvious if I had suddenly lunged for my phone. Besides, I didn't want him to know I was uncomfortable.

"Is there anything I can tell you now that would help you and the others get organized?" I asked, noting that my voice sounded higher than usual. I wanted to keep him focused on the work of running the castle.

"Not that I can think of. Cadi can figure it all out if necessary. Tell me, what exactly do you know about the other will Annabel made before she died?"

Not this again. "Hugh," I said with a sigh, "there is no will. Rhisiart had been following me and my cousin one night and I was annoyed with him. I figured that if he wanted to hear something really juicy, I would give him something. So I made up the story about a missing will, drawn up after the one that was in the lawyer's office."

He arched his eyebrows at me, clearly not believing a word I said.

"You know I can't let you leave until we know where that will is hidden, and I think you know exactly where it is," he said, his voice low and his eyes flashing. This man meant to do me harm, that much was certain.

"Hugh, how many times do I have to tell you the will doesn't exist?" I asked, my anger rising with my apprehension. I wondered if I could somehow alert Maisie to the danger I was in. I stomped my foot on the floor, hoping she could hear, but I doubted it would do any good. If she heard it at all, she would just assume I had dropped something while I was packing.

"Maisie can't hear you, if that's what you're thinking. She went outside to her car."

"Hugh, listen to me. I'm telling you the truth. Annabel loved you and your brothers. She wanted nothing more than to see you inherit this castle when she died. Of course she didn't think she would die as early as she did, but I'm sure she would be happy to know that the castle is under its rightful ownership right now."

"The problem with lying is that no one ever knows when you're telling the truth, Eilidh." Hugh's voice was calm, low, rational, but there was a malice that lay behind his words, a malice I could see in his eyes.

"And we are forced to assume that you were telling the truth the night you told your cousin about the will. And that you're lying now because you're scared. I can see that you're scared."

"I'm not scared."

"Of course you are. Listen to yourself. Your voice is shaking, you keep wiping your hands on your trousers. You're terrified. And you should be."

With that he lunged at me, hatred glittering in his eyes. I dashed around the bed and stood on the other side, away from him, watching him warily. He backed up and stood facing me across the bed, then suddenly he was leaping over the bed, scrambling to get to where I stood. I had no choice but to run away from him, but this couldn't last long. The room wasn't huge—he was going to catch me.

I ran headlong into the door. With shaking hands I somehow managed to unlock the door and fling it open. I could feel the rush of air at my back when Hugh grasped my shirt as I ran out of the room, but I wrenched it away from him.

I don't know what compelled me to run in the opposite direction of the great hall, but before I knew it I was headed toward the crumbling wing of the castle, the place where no one ever dared to go. A heavy wooden door separated me from the stone ruins of the unused wing, but to my shock and immense relief, I found it unlocked. I couldn't imagine why Annabel hadn't kept the door locked, but I forced that thought from my mind, grateful that she hadn't. Hugh was only a step or two behind me, but I thrust the door closed as he reached my location.

That only bought me a second or so of time, but it was enough for me to scramble out of the way of the door and over a pile of mossy stones that lay in my path. I was vaguely aware that there was no roof above me, and rain was falling softly. The old stone floor was wet and slippery. With a cry of rage, Hugh raced through the door behind me; he grabbed my arm and wrenched it behind me as I slid on the floor and cried out in pain.

"You couldn't leave well enough alone, could you?" he seethed between clenched teeth. "You couldn't just keep on working, minding your own business. No, you had to go around making noise about another will. Now we have to find it and destroy it before the lawyer gets wind of it and we lose the castle. And you realize, of course, that you're not getting out of here. That stupid coke-sniffing bitch is dead because of you, because you tricked me into thinking you were in the bedroom. I'm not going to make that mistake again. I've lost all the income from selling her the coke because of you." He shook my arm like a jackhammer and shoved my head hard into the floor.

"Where's the will?" he asked, low and deadly.

"There is no other will!" I grunted, trying to free myself from his grasp, my head spinning from the force of the blow against the stone.

"I should have known you'd be trouble from the minute I arrived at the castle," Hugh said, yanking me into a standing position. His arms closed around my chest from behind, squeezing, making it hard for me to breathe. "I should have killed you instead of Annabel—it would have been easier to convince her to destroy the new will."

I let out a groan. "Why did you kill her? Your own mother?" I managed to ask.

"Because she never loved us! She didn't care about us! All those times she let our father beat us senseless... It should have been her. She had a duty to protect us and she failed!"

"She loved you, Hugh. She was scared to death of your father. And she was young and made mistakes. But she loved you more than you realize. She wanted to make amends."

"Ha!" Hugh shouted, his voice ugly and ragged. I was struggling to get away from him and it was just making him angrier. Someone was pounding on the wooden door leading to the ruined wing of the castle. I glanced in that direction and saw that Hugh had wedged a stone under the door so no one could follow us.

"Help!" I cried, but my voice came out as more of a croak.

"Eilidh?" I had never been so happy to hear Griff's voice. "Eilidh, are you in there?" He rattled the door handle again. "Open the door!"

"Shh," Hugh whispered savagely in my ear. "Maybe he'll go away."

In reply, I made a noise with my throat that I hoped would be loud enough for Griff to hear on the other side of the heavy door. Hugh immediately let go of me and struck out at my face with his closed fist. I saw stars. There was a loud ringing in my ears that wouldn't stop. I stumbled back toward the door and slammed into it with my shoulder. Then I was on all fours on the floor, shaking my head and trying to get the ringing to stop when Hugh rushed over to me. Bending down, he held me in place with his arm while he kicked my abdomen repeatedly. I curled up into a ball as best I could to stop the blows, still making sure to hit the door with my feet so Griff would know I was inside.

I couldn't stand up. Hugh had tired himself out—he was bent over, his hands on his knees, taking a few deep breaths. I knew I wasn't getting back into the castle without serious injury, or worse, if I couldn't get help. I could dimly hear shouts coming from the hallway, and just a moment later Griff burst through the door, splintering the wood and heaving a heavy crow bar onto the stone floor as soon as the door opened. He took one look at what was happening and advanced toward Hugh. Hugh stood up straight, flexing his hands to let his fists fly at Griff. But Griff wasn't tired like Hugh was. He picked up a stone and hurled it at Hugh's head.

Hugh hit the floor with a sickening thud and suddenly my ordeal was over. Hugh lay unconscious amid the crumbling old walls of the castle ruins and I stood trembling by the door, crying my thanks and trying to keep my arms around my chest, protecting the bones I was sure Hugh had broken with his vicious kicks.

Griff sank to the floor next to me. I cried like a baby as he held me in his arms, waiting for the police and an ambulance to arrive.

"Could you hear what Hugh told me?" I asked between gulps of air and wrenching sobs.

"I could hear most of it. He killed Annabel, didn't he?"

Amy M. Reade

I nodded, unable to speak until I could catch my breath. He helped me shift my position so I could breathe more easily.

By the time I could relate the full conversation between Hugh and me, the police had arrived at the castle. In all their visits to the castle they had never been in the ruined wing and Rhisiart showed them where to go. Two ambulance attendants wheeled a stretcher down the hallway behind the police, but they weren't able to enter the ruins with it. They waited for me in the corridor.

Not long afterward, Sylvie ran up to the rest of us, clamoring to know where I was and what had happened to me. Sylvie broke down and cried with relief when she saw me.

Griff rode with me to the hospital in the back of the ambulance. Once I had been examined, prodded, X-rayed, and given a room, the police came in to ask questions. Griff stepped out when they first arrived, but a nurse came in just a moment later to ask the police to keep their questioning to a minimum, as I had to rest. I was thankful to have Griff looking out for me.

I told them everything Hugh had told me—that he killed Annabel, that he believed there was another will, that he had attacked Brenda thinking it was me. The officers took notes furiously while I spoke, then the nurse ducked her head in again to ask if they could come back another time to continue questioning me.

They left, but it was several minutes before Griff returned. He told me they had questioned him too, in the hallway right outside my room, and he gave them the same information I had shared with them. He was holding my hand and stroking my good arm, helping me to fall asleep, when Sylvie arrived. She started crying all over again when she saw me. The emotions across her face told me everything.

"Seamus said he's sorry he can't come to the hospital, but he's too sick," she said with a hiccup. "He's mad at you, though, for going over to the castle without him." She let out a short laugh; the tears started afresh.

"Tell him that's okay, I won't need his help after all," I said, barely able to smile through the pain in my face and jaw.

"I'm so glad you're all right," Sylvie cried, bending over to kiss my forehead. One of her tears fell on my cheek and my tears mingled with it.

"I'm fine, Sylvie. Stop crying. I'm going to be as good as new," I assured her. "I'm just sorry you had to make the trip back here."

She waved her hand at me to dismiss the thought. "We're so glad we could be here when you needed us the most," she said. "What happens next?"

The nurse had come into the room. "What happens next is that you go home," she said, "and let this poor woman rest."

Sylvie left with a promise to return later in the day and a few minutes later I was sound asleep. I didn't sleep long, though, because I got more visitors. Griff whispered in my ear, "Eilidh, Cadi and Rhisiart are here. Do you want to talk to them?"

"If I have to," I mumbled. The pair walked into my room, Cadi's hands clenched in front of her and Rhisiart running his hand through his hair. Griff eyed him warily.

"How are you doing?" Rhisiart asked.

"I've been better, but I'm going to be all right."

"I think we owe you an apology for everything that has happened," he said. Cadi nodded beside him.

"I really thought it was Sian who killed Annabel. Sian really is an avid gardener. What I told you was true. God, how I wish it had been her. I can't believe it was Hugh," she said. "I have always known him to have a temper, but not like that. To kill his own mother..." She trailed off, probably thinking about what life would be like for her after Hugh went to prison, which would surely happen. I knew a thing or two about surviving while a spouse was in prison. I knew what anguish was headed her way.

"And to attack Brenda like that, thinking she was you," Cadi continued after a moment. "I'm so very sorry for all of it."

I could do nothing but nod. Rhisiart spoke again. "Hugh was frantic when he found out there might be another will. He felt we should find it and destroy it in case Annabel had left her estate to someone else. Like you," he said, pointing to me.

"Even if she had, I wouldn't have accepted it," I said. "I don't want to live at the castle without Annabel. She was the one who made it a happy place. It's not a happy place anymore."

"So the will—do you know where it is?" Rhisiart asked. Would he never stop this line of questioning?

"Rhisiart," I said with a long sigh, "there is no other will. You can turn that castle upside-down and you'll never find it because it doesn't exist. As I told Hugh, I made up that story because I knew you were following me and Sylvie that night out by the garden and I wanted you to go fritter away your time on something other than browbeating the people who worked for Annabel. Please, no more about the will." I had exhausted myself talking.

It had obviously been a mistake to make up the story about the missing will, and I had learned my lesson well. I would never do such a thing again—the next time I wanted to get somebody to stop doing something, I would confront them myself and tell them the truth. All the pain, the violence, the death, over something that never existed, would haunt me for the rest of my life. And Brenda was dead because of the lie I had told.

I waved my hand at Rhisiart and Cadi in an effort to get them to go away, and Griff understood immediately what I wanted. "It's time for you two to go," he said gravely. "And please don't come back unless you're invited."

They nodded their assent and left the room. I opened one eye just long enough to satisfy myself that they were gone and I was asleep again in no time. Griff stayed overnight in my room and was there in the morning when the police returned, this time to deliver the most shocking news of all.

"We wanted to inform you that Maisie Wellingbottham has been arrested and charged with killing Andreas Tucker."

I gasped and struggled to sit up. Griff put his hand on my arm to keep me from hurting myself.

"You're kidding," he said.

"What happened?" I asked.

"Officers at the castle yesterday found her trying to sneak away after you had been taken away in the ambulance, miss. When they stopped her and began asking questions, it was clear that she was afraid of something in addition to what had happened in your bedroom. Upon further questioning, she broke down and admitted that she had been responsible for Mr. Tucker's death."

"But how?" I asked, unable to believe what I was hearing.

"When he left the castle the night of his death she was still there working. She heard him leave; she followed him while he took a walk down by the water's edge. She pushed him into the river," the officer answered.

"But why? Why did she do it?"

"Apparently to stop him from selling cocaine to her daughter, miss." And now that daughter was dead.

I didn't say anything. I was trying to imagine how I would react if I knew the person selling cocaine to my own daughter, trying to get her hooked, ruining her young life. I had to admit to myself that I might do the same thing under the same circumstances. Finally I said softly, "She was just trying to save Brenda."

"We know that, miss."

The officers left and Griff held my hand as tears coursed down my cheeks—tears for the pain Maisie had lived with trying to keep her daughter off drugs, pain for her future, and pain for Brenda, for her life snuffed out because of a lie I had told.

Chapter 21

Over the next few days as I recuperated in hospital, several things were revealed to me by the police. Most importantly, Hugh had officially admitted to killing his mother and Brenda.

"How did he poison Annabel?" I asked.

"He ground up the wolfsbane and put it in her favorite body lotion and her lip balm." My mind snapped back to the day of Annabel's death. I had given her lip balm because her lips were so dry. I had inadvertently killed Annabel. I blurted this out to the officer.

"The medical examiner, Dr. Thomas, determined that the dosage in the body lotion was more than enough to kill her. The dosage in the lip balm was much lower. In other words, she would have died from the wolfsbane even if there had been no poison in the lip balm. So don't lead yourself down the road of believing you killed her. You did not."

I wouldn't have been able to bear the guilt if I had been responsible for Annabel's death, so the officer's assurances that I didn't kill her were a salve on my frayed nerves.

"How did Hugh know about wolfsbane?" I asked. "Why didn't the police find any information on his computer?"

"He got his information the old-fashioned way—at the library. He went and looked up the information he needed in a book."

"But he was so keen to have an autopsy performed on Annabel," I said.

"He was just trying to deflect suspicion away from himself," the officer replied. "He figured it wouldn't be discovered and that Annabel's cause of death would simply be heart failure. And if it was discovered, he thought he wouldn't get caught. Typical bloke with a big ego."

"He did all of this because he hated his mother?"

"Apparently he did hate his mother, but he and his wife Cadi were also experiencing serious financial problems. He thought he was safe with one-third of his mother's estate, especially if it turned into a center for horse breeding. But when he suspected there might be another will that left the estate to someone else, he panicked. He had already been dealing drugs to make extra money—he took over where Andreas left off, as you know—but that wasn't enough."

"Brenda wouldn't tell me that she was getting her drugs from Hugh," I said in a quiet voice.

"I can explain that, too," the officer replied. "Apparently she knew her mother was responsible for the death of Andreas Tucker. She didn't want her mother to lash out at Hugh, too. There's been way too much death in this family."

I was dumbfounded. Brenda had known her mother was guilty of killing Andreas?

It would be a very long time before I could make sense of everything I had learned.

One day Cadi came to see me. She called first to ask permission, as she had promised to do, and I consented to a short visit. She showed me a letter Sian had found when she was cleaning out Annabel's desk. Cadi handed it to me and stood at a distance while I read it.

My darling boys,

You will never know the suffering I have endured because I haven't been able to take care of you the way a mother should. Your father threatened to kill you all, and me, if I revealed the extent of his brutality, so I stood by, meek and useless, as he continued his despicable behavior. I figured it was better for you to be hurt than dead.

I want you to know that I did everything I could to protect you, though I'm sure there were other things I was too timid to do. I took blows and beatings meant for you in exchange for leniency by him toward you three, but it was never enough.

In the end, it was I who watched him die in the throes of an alcohol-fueled stupor. He demanded help through the fog of his drunkenness, and I ignored his pleas. I killed him by my inaction. I have never regretted letting him die before my eyes because I knew his death spelled the end of the horror you faced as children. My only regret is that I didn't do it sooner. You can never know how much love I have for all of you and how I have suffered from my own shortcomings.

Love,
Mum

So Hugh had killed his mother without the knowledge of how much she suffered for him and without knowing that she was the one who, in the end, allowed her husband to die an agonizing death, all for Hugh and his brothers. I thanked Cadi for showing me the letter and she left. There was nothing more I could say to her. It had all been so senseless.

By the time I left hospital the doctors were concerned that I had sunk deep into a depression for which I would require further treatment. Rhisiart and Sian had given me permission to live in the coach house for as long as I needed, and Sylvie and Seamus had to return to their lives in Scotland. I hated to see them go, but it was time. They had done all they could for me and I had to face the future without them.

But I didn't have to face the future alone. Griff stayed with me in the coach house until I had healed physically, then he stayed on until my mind began to heal, too. He had quit his job at the castle stables and had found work at another stable near the village.

I knew the best thing for me was to get a new job. If I could get back to work, to give myself something to do every day, then I knew I would begin to feel better. I visited Maisie whenever I could, but often my mood prevented me from going to see her. She had plenty of her own troubles— she didn't need me showing up in a melancholy, self-blaming mood at the prison where she was being held until her trial.

I still had a hard time believing Maisie had killed Andreas, but I couldn't condemn her for it. She had only done what I imagined I might do under similar circumstances—protect her daughter at all costs. Maisie and I talked about it when I visited her the first time, after I had had a chance to sort out my thoughts. She cried when I told her how I felt, relieved that I understood how she could kill Andreas because of the anguish and harm he was causing Brenda.

Though I appreciated being able to stay on the castle property rent-free, I didn't want to stay there any longer than I had to. The day came when I knew I had to move out of the coach house and into a flat of my own. Griff begged me to come live with him in his cottage in the village, but I knew I needed to be able to survive on my own before I could think about living with him.

So I let a flat in the village over the dress shop Annabel had loved to frequent. It seemed right that I shared that connection with her even after she had died and I had moved away from the castle.

But there was another connection, too. As the months passed and I got better, Griff and I continued to grow closer. I was still looking for a job, but nothing had opened up and I was trying to find other jobs that I might be able to do, including working part-time at the dress shop. But Griff had another idea. Rhisiart and Sian, who both continued to live in the castle, remained hell-bent on their scheme to convert the castle and its surrounding property into a racehorse breeding center. They decided to sell all of Annabel's horses and replace them with younger racing horses and valuable studs. When Griff got wind of their plan, he used all his savings and I chipped in much of mine to buy the horses. In exchange for doing some extra work around the stables where he worked, he was allowed to board Annabel's horses there.

His plan was to buy a farm and raise horses. There could be no more perfect job for him, and when he asked me to share his life and his dream with him, I was over the moon. We were married in a tiny ceremony in the village hall, with only a few others present. We honeymooned on a farm where Griff had agreed to do some menial chores each day for a week in exchange for a small room over the stables that we referred to as our "honeymoon suite." It was perfect—not a traditional honeymoon, but nothing about myself or my life had been traditional since I left Scotland. And it suited me perfectly.

Discussion Questions

1. Do you think Hugh had feelings for Sian? Was that part of the reason Hugh and Andreas didn't get along?

2. Did Sian know about Andreas's drug dealing? Did Cadi know that Hugh took over Andreas's clients after Andreas was killed?

3. Why did Annabel wait so long to ask her sons for forgiveness for failing to protect them when they were children?

4. Did her sons lie when they said she was forgiven for her inaction when they were young? If so, why?

5. Why do you suppose Annabel didn't give her sons the letter that was found in her desk?

6. How do you feel about Maisie's involvement in Andreas's death?

7. How do you feel about Annabel's involvement with Arthur's death?

8. What do you think the future holds for Eilidh and Griff?

9. Do you think Sian will continue to live at Thistlecross Castle, or will she eventually return to London with André?

10. What do you think the future holds for Cadi and Rhisiart?

**If you enjoyed *Murder in Thistlecross*, be sure
not to miss Amy M. Reade's other Malice novels,
including *Highland Peril*.**

*Trading the urban pace of Edinburgh for a tiny village overlooking a
breathtaking blue loch was a great move for budding photographer Sylvie
Carmichael and her artist husband, Seamus—until a dangerous crime
obscures the view...*

Sylvie's bucolic life along the heather-covered moors of the Highlands is
a world away from the hectic energy of the city. But then a London buyer
is killed after purchasing a long-lost Scottish masterpiece from Seamus's
gallery—and the painting vanishes. As suspicion clouds their new life,
and their relationship, Sylvie's search for answers plunges her into an

unsolved mystery dating back to Cromwellian Scotland through World War I and beyond. And as she moves closer to the truth, Sylvie is targeted by a murderer who's after a treasure within a treasure that could rewrite history… and her own future.

Keep reading for a special excerpt!

A Lyrical Underground e-book on sale now.

Chapter 1

As much as I love Seamus, he can make me crazy.

Don't get me wrong—living in the Scottish Highlands suits me better than I ever dreamed it would when he first suggested we leave Edinburgh. I enjoy working in the antique shop and I don't even mind running the gallery when he's been bitten by the painting bug and can't tear himself away from his latest creation.

But when he asked me to "whip up a wee snack" for him and a client, I had to put my foot down.

"I'm not your maid, Seamus. Whip something up yourself."

He spread his big hands out, pleading. "Please. Sylvie. I don't have time."

"Neither do I. Just take him over to the pub."

"It's pouring out. There's no need to go out in this weather when we have stuff to eat here. I promised him real Scottish food."

"Well, that's your problem. You know I can't cook anything, let alone anything Scottish."

"Just slice up some of the haggis in the fridge and fry it."

"I'll burn it. Remember what happened last time?"

He nodded, grimacing. "It was as hard as a rock."

"Why do we need to feed him, anyway? What's so special about him?"

"Keep your voice down," Seamus cautioned, looking over his shoulder through the door to the shop. "He's up from London. Looking for a painting that reminds him of his childhood. There's one he seems to like, but it's expensive and I'm trying to butter him up."

"Well, you'll have to butter him up without haggis, I'm afraid."

"Fine. Just get us a couple drams, would you?"

I glared daggers at my husband. "All right. But if you sell that painting, you have to take me shopping in Edinburgh."

He smiled. "You know I will, love."

"You're lucky I'm so nice."

He chuckled as he walked back into the shop, shaking his red head. "Care for a dram?" I heard him ask the man from London.

I went into the house and poured two measures of whisky, put them on a tray, and carried them back into the shop. Seamus was pointing out a small detail on a painting when I walked in.

"Ah, here's the whisky, along with my wife. Sylvie, I'd like you to meet Florian McDermott. He grew up in the Highlands and lives in London now. He's looking for a special painting. Florian, meet Sylvie."

I set my tray down and shook hands with the man, who was wispy and pale. His hand was cold in mine, though his eyes were warm.

"I'm looking for a painting that reminds me of my childhood in the Highlands," Florian explained.

"You must have fond memories of your childhood."

"What makes you think that?" Florian asked.

"Um, I guess…"

"It was awful."

I was at a loss for words. I looked to Seamus for help.

He just smiled and reached for the two glasses. Handing one to Florian, he raised his own in the air and said in a booming voice, "Here's tae ye!"

Florian raised his glass in silence, nodded, took a tiny sip of the whisky, and began to cough. He hacked away while Seamus grabbed his glass and I hurried for the pitcher of ice water I kept in the gallery. He was still coughing when I returned. He drank the water right from the pitcher, though I had meant for him to add it to the whisky to cut its strength.

"Are ye all right, man?" Seamus asked. Florian gasped for air, nodding, his previously pale face now a mask of hot pink.

"Sorry about that," he gasped. "It was a bit stronger than I expected."

"A *bit* stronger?" Seamus asked. "It must have gone down your throat like flame. I'm sorry. If I'd known, I would have had Sylvie get you something milder."

I glared at him. *If I'd known, I would have made you get your own whisky,* I thought.

"No, no. I just wasn't expecting it, that's all," Florian assured us. "I'm not much of a drinker."

"Ginger ale for you?" Seamus asked.

"No, thank you. I think I'd like to go back to the bed and breakfast where I'm staying and think about this for tonight."

"No problem at all," Seamus replied. He handed Florian a business card. "I look forward to hearing from you."

Florian nodded, his face returning to its former ghostly hue. He left without another word.

"He's a strange one, that's certain," Seamus said after Florian had disappeared from view.

"Did he say why he wants to get a painting to remember something he thought was awful?"

Seamus shrugged. "He didn't make much sense."

"Quite a loon," I said.

"I don't care if he's from outer space as long as he buys that painting. I've had it for three years now and nothing I can say will convince anyone to buy it. It's just too expensive."

"Why not lower the price?"

"Because it's by William Leighton Leitch, a famous Scot painter. So it's worth a lot of money. It's just a matter of waiting for the right buyer to come along."

"Well, maybe you've finally snared the right person."

He chucked me under the chin. "I didn't *snare* him. I just let the painting do the talking."

I smiled at my big, burly husband. "That painting must have quite a way with words, then."

He busied himself in the back of the shop while I returned to the gallery. No one had come in while we were speaking to Florian. We didn't get a lot of visitors, but when we did it was usually a serious buyer who came specifically to buy one of Seamus's paintings.

When we lived in Edinburgh, Seamus painted urban scenes with great success. In Bide-A-Wee house, where we lived with my sister, Greer, and her little girl, Ellie, until our marriage, Seamus had made part of the sunny, bright living room into a studio. He sold paintings online and in Edinburgh galleries. He had also been invited to show several of his paintings in some of the smaller London galleries, where they nevertheless had a larger audience and fetched higher prices. Once we were married we moved into our own flat near Bide-A-Wee and he continued painting there, until the weekend we went camping with friends—against my better judgment—in the mountains of the Scottish Highlands.

Seamus was hooked. The raw, rugged beauty of that part of Scotland appealed to both the artist and the outdoorsman in him, and he couldn't wait to leave Edinburgh and head north. He longed for a change from the scenery of the city.

But I didn't want to go. I loved the city, with its moods, weather, wonderful and sometimes quirky inhabitants, and its cultural events and history.

We were at loggerheads—a rather inauspicious way to begin married life.

But repeat trips to the Highlands on our days off and Seamus's constant discussion of how wonderful life would be if we moved finally began to wear me down. I found myself looking online at homes for sale. I began to actually look forward to our day trips and short overnights to the mountains.

But what clinched it for me, what made me finally agree to leave Edinburgh (with promises from Seamus practically written in blood that we would return to the city often) was a gift.

Seamus gave me a camera for my birthday that year, just a few months after that momentous camping trip. Previously I had used my mobile phone for photos and it wasn't very good. The camera unearthed a passion for photography I never knew I had. With that camera in my hand, I found I could make the Highlands come alive. I could see the interplay between light and shadow, between color and white space, that other people missed when they looked at a landscape.

So I started taking that camera with me wherever I went, and my favorite photos were the ones I took on our drives up to the Highlands. The craggy mountains capped with snow, the purple heather-covered moors, the dark peaty bogs, the deep blue lochs—I took pictures of everything. My cousin Eilidh convinced me to start selling my photos online and before I knew it I was making an income, however small, with my passion for photography. I had never had a job I loved: I had graduated from university with a degree in business and hopped from one boring office job to another for years until I discovered photography. Between Seamus's gift and the beauty of Scotland's breathtaking landscape, I had finally found more than a job—I had found a career that made working exhilarating and fun.

Seamus's feet didn't touch the ground for a week after I told him I was ready to make the move to the Highlands. He was thrilled and quite willing to do anything I asked in return.

So I made the one request I'd been mulling over: I told him I wanted to live in the tiny village where Eilidh and her husband, Callum, lived. Seamus agreed in the blink of an eye. Having lost his own parents in a house fire, Seamus heartily embraced my family—from Eilidh and Callum to Greer and Ellie to my mum, whom he loved as his own. He had been an only child, so having an extended family was new and wonderful to him. He loved the idea of living just a stone's throw from my cousin and Callum.

And that's how we came to live in Cauld Loch, a wee village clinging to a steep hill overlooking a loch of the same name, a small mountain lake with icy dark blue water. There was only one place for sale in the village, a house with a large attached shop, and we bought it. We named it Gorse Brae, after the gorse that grew in the front yard. We divided the shop into three parts: an antique art shop, a studio where both Seamus and I could work, and a gallery to display his paintings and my photos. We had been looking for a shop because just as I found a passion for photography, Seamus had found a passion for antique artwork. He had begun amassing his collection before we were married and finally decided he wanted to start selling it, too.

Seamus had invited Eilidh and Callum for dinner the night of Florian's visit, and the four of us pondered the mysterious stranger over our lamb stew.

"If he doesn't like the Highlands, why come all the way up here to find a painting? There are lots of places to find Highland art in London," Eilidh said.

"He didn't say," Seamus answered.

"How did he hear about the shop?" Callum asked.

"Saw one of my paintings in London and asked the gallery owner about me. I guess he likes the style of my paintings, but he wanted something old, something that had a previous life. And when the gallery owner told him I have an antique art shop up here, he took a chance that I sell the same types of artwork I paint, so he came up."

"He must be pretty serious about finding just the right painting," Eilidh noted. Seamus nodded, his mouth full. Finally he swallowed. "Aye, and this one seems to be just what he's looking for. I've had nary a nibble on it in a long time."

"What's it called?" I asked.

"It's unnamed. I call it 'Old Kirk in the Field.'"

"So it's a picture of a church?"

"Yes, but there's an old woman stooped over in front of the kirk. It looks like she's picking flowers."

"I wonder why that reminds him of his awful childhood."

Seamus shrugged. "I've no idea."

"If William Whoever was such a famous painter, why do you have one of his works in your shop? Shouldn't it be in a museum somewhere?" Eilidh asked.

"It's William Leighton Leitch. When he died in the late eighteen hundreds, he left behind just a few paintings and drawings. Somehow this one ended up in a shop in Edinburgh. I bought it for a bargain because it's not in great shape."

"What's wrong with it?" Callum asked.

"There's a small tear in one corner and the paint is quite faded. Still, it's a steal. A famous painter, a painting that was lost after his death—it's all very exciting."

"It's too bad the painting isn't in good shape. If it was you could sell it to a museum instead of Florian and get a bundle for it," I said.

"Maybe," Seamus said, sitting back in his chair, "but I don't really have the time to restore it right now, and I don't want to pay for its restoration if I can get someone to buy it from me as is. Someone like Florian."

The phone rang in the gallery. We normally didn't answer the gallery phone after hours, but Seamus pushed his chair back from the table and hurried through the door into the gallery, saying over his shoulder, "Maybe that's Florian."

He was gone several minutes. I cleared away the dishes and was setting out bowls of berries and cream when Seamus came back in, shaking his head.

"Was that Florian?"

"You won't believe this," he said. "It was some guy wanting to look at the Leitch painting. The same one Florian is interested in."

"You're kidding."

"No," he said, rubbing his beard. He did that when he was thinking. "He said he heard I might have an old beat-up William Leighton Leitch painting in my shop, one with a stooped old lady at a church, and that he'd like to come up tomorrow to see it."

"What did you tell him?"

"I told him I might already have a buyer for it and that person gets first dibs." He turned to stare at me. "Can you believe it? I've tried to sell the thing for three years with no bites, and all of a sudden I have two potential buyers."

"What did he say when you told him he's second in line?"

"He didn't say anything about it. Just asked if he could come up tomorrow to see it. I'll have to call Florian and tell him about this. Maybe get him to make up his mind a wee bit faster."

"Do you think he will?"

"How do I know?" Seamus hates it when I ask unanswerable questions.

He drew Florian's business card out of his back pocket and punched some numbers into his mobile phone.

"Hi, Florian? It's Seamus Carmichael from Highland Treasures. I've received a call from a man who wants to have a look at the Leitch painting tomorrow. I told him you have first dibs on it, but you might want to make a decision soon."

Florian said something on the other end.

"Aye, great. It'll be ready."

Seamus ended the call and swooped me up in his arms, swinging me around the kitchen. "Florian'll take it! He's coming over tonight to pick it up! We finally sold it!"

I tilted my head back, laughing, already looking forward to my shopping trip in Edinburgh. Ignoring the berries, I cracked open a bottle of sparkling wine and the four of us raised our glasses to Florian. Seamus disappeared into the shop to wrap the painting, then joined the rest of us for dessert. After Eilidh and Callum went home Seamus waited by the shop door, watching for Florian's headlamps to sweep up the road.

"Sylvie, come here," he said after a few minutes.

"What?"

"Just come here."

I joined him at the shop door as he shut off the lights. "What are you doing that for? What if Florian can't find the shop?"

"Look," he said, pointing outside. A dark car crawled along the road just fifty meters from the shop, its lights off.

"Do you suppose that's Florian?"

"I don't know. I wonder why the driver doesn't have the headlamps on."

"Why did you turn off the shop lights?"

Seamus shrugged. "So whoever it is can't see us watching."

"It's a bit creepy, don't you think, standing here watching someone in the dark?"

He didn't answer.

The car slowed to a stop in front of our house. After just a moment, a slight figure stepped out of the car and stood looking up at the shop.

"That's Florian," Seamus said, his voice low. "Even in the dark I can tell him by his size and shape."

I nodded. Seamus took my elbow and we returned to the kitchen. "Why are we sneaking around our own house?" I complained.

"Something's a bit off about this whole thing," Seamus said, stroking his beard again. "Why would Florian drive around without his headlamps on?"

We stood in the kitchen, looking at each other, until the shop doorbell rang. Seamus returned to the shop, flipped on the light, and opened the door. I followed him, and together we watched as Florian skittered into the shop, checking over his shoulder.

"Is the painting ready?" he asked.

Seamus pointed to the large package on the shop counter. "Aye, it is. Say, Florian, did you realize your headlamps are out?"

Florian, who had been looking around the shop, jerked his head toward Seamus. "Is that so? That's funny. I didn't even realize it. I'll have to remember to switch them on when I go back."

"How far away is your bed and breakfast?"

"Just a few miles."

"It's dangerous to drive around here without headlamps. Lots of twists and turns in the roads. Be careful," Seamus cautioned.

"I will," Florian assured us. He pulled out a thick envelope. "How much do I owe you?"

Seamus quoted a high number and Florian opened the envelope. Rifling through its contents, he pulled out a wad of notes and handed them to Seamus, who watched him with wide eyes.

"Och, man, do you always carry that much cash wi' ye?"

Florian looked straight into Seamus's eyes with a boldness that seemed uncharacteristic. "Not usually." Seamus took the hint and looked away. Strange that such a meek little man could make Seamus feel self-conscious. Seamus had done time in prison, for heaven's sake, for injuring a man in self-defense. He wasn't afraid of anyone.

"Well, thank you for stopping by on such short notice," I said, hoping to hasten Florian's departure. "Good luck with your painting."

Florian gave me a long look and nodded, then left the store carrying the large painting with both hands.

"I'm glad he's gone," Seamus said as he locked the door and turned off the lights.

"Should you call the other man and tell him the painting is gone?"

"I can't. He hung up before I could get a mobile number from him."

"We really should get a caller ID service."

We stood by the door and watched Florian drive away, once again without the use of headlamps.

"He's going to get killed on these roads," Seamus muttered.

"He is a strange one, that's for sure."

Meet the Author

Credit: John A. Reade, Jr.

USA Today bestselling author **Amy M. Reade** is a former attorney who now writes full-time from her home in southern New Jersey, where she is also a wife, a mom of three, and a volunteer in school, church, and community groups. She loves cooking, traveling, and all things Hawaii and is currently at work on the next novel in the Malice series. Visit her on the web at www.amymreade.com or at www.amreade.wordpress.com.